HONOR'S FLIGHT

HONOR'S FLIGHT

(Fallen Empire, Book 2)

LINDSAY BUROKER

FOREWORD

Thank you, good reader, for coming back for the next installment in the Fallen Empire series. I'm having fun writing these adventures, and I hope you're having fun reading them. Before you jump into Book 2, please let me thank my editor, Shelley Holloway, for sticking with me in what's turning out to be an ambitious release schedule. Also, thank you to Sarah Engelke for beta reading under a deadline and Tom Edwards for the cover design.

CHAPTER ONE

Alisa Marchenko, captain of the *Star Nomad*, the only Nebula Rambler 880 in the galaxy that hadn't been scrapped decades earlier, fiddled with the flight stick as the planet Perun grew larger on the view screen. Nothing had happened yet to justify the queasy feeling in her stomach, but anticipation was making her hands sweat.

This had been home once, the planet where she had gone to school and met her husband, but that had been before she had chosen to join the Alliance army, serving as a fighter pilot to help take down the empire. Perun was all the empire had left of the dozens of planets and moons it had once controlled. Odds were they wouldn't be happy with her, knowing she had flown for the Alliance. But Alisa had no choice but to land on the planet. Somewhere down there, amid the vast oceans and the populous cities that sprawled across several continents, her daughter waited for her.

A clang sounded behind her, and a tall figure stooped and came through the hatch and into NavCom. Tommy Beck, her security officer, wore his white combat armor, the full body suit and magnetic boots, everything save for the helmet.

"Are you planning to take a walk?" Alisa asked, waving outward to indicate the exterior of the ship.

Beck turned, his nose to the window as he slid the hatch shut, and he didn't notice her gesture. "Mind if I make some privacy for us, Captain?"

"I don't know. You're not really my type, Beck."

From the way he turned his head and wrinkled his brow, he either didn't get the joke or hadn't ever considered her in a sexual manner. She decided not to find the notion of the latter depressing, especially since dating was the last thing on her mind. It had only been five months since she had woken from weeks in a medical regeneration tank to learn that her husband had been killed during an attack on Perun. They had been married for nearly ten years, and she hadn't expected to ever have to think of dating again.

"Oh?" Beck said. "What's your type?"

"My husband was a slender scholar rather than a big muscly man. He was smart, quick-witted, and always made me laugh. His jokes never had an edge. They were never designed to make a person hurt." Her voice lowered, and her gaze shifted toward the dark side of the planet that they were approaching, the clumps of city lights growing visible. "Not like mine. He was a better person than I am."

"Was? He's gone?"

Alisa winced, reminded that she hadn't shared the details of her past with anyone except Mica, neither mentioning Jonah's death nor that her daughter was the reason she had come to Perun.

"Yes," she murmured, her response barely audible.

"Sorry about that," Beck said, "but I'm closing the door so that Lord Colonel Enhanced Ears doesn't hear us."

Alisa pushed away her memories. "Oh? Are we going to have a secret conversation about Leonidas?"

"Leonidas." Beck grunted. "Right."

He came forward and perched on the edge of the co-pilot's seat, clunking the broad shoulders of his armor on equipment as he did so. He nearly clunked Alisa with one of his knees too. Combat armor was spaceworthy and meant to withstand a lot of damage in battle; it wasn't meant for helping a man into tight spaces.

"Why are you wearing that now?" Alisa asked, ignoring the comment about Leonidas.

As she had found out about a week ago, his real name was Colonel Hieronymus Adler, but she preferred to think of him by his call sign. A call sign wasn't a constant reminder that he had been the commander for the imperial Cyborg Corps. The enemy. A very feared enemy. Leonidas had saved her life back in the Trajean Asteroid Belt, and even if she sometimes still felt uneasy around him, she had offered him a permanent place on her crew as another security officer. Of course, he hadn't accepted that job offer yet, and she did not know if he ever would.

"I'm not stepping foot on Perun without proper protection," Beck said. "We'll be lucky if they don't shoot us as soon as we walk off the ship."

"I wasn't planning to announce that we were Alliance soldiers during the war."

"The imperials will find out."

Alisa had that fear, as well, but she hoped they might slip down there under the guise of merely being a freighter crew. Was that naive? She, Beck, and her engineer Mica Coppervein had all fought for the Alliance. If the imperials found out, would they arrest them? The *Star Nomad* had been sitting in a junkyard during the war, so *it* wouldn't rouse suspicions, but what if the imperials demanded IDs? Should she have looked into buying altered ones?

"We'll do our best not to tell them," Alisa said. "It's not like they have the resources of an entire system at their disposal anymore. They probably don't even have sys-net access anymore."

A couple of satellites showed up on the sensors, but who knew if they were connected to the system-wide grid? Alisa certainly would have removed the imperials' access if she had been in charge after the war.

"I wouldn't count on it," Beck said glumly, rubbing the breastplate of his armor. "But I want to tell you what I've learned about *Leonidas*." He put that emphasis on the pseudonym again as he laid a netdisc on the control console in front of him. "I looked him up."

"Is he *your* type?" Alisa asked.

It was a bad joke, and she wasn't surprised when Beck gave her an incredulous look.

"Never mind," she said.

"No, and I hope he's not yours either."

"He has even more muscles than you do."

"Thanks for the reminder." Beck grimaced.

He tapped the disc, and a holodisplay appeared above it with Leonidas's head and shoulders floating in the center. He looked a couple of years younger than the forty or so that Alisa guessed him to be now. He wore a black imperial army officer's uniform, and his hair was very short, very military. In the picture, his blue eyes were intense with determination, harder than they were in person. Or perhaps it was his attitude that had changed in the intervening years. He was still intense, still determined, but she had caught a wistful, almost morose expression on him from time to time.

"Colonel Hieronymus Adler," Beck said, swiping a finger along the bottom of the image so that the name popped up, along with a paragraph of text underneath it. "Former commander of the 22nd Infantry Battalion. Cyborg Corps."

Alisa nodded. "I know this. I was there when Doctor Dominguez told us, remember?"

"Yes, but he didn't mention this." Beck enlarged the small text under Leonidas's picture. "Wanted alive, two hundred thousand Alliance tindarks. This alert was issued by our government."

Alisa's mouth dangled open as she realized she was looking at a wanted poster. "There's a reward for him?"

"A *big* reward." Beck glanced toward the hatch, perhaps reassuring himself that Leonidas was not standing there and looking in the window. "With that kind of money, I could pay off the White Dragon mafia. Get them off my back. I might even have another shot at starting a restaurant."

Alisa rubbed the back of her neck, floored that someone was willing to pay that much for Leonidas, and bemused that her security officer thought that turning bounty hunter was a good way to fund his culinary ambitions.

"Does the Alliance even *have* that much money?" she wondered. "I know our government gets some of the taxes that once went to the empire, but only on the three planets and handful of stations we had the resources to secure. And during the war, we were poorer than a depleted asteroid after three centuries of mining. Remember the ships we had to fly? Some of them were practically museum pieces."

Beck's gaze flicked toward the ceiling, but he did not point out that the *Nomad* could also be in a museum. Wise choice.

He pulled up some more text in the holodisplay. "It says here that they have the money. If you bring him in, no questions will be asked. They're offering *physical* coin for him."

"How old is that poster?" Alisa peered closer to read the text. "Maybe it was something put out at the beginning of the war, when he was commanding the Cyborg Corps."

Even as she spoke, she wondered if that made sense. Would someone pay that kind of money just to take an enemy officer out of the equation? Leonidas might have been good at his job, but surely the imperials would have replaced him with another officer if he had disappeared.

"Nope." Beck prodded a line, enlarging the text. "The issue date is less than six months ago."

He was right. This hadn't come out until three days after the treaty had been signed and the war had officially ended.

"It doesn't say what he did? Or why he's wanted?"

"Nothing about it." Beck shrugged. "We don't know what he was looking for in that cybernetics lab, but it might have been something a lot more important than a few parts upgrades."

Alisa leaned back in her seat. It was true that Leonidas had never explained what he sought there, only that he had wanted to talk to the head research scientist, a man they had found dead on the floor of his lab. Leonidas had collected some files from the computer before leaving, but he had never shared what they were about.

"Two hundred *thousand*, Captain," Beck said. "If you helped me, we could split it. You could buy a brand new ship with that, or at least put a real substantial down payment on one. A bigger one. One that would let you haul a lot more freight in a single run and make more money."

As if money was what motivated Alisa. Oh, she wouldn't mind having more of it, especially since her Perunese bank account had likely disappeared along with everything else after the war, but for now, all that mattered was getting Jelena back. Something that should *finally* happen soon. It made her giddy to realize that by this time tomorrow, she should have landed and found her sister-in-law and her daughter.

Would Jelena like the cabin Alisa had made up for her? Remembering how much she had enjoyed *Andromeda Android*, Alisa had downloaded some stencils, printed them out, and painted the walls with characters from the cartoons. The family had chatted over the net as often as possible when Alisa had been away, and she thought she recalled Jelena still quoting the heroine

LINDSAY BUROKER

in their most recent exchange, but that had been months and months ago, so she could not be sure. She worried that Jelena's tastes might have changed and that she would be too mature for cartoon characters now.

Realizing Beck was gazing intently at her and waiting for a response, Alisa said, "How would we subdue a cyborg and transport him to an Alliance planet? He could kill either of us any time he wanted. Surely, you remember how your first time trying to shoot him went."

Beck had the self-awareness to squirm in his armor and flush a deep red, which was noticeable even with his bronze skin. "I do remember that, Captain. That's why I came up here to enlist your help."

"You want him to bend my gun in half too?"

She wasn't even wearing her Etcher, having left the holster in her cabin. Though she did not fully trust Leonidas or Dr. Alejandro Dominguez—someone else who had admitted to being loyal to the empire—she doubted either would charge into NavCom and strangle her while she piloted. One of the perks of being the only pilot on board was that people who wanted to see land again rarely threatened her.

"No, but you're a schemer," Beck said. "You could come up with something. Maybe we could drug his food and strap him down, lock him in his cabin until we got to Arkadius."

Given the athletic feats that Alisa had seen Leonidas perform so far, she doubted a locked hatch or chains would keep him immobile for long. And the *Star Nomad*, designed only to transport cargo and a handful of passengers, did not have a brig with forcefields. The old freighter did not even have weaponry—it had always been illegal on civilian ships when the empire had reigned.

"I'll think about it," Alisa said, more because she didn't want Beck to come up with some harebrained idea on his own than because she wanted to betray Leonidas.

A beeping sound came from the sensor display to the left of her seat. Three ships had broken orbit and were heading in their direction.

Alisa licked her lips, her nerves jangling anew. She tapped a button to bring up the starboard camera feed on the view screen, so they could watch the ships' approach. She glanced at the comm panel, expecting one of them to contact her. Those were imperial warships, one dreadnought and two escort cruisers, all heavily armed. She tried to tell herself that there were signs of old battle damage on the hulls, maybe even a rusty patch or two, but it might have been her imagination. From what she had heard, the empire still claimed ten or fifteen warships with which to defend its sole remaining planet.

"It's hard not to see those big ships without getting a little twitchy," Beck said, his gaze locked on the view screen. "The last time I saw them... well, my last battle didn't go well."

"Mine, either. Technically, we won—it was the battle for the Dustor 7 Orbital Shipyard—but my little Striker got pulverized by a kamikaze imperial Cobra right at the end. The bastard was determined to do as much damage as he could and go out in a fiery mess. His people had already surrendered at the time."

Alisa gritted her teeth as the memory of that Cobra hitting her leaped out of the recesses of her mind. She had lost control of navigation and crashed soon after. She remembered nothing after that, except waking up on Dustor weeks after the war ended, the primitive medical facilities there taking their time in rejuvenating her macerated organs and spine and getting her off life support.

"You look even grimmer than me, Captain."

"Maybe we can swap war stories sometime." That crash had been a nightmare, one she had no wish to relive, but she had other stories that she would gladly share, stories where her flying had kept her alive and destroyed enemies attacking key personnel. Those were worth remembering.

"To be honest, I'd rather swap barbecue recipes."

"You're a strange security officer, Beck. Anyone tell you that?"

"Lots, but usually while they were asking me to make ribs and my famous honey-glazed biscuits. You get the oven in the mess working, and I'll make a pile of them." His words were coming out rapidly, nervously, his eyes still locked on the approaching ships.

Alisa noticed that her own palms were sweating. Speaking of nerves...

She wiped them while glancing at the comm again. What if the empire had quarantined Perun and was not going to let anyone in? What if they somehow knew that half of her crew had fought in the war? What if—

The comm light flashed, and a beep sounded.

Even though she had expected it, Alisa twitched with surprise. She reached for the button slowly, composing herself so that her voice would come out as calm and indifferent. She had no reason to sound nervous, right?

"State your purpose for approaching Perun, unidentified Nebula Rambler," a cool female voice said. Was that a haughty sniff at the end of the statement? Maybe she knew about the shag carpet in the rec room and wasn't as impressed as Alisa that there was a Rambler still flying.

"This is the captain of the *Star Nomad*," Alisa said, deliberately not using her name in case they had a list of Alliance army officers in their database somewhere. "We are a peaceful freighter with passengers to drop off in Perun Central. We're also hoping to pick up some cargo if that's allowed." She made a note to herself to later check and see if anyone *was* trying to get goods off the planet. Once she had her daughter, she would have to turn into a legitimate businesswoman and find a way to pay for fuel and food.

"What is your name, captain of the *Star Nomad*?" the woman asked dryly.

Alisa blew out a slow breath.

Did she lie and hope for the best? That the empire was, indeed, cut off from the system as a whole and wouldn't have access to the global database of imperial subjects that had once existed?

"Alisa Marchenko," she ultimately said.

Life would only get more difficult if she lied and was found out. Besides, the war was over. Part of the treaty said that there would not be reprisal against civilians, former military or not, by either side. Of course, that apparently didn't apply to everyone since there was a warrant out for Leonidas's capture.

"Access to Perun is denied," the woman said scarce seconds later. Had she even had time to look up Alisa in a database?

"Pardon?" Alisa asked. "We have passengers that paid good money and traveled all the way from Dustor to land here. They're imperial subjects." She thought about pointing out that she had lived on Perun for more than ten years, but she did not want them snooping into her past. Or her present.

"Access is denied," the woman repeated. "You will turn around and leave the vicinity, or we will force you to do so."

Alisa muted the comm and muttered, "Very brave of you to threaten an unarmed freighter, assholes." She turned off the mute and tried to force a smile into her voice. "May I inquire as to why? Our passengers didn't inform us that there was a quarantine or any reason that we wouldn't be allowed to land."

Though…now that she thought about it, she remembered that none of the other ships that had been leaving Dustor at the same time as the *Nomad* had been heading to Perun. She distinctly remembered Alejandro mentioning that he had been waiting a while for a ride.

"Only loyal imperial ships are allowed access to our world."

"We could be loyal," Alisa said. "I just want to run freight. Is there a license I can apply for?"

"A loyalty license?" The woman really did have the driest voice. Even Leonidas, who did dry quite well himself, would have been impressed.

"Yes, I'll take one. I want to run freight all over the system. May I land and apply?"

A new voice came over the comm, and Alisa had the impression of a senior officer leaning over the communications officer's shoulder. "Was that lippy mouth appreciated by your superiors in the Alliance army, Captain Marchenko?" he asked, his tone as dry as the woman's.

Alisa had the distinct impression that the man referred to her military rank rather than her status as a freighter captain. It seemed someone had looked her up.

She should have shut up, but she could not resist responding. "Oh, absolutely. My wit regularly left the senior officers in guffaws." She ignored the incredulous look Beck shot her way. "It's well known that the ability to appreciate humor was what won us the war."

"Alcyone knows it wasn't honor," the man muttered darkly.

Alisa sighed and leaned back, muting the comm again.

"What?" she asked to the stare Beck was still leveling at her. "It's not like they were going to let us in, anyway."

"Access denied," the man repeated. "Leave now."

Alisa resisted the urge to add that the utter *lack* of humor had surely been what resulted in the empire losing the war. But, in truth, her senior officers had not truly appreciated her wit that much. They had appreciated her piloting skills, but that was about it. Only Jonah had regularly laughed at her jokes, whether they were funny or not.

A knock at the hatch kept her mind from traveling down tunnels of nostalgia and regret.

"It's Leonidas," Beck said, grabbing the netdisc off the console, even though he had turned off the holodisplay several minutes before. There was no condemning evidence floating around to alert Leonidas to the treachery in his mind.

Alisa punched a couple of buttons to alter their course—not away from the planet, not yet, but along a lateral trajectory that would not take them any closer. Then she rose to open the hatch. Like most of the doors and controls on the old ship, everything had to be done manually. She unlocked it and slid it open. Leonidas and Yumi, one of the passengers who had paid in advance for a ride to Perun, stood in the corridor.

"Any chance you can dress up in your red armor and get us an invitation down to the planet?" Alisa asked Leonidas, not ready to give up yet.

Even without his combat armor, Leonidas was intimidating: tall, broad-shouldered, and brawny. His bulging arm muscles were on display in the sleeveless vest that he wore today. As Alisa had noted before, he looked entirely human, albeit extremely fit and developed for a human, but she'd seen him hurl big men twenty meters across a shuttle bay and drop from great heights to land easily on his feet. There was no doubt as to what he was.

His gaze flicked toward the ships on the view screen. "The doctor's name might be more likely to gain you entrance. I'm not anybody anymore."

Uh huh. And that was why someone had a ridiculously large bounty out for him.

"You didn't try giving them my name already, did you?" Leonidas added.

"No, I gave them my name, and they didn't like it," Alisa said. "Given what a fine name it is, I couldn't imagine anyone else's performing better."

He frowned down at her, probably not sure if that was pure sarcasm or if there was a useful answer in there.

"I see you haven't learned to appreciate my humor yet," Alisa said.

"Was that what that was? Humor?"

Yumi snickered softly, her dark eyes twinkling. Those eyes looked a little odd, the pupils dilated, and Alisa wondered what she had been smoking, chewing on, or snorting this time.

"I'll work on my jokes," Alisa said. "Would you mind asking the doctor if he'll come up here and talk to the imperials?" She stopped herself from saying that she would get him herself if his brawny bigness were not blocking the corridor. She didn't truly want to annoy him. It was her reflex to be snarky to the enemy—better than letting the enemy see one's fears and weaknesses. But somewhere between the T-belt and here, she had stopped thinking of him as an enemy. She hoped that was not a mistake.

Leonidas lifted a hand and headed toward the passenger cabins.

"Same offer goes for you, Yumi," Alisa said.

"Pardon?"

"If you have any sway on Perun and can get us down there…" Alisa extended her palm toward the ships filling the view screen.

"Ah. I don't think the empire has reason to dislike me, but unless they're in need of science teachers, I'm not certain what value I would have in their eyes."

"You do have that flock of chickens in the cargo hold."

"You think there's a chicken shortage on Perun?" She smiled, pushing a long braid of black hair behind her shoulder.

"It does have a large population with cities stretching for hundreds of miles along the coasts. I wouldn't be surprised if food became a problem for them eventually."

"A problem my ten chickens can doubtlessly help them with."

"I've heard chickens like to make more chickens."

"Not with the way that Tommy is demolishing their eggs in the mornings."

Beck lifted his hands. "You said they were free for all. And I've shared my large omelets."

The comm light flashed on the console again. Even though Alisa had altered her course, the imperial ships were shadowing her. She expected another threat, or for someone to point out that flying parallel to a planet was not the same as flying *away* from a planet.

Leonidas returned. "The doctor says he'll request that they let us through, but he wishes to communicate from the privacy of his cabin."

"Does he," Alisa murmured, wondering what secretive things Alejandro intended to say. She supposed it did not matter. Once they landed, he wouldn't have a reason to return to her ship. He would depart and do whatever he needed to do here, he and that strange glowing orb that he protected like a mother with a newborn babe. After that, she would never see him again.

Alisa flicked a couple of switches to give Alejandro comm access from his cabin. He could be the one to deal with the imperial officer's insults too. Then she slid into the pilot's seat and drummed her fingers. It crossed her mind to eavesdrop, and she might have done just that if she hadn't had so many witnesses. Nothing like witnesses to help one rein in tendencies toward moral ambiguity. Still, she wouldn't have felt that wrong for eavesdropping, not when she suspected Alejandro and his orb were at odds with the Alliance. More than once, it had crossed her mind to report him and what she had seen once she reached an Alliance world.

Leonidas stepped to the side, and Alejandro appeared behind him.

"Any news?" Alisa asked.

"We're to be allowed to land at the Karundula Space Base. A civilian station." Alejandro said those last words firmly, making Alisa wonder if there had been an argument over that matter. Had the imperials wanted to direct them to a military facility? Where they would be more easily monitored or even locked down?

"That's excellent," Yumi said, clapping her hands together. "The girls will enjoy getting out."

"Yes, finding sunlight for your chickens was my primary concern too," Alisa said, watching as the dreadnought veered away. The two cruisers moved toward her, assuming a flanking position. "Oh, goody. We get escorts."

"Better than being shot at," Leonidas said and headed toward the rear of the ship.

Beck pushed himself to his feet and rapped his knuckles on his breastplate. "Guess I better find my helmet."

Yumi wandered away, too, leaving only Alejandro gazing at the planet, a mix of emotions on his face, none of them easy to read.

"What did you say to convince them to let us land?" Alisa asked.

"I simply gave them my name."

"No mention of the specialness of your orb?" She smiled and quirked an eyebrow.

Alejandro frowned at her. "If they interview us, speak nothing of that." The order seemed strange coming from him, a mild-mannered man in the gray robe of a disciple of the sun gods. Perhaps he realized it, because he added, "Please."

Alisa waved an indifferent hand. "I'm just relieved they're letting us land. Yumi's chickens need sun, you know."

"Is *that* why they've been complaining so much," he murmured.

"Either that, or because Beck is stealing all of their eggs."

Movement on the screen drew Alisa's attention back to the controls. The two imperial cruisers were veering off. As the *Star Nomad* angled toward the surface of the planet, they shifted into an orbiting path again.

"I guess they decided we weren't interesting enough to escort, after all," Alisa said, more relieved than concerned. She hoped the imperials would not call ahead to the base and alert the locals about suspicious Alliance sympathizers en route.

Alejandro frowned but did not reply.

A couple of minutes passed, the imperial ships turning into white dots in the distance. As Alisa took them down toward the largest of Perun's continents, something slammed into the freighter. She did not have her harness on and was hurled forward, the flight stick smashing into her stomach as her head nearly cracked the view screen.

"What in the hells?" she blurted as she hit the button for the shields.

Alejandro lay crumpled on the floor between the seats and only groaned as a response. She checked the sensors. If there had been a ship or any type of object that could hit them, the proximity alarm should have gone off.

"What's going on up there?" Mica asked over the comm. "You're bruising my ship."

"As soon as I figure it out, I'll let you know." Alisa's hands flew over the controls, getting damage reports and also cycling through the exterior cameras, trying to see with her eyes what the sensors had missed. "And it's *my* ship. You said you were leaving me for a better job as soon as it came along."

Something struck them again. This time, the *Nomad* merely shuddered slightly, the shields protecting them, and on one of the cameras, Alisa glimpsed a blast of blue energy striking them.

"E-cannon," she growled. "Someone's firing at us."

She squinted into the darkness of space, trying to see where the blast had come from.

Alejandro pulled himself into the co-pilot's seat and fastened his harness. Alisa should have done the same, but she was too busy scowling and peering.

"The imperial ships?" Alejandro asked, bewildered.

"No. Though they sure departed in a timely manner. Look. Do you see that? That dark, angular blob?"

"Angular blob?" From the way he still sounded dazed, he might have hit his head.

"Yes, there's definitely something there."

As if to agree with her, the sensors finally gave a tenuous beep.

"Twenty tindarks says that's a Stealth Fang." Alisa had fought against them during the war. They were usually imperial ships, but they were also popular with the criminal element since they did not show up on sensors until they were right on top of an enemy.

"I don't take bets, Captain." Alejandro had recovered enough to grip the console and peer at the screen.

"Because your religiosity forbids it?"

"Because my financial acuity forbids it."

"What's going on?" Leonidas asked, walking up the corridor with Beck.

Something made the ship shudder again. This time, Alisa did not see the fire from an e-cannon, but her control panel lit up in complaint.

"Beck may get to use his armor," Alisa said, nudging the *Nomad* to maximum speed, hoping to escape their near-invisible pursuer.

Leonidas looked sharply at her. "Someone's trying to board us?"

"That was a grab beam. They're going to have to get closer to catch us, but…" Alisa eyed the sensors where their enemy now showed up as a fuzzy green blip. "They're faster than we are, so it seems likely that could happen."

"Can we get down to Perun first?" Alejandro asked.

She did not need the computer to run the calculations comparing the distance, their speed, and her speed. "No."

CHAPTER TWO

They couldn't make atmosphere and definitely couldn't reach Karundula Space Base before the other ship caught up. Alisa changed their course, all too aware of the agile way the Fang followed them. The angular ship was hard to see, its body all black with no running lights, and a sensor-dampening system camouflaging it until it was close enough to strike. But she knew what she was dealing with. The triangular craft was as sleek and maneuverable as a Delgottan cheetah. She knew its range for that grab beam too. Another minute or two, and it would be close enough to get the beam to stick, to capture the *Nomad*.

Leonidas and Beck had charged back to their quarters to fully suit up. Having a cyborg on their side should help even the odds if they were boarded, but Alisa would prefer not being captured at all. Where had those imperial ships gone?

"You doing all right, Alejandro?" she asked.

His eyebrows were pinched together, and he gripped his waist, like he might have clunked his ribs hard when he fell.

"You're not going to die, are you?" she added, wishing she had a field full of asteroid debris to fly through so it might slow down their pursuers.

"Rebus-de teaches us not to fear death, that our souls live on for eternity, floating in the Dark Reaches and finding peace with the cosmic essences that were born with the universe and that shall continue on forever."

"I think you can find cosmic essences in Yumi's cabin, if you want to commune with them preemptively." Alisa should not have mocked him, especially if he was quoting scripture to reassure himself, and raised an apologetic hand as soon as the words came out.

"I do not believe you," Alejandro said.

"Pardon?"

"When you said that your Alliance superiors appreciated your wit, I do not believe that you spoke the truth."

"You imperial folk are so mistrustful." Alisa grinned at him, but it was a short-lived gesture. Their pursuers tried to envelop them with their grab beam again.

The ship lurched as a tenuous hold grasped them. Alisa accelerated, decelerated, and dove downward, trying to shake them. The Fang wasn't close enough yet. That grip *shouldn't* be a solid one.

There. Adding a clumsy barrel roll to her dive did the job.

"Shook them for the moment," Alisa said. "But that slowed us down too."

She corrected their course, heading in the direction the imperial ships had gone instead of down toward the planet. Unfortunately, she could not see those ships anymore. They had taken off quickly. It was as if they had been running from the trouble. Or intentionally leaving the *Nomad* to its fate.

"Should we try communicating with them?" Alejandro asked.

"The imperial ships?"

"The people chasing us."

"I think they effectively expressed what was on their minds when they fired at us," Alisa said.

Something they hadn't done again, interestingly. The Fang was close enough. It could have fired numerous times by now. The *Nomad* had sturdy shields, but they would not hold up indefinitely. But the Fang did not want to obliterate Alisa's ship. Clearly, it wanted to capture them. Maybe the Fang's crew had hoped to disable the *Nomad* with that first surprise strike. The helmsman over there probably was not too concerned that it had failed. There was no need for concern. They had the faster ship.

Alejandro hesitated, looking at her, then pushed the comm button. Was he worried she would object? If he wanted to chat up the people chasing them, that was fine with her. She was too busy flying to care. Ah, *there* were those two imperial ships. The white dots that represented the cruisers had come into view.

"Unidentified ship that is attacking us, this is Dr. Alejandro Dominguez. Please explain your actions. We are a peaceful and unarmed freighter."

Alisa thought of Beck and Leonidas. They were not *entirely* unarmed, though the handheld weapons would be of no use until intruders forced their way onto the ship.

Alejandro received a response by way of a red beam of energy that lanced past the starboard wing. It did not strike them, but it might have shaved some paint off the hull.

"I don't think they want to talk," Alisa said. "Why don't you see if you can raise those cruisers? Tell them that you're about to be captured or killed or tortured or worse and that we could use an ominous imperial presence to loom scarily at our backs."

Alejandro hesitated, and she wished she had eavesdropped on his conversation with the imperials. If they were buddies, as she had suspected, he shouldn't hesitate to ask for help now, should he? And they would gladly give it…They wouldn't veer away and pretend he wasn't in trouble. Such as they were doing now. Hm, he hadn't blackmailed or otherwise coerced them, had he?

Alejandro tapped the comm, directing the signal ahead of them. "Captain Ravencraft? This is Dr. Alejandro Dominguez. There are unfriendly ships in your planet's orbit, and we're being attacked. We are in need of—"

The comm beeped at him, and a red warning light flashed.

Alisa cursed and thumped her fist on the console, as if that would help. "The Fang is jamming our communications."

"Is there a way to override them?"

"Not unless you want to climb up on the roof and realign the comm dish."

He looked at her, maybe thinking she was serious.

"It's a joke. That wouldn't help. Besides, you might interfere with my reception of *The Fiery and the Glamorous*. We've already missed two weeks' worth of episodes by being way out on the edge of the system."

"Perhaps they'll *see* that we're in trouble," Alejandro said, ignoring her joke.

The white imperial ships had grown on the screen, their cylindrical details now visible.

"Oh, they can see." Even if the Fang was still invisible to their sensors, the imperials would have detected those energy shots being fired, and they would see Alisa's evasive maneuvers. "I think they're just not interested in helping. Do people here not love you as much as I thought?"

"Politics are always complicated."

She glanced at him. "Are you implying that the Fang is from a different faction on the same side? Another imperial ship?"

"I can't know that. I only know that some people may not be pleased about the existence of the orb, as you call it."

"What do *you* call it?"

Alejandro pressed his lips together and said nothing.

Another beam of energy shot out, this time hammering into their aft shields. An alarm flashed the percentage of shield power remaining. Apparently, the warning shots were over. Maybe the Fang had realized where they were running and worried that Alisa might get help.

"Mica," she said over the internal comm. "Can you get any more power out of the engine? Going faster would be excellent for our health right now."

"I gathered that." Some clanks and a grunt followed Mica's words.

Alejandro glanced at Alisa.

"That's the Alliance equivalent of *yes ma'am*," she explained.

"Sometimes it seems unfathomable that your side won the war."

"Even though you say things like that, I'll still offer to buy you a drink after we land." Another energy beam slammed into the back of the *Nomad*, this time with enough force that the ship bucked, even *with* the shields up. "*If* we land."

The shield power dropped below fifty percent.

Alejandro clasped the three-suns pendant that dangled down the front of his robe and closed his eyes.

A little more juice filtered into the power display next to the flight stick. Alisa did not hesitate to boost their expenditure and push them into the red. The deck plating rattled under her feet, and the ship's voice promised dire consequences if she did not ease back, but the imperial ships grew closer, their white and gray hulls filling the screen.

As soon as she was close enough, Alisa zipped past one's thrusters, slowing enough to maneuver. She weaved between them, as if claiming them for dance partners at the Tri-Eclipse Ball.

"What *are* you doing?" Alejandro asked. "Trying to annoy them?"

"Not exactly."

The Fang did not follow her, instead slowing down at the edge of the cruisers' firing distance. Good. If Alisa had to, she would hide between the two ships until their pursuer got bored and left, or she would go with them all the way down to the planet if that was where the imperials were headed.

Unfortunately, the Fang did not hesitate for long. The sleek ship swooped into the view of her rear cameras again, and she could tell it was trying to target her without bothering the cruisers. The other captain's audaciousness floored Alisa, and she thought Alejandro might be right, that these ships were all on the same side. The Fang certainly did not seem worried that the imperials would see it and fire.

Alisa guided them in close to one of the cruisers, almost bumping wings as she kicked up the acceleration. The cruisers raised their shields, and the *Nomad* shivered as her own energy field bumped against theirs. Giving them a little more room, Alisa piloted her craft in front of one cruiser's nose an instant before the Fang fired. A red energy beam streaked through the air between the imperial ships. Had she remained where she had been, it would have struck them, but it zipped past without hitting its target.

As she took the *Nomad* under the belly of the same cruiser, the comm panel flashed.

"How much do you want to bet that's the imperials, whining about us using them as asteroids in a Seek and Find game?" Alisa asked.

"I told you, I don't gamble. But if I did, I wouldn't take that bet." Alejandro tapped the comm button. "Captain Ravencraft, are you now interested in coming to our assistance?"

"Who in the hells are you?" a man's voice snarled.

"As I informed you previously," Alejandro said calmly as Alisa continued diving and weaving, "I am Dr.—"

"Admiral Benton said we can't fire on you, but if you don't get your loathsome tick of a ship off my belly, I'm going to knock you into the farthest sun."

"*Loathsome?*" Alisa snarled, almost missing another attack from the Fang. She danced toward the belly of the other ship to avoid it. "The *Nomad* isn't loathsome."

"If you would simply deter the Fang from attacking us further, we would be delighted to leave," Alejandro said.

"More than delighted," Alisa grumbled.

A new plan jumped into her head. Maybe the imperials needed more of an incentive to attack the Fang.

So far, she had been using the other ships to stay out of their attacker's line of sight, but now she swooped out from underneath one and drew closer than wise to its thrusters. Making sure the Fang could see them, she pretended to get too close to one of the big housings. As if they had clipped the hull of the ship, or perhaps the shield, she threw the *Nomad* into an artful roll. The view spun, but in her mind, she kept precise tabs on where the cruiser was and where the Fang was. For a moment, their attacker had an easy shot.

"Captain?" Alejandro asked, gripping the console with both hands.

She couldn't tell when the Fang was about to fire, so she had to guess. Where was the perfect spot? Her belly would be most vulnerable, so when it was exposed to them, she reached for the thruster controls. She waited, trying to time it just right, to judge when the weapons person over there would shoot. The ruse would only be good for one shot.

"Now," she whispered and summoned full power.

The *Nomad* surged forward, losing the roll as she streaked into space. Alisa decelerated almost immediately, not wanting to be too far from cover if this failed.

The rear cameras caught the red beam lancing out and striking just where she had wanted—one of the thruster casings of an imperial ship.

"Hah," she said.

The shields were up on the cruisers, and that shot would not do any damage, but she hoped…

A fiery ball of orange shot out from the cruiser's rear e-cannon. It slammed into the side of the Fang, briefly lighting up all of its black contours.

Alisa grinned. The Fang would have shields, but those cruisers were big, powerful ships with big, powerful weapons. At that close of range, that cannon blast should have made quite a dent. To her delight, second and third shots followed after the first.

The Fang veered away, its tail between its legs. With that sensor-dampening camouflage, it soon disappeared from sight—and from the sensors—but in her imagination, Alisa pictured plumes of smoke wafting from its scorched hull.

"All right," she said, adjusting their course, "I'm taking us down to dock before any more trouble finds us." Such as if the irritated captains of the cruisers turned their cannons on the *Nomad*.

"A good idea." Alejandro tapped the comm. "We thank you for your gracious assistance, Captain Ravencraft."

"Get your tick off our belly," came the less than gracious response.

Alisa sneered at the comm, remembering the days when she had flown a combat ship and could have sent a few torpedoes up his nose for saying such snide things about her vessel. Alejandro closed the comm channel without comment.

"Are you done dogfighting up there, Captain?" Mica asked over the comm.

"Yes, thank you for your help. Are you sure you want to leave my ship to take an engineering job down on Perun?"

"More sure than ever."

"You wound me, Mica. Nobody else will appreciate you the way I do."

"If that's not a lie, it's an awfully depressing truth."

Alisa looked at Alejandro. "I'm not sure if I was just insulted or not."

"Alliance," he muttered, gazing at the view screen as they flew down toward the city-lit continent on the dark third of the planet.

She brushed away the insults, implied and perceived, and focused on getting them down to land. She had no idea if reaching Karundula Space Base would provide any measure of safety. Someone was after Alejandro and his orb, a mafia outfit wanted her security officer dead, and Leonidas had the kind of reward on his head that could buy a person a small island. Even Yumi, Alisa recalled, had cast a few nervous backward glances over her shoulder when she had first boarded the *Nomad* back on Dustor. How in all three hells had she ended up with so much trouble on board? She and Mica might be the only ones here that nobody wanted dead, at least not badly enough to do something about it. And Mica was threatening to leave her.

Alisa should have felt exhilarated after escaping an uncertain fate with that Fang, but it was bleakness that rode down to the planet in her heart.

CHAPTER THREE

Alisa trotted down the metal steps into the cargo area, anticipation and trep-
idation warring for prominence in her mind. She worried about stepping
foot on the planet and about the trouble that her crew and passengers were
carrying with them. But she also felt nearly giddy as she pictured walking up
to her sister-in-law's apartment, smiling brightly, and saying she was there to
pick up her daughter.

It had been so long since she had seen Jelena in person, well over a year
since her last leave and her last time visiting. And more than four years since
she, Jelena, and Jonah had lived together as a family. The video chats had
helped to keep Alisa up to date on the goings on back home, but it had been
nine or ten months since the last one, and Alisa worried that Jelena would
feel she had been abandoned. Alisa hoped they could make up for lost time
in the future. They could travel among the stars together, share in Jelena's
studies, play games, and find the ingredients to make chocolates by hand, as
they had often done before the war. Alisa had done similar things with her
own mother when growing up on the *Star Nomad*. Sometimes, it had been
a lonely life for a girl, but there had been interesting passengers now and
then, and she had played with other children when they'd been in dock or
planet-side for a few days. Alisa had many good memories of those days
and hoped Jelena wouldn't begrudge her new future, that she would learn
to appreciate it.

Alejandro turned toward Alisa as she reached the bottom of the
steps. He stood by the hatch, a satchel slung over his shoulder but not
his duffel bag.

"You're not taking everything with you?" Alisa asked.

He hadn't left that orb in his cabin, had he? She couldn't believe that, not when she was fairly certain he slept with the thing. He must have it in the satchel. She did not feel it, though, not the way she had on that pirate ship, when it had lain on the table, the four interlocking pieces glowing like miniature suns and raising the hair on her arms as it pulsed with some strange power she could only guess about.

"Not unless you're denying me further use of the ship," Alejandro said mildly.

"No, the cabin's yours until we leave. But if you're still here then, I'll have to charge you for the next leg of our journey." Alisa smiled, not expecting him to take her up on the offer. He'd been waiting weeks, if not months, to come to Perun.

But he tilted his head curiously. "Where are you going next?"

"I had Arkadius in mind." The seat of the Tri-Sun Alliance government and a planet as populated as this one. No place for an imperial loyalist.

"Arkadius is reputed to have an excellent library," he mused.

"Uh, yes, and the Floating Gardens of Scinko Terra too. One of the thirty-seven wonders of the system." Or so the tourism pamphlets promised. Alisa was fairly certain it was the orgies that happened in the heated pools that rested on those floating terraces that made the place popular.

"I've seen the wonders. I haven't seen all of the libraries."

"Is that where you're heading here? To the library?" Since they were in the capital, she assumed he would go to the university's Staton Hall Library. It boasted forty levels filled with books and computer terminals stuffed with data from centuries past, some of the systems dedicated to reading formats that had long ago been forgotten, information that nobody had bothered scanning and modernizing.

"Perhaps," Alejandro said noncommittally and smiled.

The lack of trust went both ways around here. Not that she could blame him. Whether the war had ended or not, she was Alliance, and he was imperial.

"Make sure to stop at the Black Bomber on the first floor. They put adreno-shots in their espresso. The students love it. It makes your hair stand on end."

Much as his orb did. She didn't mention that.

"When I was a surgeon, I occasionally had to perform emergency heart procedures on people who drank too many drinks like that," he said.

"Students will go to great lengths to buy themselves more time to study," Alisa said.

"I suppose open-heart surgery would pass for a medical bye. How long do you plan to remain here?"

"On Perun? Assuming the imperials don't kick me out, a few days probably." In addition to collecting her daughter, she needed to find cargo and buy supplies for the ship. She was well aware of the paucity of her funds and how she had to pay Beck with them as well as keeping the *Nomad* in the sky. She would soon have another mouth to feed, as well, but she smiled, not thinking of Jelena as a burden.

Clanks sounded on the steps, Beck tramping down in his full combat armor, including the helmet, with two rifles slung over his back in addition to the built-in weaponry of his suit. Oh, yes. The authorities were going to let him walk off the ship and into the world without any trouble whatsoever.

Leonidas appeared on the walkway and came down the steps after him. He wasn't wearing his armor, carrying only his destroyer in a hip holster, the weapon barely noticeable under his old military jacket. Apparently, he wasn't worried about people shooting at him as he walked off the ship. Did he even know about the bounty? Alisa wagered a lot of loyal imperial subjects would be happy to turn on one of their own for two hundred thousand tindarks.

Interestingly, Leonidas had not packed up and also was not carrying his belongings. Was he still considering her job offer? Alisa had the impression that he had business here on the planet, but not surprisingly, he hadn't spoken of it.

Mica and Yumi walked down the steps after him. The chickens penned in the corner of the voluminous hold squawked with excitement at Yumi's appearance, even though she did not head toward their feedbag. She wore her dress and boots, but not a purse or anything that might suggest she intended to go out.

Was it odd that none of Alisa's passengers were in a hurry to leave? Given all the danger they had been in during the last two weeks, she would have expected them to bolt as soon as the hatch door opened.

"Not going out?" Alisa asked as Yumi strolled up with Mica.

"Not currently," Yumi said. "Mica and I are going to scour the planetary network and hunt for jobs."

"You're not going to take my offer of a job as science officer, eh?" Too bad. It had crossed Alisa's mind that Yumi might be talked into tutoring her daughter. Oh, she might not be the best influence on a young girl with her interest in psychedelics, but so far, she had proven knowledgeable and useful, and she kept to her cabin when she was pursuing non-academic hobbies.

"I don't think so," Yumi said. "You hardly need a science officer on a freighter going back and forth in the shipping lanes out there. Though I must admit that traveling with you thus far has been stimulating."

"Likewise. I'll figure out a way to pay your salary if you change your mind."

"Thank you. I'll see what the job market is like here. It's a populous planet, I understand, so teachers should be in demand."

"You've never been?"

"No," Yumi said. "I grew up in a small village on the northern continent of Arkadius. I've traveled to many places to further my education and explore, but I've rarely been drawn to the great metropolises. I hope to find something in a smaller country here on Perun."

"Not me," Mica said. "I want a job in the city here. I imagine they're rebuilding, so there should be chances to put a stamp on the infrastructure of the capital that could last for centuries to come."

"You're not staying with the ship?" Leonidas asked Mica.

Alisa wondered if his interest—or was that concern—stemmed from the fact that he was seriously considering her job offer. She had made it before learning about that warrant. Should she revoke it? Having a wanted man on the ship where she intended to bring her daughter would not be a good idea.

"Jelena first," she murmured to herself. She could worry about the rest later.

Leonidas looked to her, his brow creased. She had forgotten about his enhanced hearing.

"Mica doesn't think keeping the *Nomad* in the air is intellectually stimulating enough," Alisa said, "so I'll be looking for a new engineer while I'm here."

"Oh?" Leonidas asked. "Your ship is attacked regularly. It seems that an engineer would find a great deal to stimulate her here."

"I'm hoping those days have come to an end," Alisa said, glancing at Beck and Alejandro and thinking of the Fang. Maybe her hopes were delusional.

Alisa hit the button to open the big cargo hatch and lower the ramp. They had been cleared to land, the air traffic controller making no comment about the battle up in orbit, and she assumed that meant they were cleared to depart the ship, too, but she watched warily as the ramp lowered. She would not be surprised to find an armed escort waiting for them.

The blue sky that came into view made her heart sing, even if it was hazy with pollution. Dustor's sky had been red and usually full of storm clouds or sand as the wind scoured the surface of the planet. Before that, she had been in space for a year. It was good to see a bright sky again, the sky of one of the few planets in the system that hadn't required terraforming to be habitable to the occupants of Earth's early colony ships.

The hordes of people striding through the concourse, hurrying along the moving sidewalks or crossing on hover bridges, didn't set Alisa at ease the way the sky did, but she expected them. Perun, its capital city included, had been bombed during the last year of the war, but it could not have put much of a dent in the population on a planet that housed billions. The capital city alone held more than ten million people. Somewhere in the crowd, someone or something with a loud mechanical voice promised specials on everything from fresh lettuce to grav boosters at the ZipZipMart on the third level of the embarkation station.

"Captain," Yumi said, "if you happen to see any chicken feed while you're out, I could use some. And also some compost for the potted plants and mushroom logs I started in my cabin."

"You're *sure* you're leaving?" Alisa asked.

Yumi smiled, her cheeks dimpling. "Not entirely."

"I'll fetch your feed and compost," Beck said, smiling at Yumi. How a man managed a shy smile while wearing all that imposing combat armor, Alisa did not know, but he did it.

"Thank you," Yumi said.

Alejandro flicked his hand in a farewell and strode down the ramp. Alisa supposed it was cowardly, but she watched to see if anyone would leap out to apprehend him before venturing out herself.

The crowds of people did not take any notice of him as he glided into the stream. His gray robe did not stand out among the eclectic attire of the cosmopolitan populace.

"You going to look for cargo, Captain?" Beck asked, stepping up to her side.

"Eventually, yes. I have a personal matter to attend to first."

"I'll come with you." He patted the strap of one of his rifles.

Alisa blinked in surprise. "Thank you, but that's not necessary. You don't even need to leave the ship if you wish." She kept from pointing out that it might be a good idea if he *didn't* leave the ship. She did not pay attention to mafia happenings and did not know if the White Dragon had a base here, but she would not be surprised. The news often mentioned that some of the big mafia empires spanned the entire system.

"Might be dangerous out there for you, and you hired me to protect you."

"I hired you to protect the ship," Alisa said as Leonidas stepped up to the top of the ramp. His brow was creased as he watched Alejandro's back as the older man disappeared into the crowd. Had he expected to be invited along? "From pirates trying to force their way aboard and steal my cargo."

"If you get mauled or kidnapped while walking along the street, who's going to get us a cargo?" Beck asked.

"I suppose that's a valid point." Alisa had never worried about being mauled or kidnapped in the years she had lived here before, but that had been when she had been an imperial subject with no allegiance—at least nothing on paper—to the budding Underground Alliance. Besides, she had no idea if the empire had managed to maintain the police force that had once patrolled the city and protected its people. She didn't even know if they were still calling themselves an empire. Could a single planet be considered an empire? When the emperor himself was dead?

"I need to pick up some spices for my marinades too," Beck said, "and some fresh meat. The bear's about gone."

"Ah." Alisa hadn't planned on a shopping side trip, at least not for minutia such as spices and chicken feed, but she supposed they could stop on the way back. Maybe Jelena would enjoy the Pan-System Market. "I accept the offer of your company then."

"Gracious, Captain."

"Someone needs to carry the chicken feed."

"Easy enough." Beck pretended to flex his armored biceps.

"Keep an eye on the ship," Alisa told Mica with a wave, but paused before she started down the ramp. She turned and trotted over to Mica. "You said you'll be on the computer, right? Looking for employment?"

"Yes." Mica squinted at her.

Alisa leaned close, keeping enhanced cyborg hearing in mind this time. "Look up a Colonel Hieronymus Adler, will you?" she whispered. "Find out anything you can. There's a warrant out for him, and I'd like to know why."

"Is that our cyborg?" Mica murmured, eyeing Leonidas over Alisa's shoulder.

He stood at the top of the ramp, looking out at the crowd, and did not appear to be concerned about their conversation.

Alisa nodded.

"Did he become a cyborg out of bitterness that his parents gave him the name Hieronymus?" Mica asked.

"Possibly so." Alisa waved again before joining Beck.

They headed down the ramp. To her surprise, Leonidas followed them.

"You're not coming with us, are you, mech?" Beck frowned over his shoulder.

Alisa winced. Even if she had called Leonidas "cyborg" for the first week she had known him, she'd come to think of him as a regular person, and she wished Beck would stop calling him by that name.

"Just heading in the same direction." Leonidas nodded toward a sign for a transit station at the end of the concourse, not obviously offended.

"You're probably going somewhere more interesting than we are," Alisa said, fishing a bit. She doubted he would tell her anything, but she was surprised that he wasn't heading off to the library with Alejandro.

"Doubtful," Leonidas said.

So much for fishing.

At the transit station, they ran into trouble when Alisa tried to pay with her four-year-old swipe card. She was not surprised when it was rejected, as she'd suspected her bank account might have become a victim of the war, but there wasn't a human operator to talk to, nor would the robot at the turnstile accept the physical currency that Alejandro had paid his passage with.

After observing for a moment, Leonidas stepped forward and waved the palm of his hand at the currency scanner. A blue light flashed, reading the subcutaneous chip that most imperial subjects possessed. Because of her itinerant youth and her mother's fear of being on the grid, Alisa had never gotten one.

"Three," Leonidas said, paying for fares for all of them. "Looks like I'm joining you, after all," he said dryly.

"For someone who was squatting in a junked freighter when we first met, you're certainly bursting with cash," Alisa said, then wished she had thanked him instead. Why did she have such a hard time doing that?

"Only on this planet," he said, his blue eyes growing a touch stormy as he pushed through the turnstile.

She shouldn't have reminded him that his government and his way of life were gone. She wondered again if he knew about the bounty out for him. Should she tell him?

"Think he'll buy us some chocolate-covered peanuts on the train?" Beck said brightly, apparently not worried about Leonidas's problems.

"Maybe if you stop calling him mech," she said, following Leonidas to the floatalator leading up to the elevated boardwalk.

"Not sure peanuts are worth that."

———

Alisa got off the train a stop early, wanting to walk past the apartment building her family had once lived in. Maybe she shouldn't have, since her sister-in-law had warned her that it had been destroyed—the bombing had been what resulted in Jonah's death—but a morbid need to see the area for herself filled her. Besides, it wasn't that far from her destination, and the afternoon was young. Jelena would probably still be at school.

"They're rebuilding quickly, aren't they?" Beck asked, walking at her side, not questioning her early departure from the train. "I didn't see nearly as many bombed-out buildings as I'd expected when we rode through the city. Just the capital building. Someone left an impressive crater there."

Leonidas walked a few paces behind them, not participating in their conversation. She still hadn't thanked him for paying for their passage, but he hadn't sat next to them on the train, so the opportunity hadn't arisen. She had a feeling that Beck was an anti-magnet, at least when it came to cyborgs.

"I wasn't involved in the fighting here, but I know our people picked their targets carefully." Alisa's commanders had kept her away from her home of record, doubtlessly knowing that she would have struggled to fire upon the city where her family lived. Busy preparing for the Dustor mission, she hadn't even learned about these bombings until after they had been carried out. If she had known, she might have found a way to warn Jonah of the attacks, to tell him to find an underground shelter. "For the most part they did," she amended quietly. "There were mistakes."

Like her family's home…

The streets they walked now weren't nearly as familiar as they should have been. Shells of buildings, sometimes only a wall or two standing, rose like headstones in a graveyard. Some of the streets were in the process of being rebuilt. Others were cracked and riddled with potholes. Still others were gone altogether.

Off to one side, a group of boys was playing around a crane and a stack of giant pipes, chasing each other in and out of them. One picked up a warped piece of metal and threw it at another. Alisa was tempted to yell at them to go play somewhere less dangerous, but was distracted by looking at their faces, wondering if she had known any of them four years earlier. Jelena had been too young to go out and play unsupervised with the neighborhood kids then, but there had been numerous children who lived in her building. Were any of these boys residents who had survived?

"Look," one of them blurted and pointed in her direction.

Several other dirty faces turned toward her little group. Alisa's first thought was that they recognized her, but they were pointing at Beck. He still wore his full suit of combat armor, helmet included. He had drawn a few curious looks, but surprisingly, the authorities hadn't shown up yet to question him about his weapons. During the empire's heyday, civilians hadn't been allowed to carry firearms on the more populous and civilized planets, Perun included. From the paucity of the cube-shaped "spy boxes" that usually floated along the streets—years earlier, they had been everywhere, like swarms of bees—Alisa guessed that there weren't as many resources for monitoring the population as there once had been.

The boys abandoned their play and raced toward Alisa and the others. She lifted a hand, half-expecting Beck or Leonidas to be alarmed and reach for a weapon. None of the kids looked to be older than ten, but she'd come across many soldiers with twitchy reflexes, and from the way bangs and thumps came from Leonidas's cabin at night, she suspected that his mind wasn't always a predictable place to live.

But neither man reached for a weapon. Leonidas watched the kids approach, but not with any more scrutiny than he watched the rest of the street. His gaze was constantly roaming, alert even here, in what should have felt like a safe harbor for him.

"Is that real combat armor?" one of the boys asked, skidding to a stop in front of Beck.

"Of course it's real," a gangly kid who could not have been more than eight said. "That's one of the Bender Farrs, a Dex 7560T. It's blazing! I've got the model. It's got rear cameras, trans-titanium casing, *and* quad guns. Nothing's getting through! Do you have the grenade launcher attachment, mister?"

The kids gathered around Beck, fearless as they gazed at him. A few dared touch his armored exterior. Leonidas stood back, his arms folded over his chest. Alisa was surprised he was still with them and hadn't veered off to pursue his own mission, whatever it was.

"Used to have the grenade launcher," Beck said. "But it got blown off in some action on a transport ship near Stardock 18. We were fighting—" he glanced at Leonidas, "—fearsome enemies."

"*Stellar*," several of the boys whispered.

"Are you planning a hit? Can we watch?"

"A what?"

"You know, killing someone." The boy waved toward a building shell, the windows all blown out and one of the corners crumbled. "That happens sometimes now. The gangs run around here. They perch in the old buildings and ambush each other. But you'd be invincible with combat armor, right?"

"Against snipers in windows?" Beck asked. "Most likely."

Other boys peppered him with questions. Leonidas shifted, like he meant to continue past and wait for them farther on—or perhaps he *wouldn't* wait for them—and the young boy who had named the armor stats noticed him. His eyes widened as they locked onto his jacket, on the patch that proclaimed he had been a part of the Cyborg Corps.

He nudged an older boy next to him with similar dark hair and eyes, a brother perhaps. Before, he had been articulate, but all he did now was whisper, "Peter, mech."

The older boy looked at Leonidas's jacket. He nudged two more boys. Soon the group fell silent aside from whispers and stares. At first, Alisa thought they might treat Leonidas similarly to Beck, being curious about his abilities and whether he was here for "a hit," but there was fear in their eyes, not awe. Leonidas continued observing their surroundings and pretended not to notice it, or maybe he was indifferent to the reactions.

"We gotta go," one of the older boys said, backing away and waving for the others to follow.

"Hope you get a new grenade launcher soon," one of the more garrulous ones said, but then they were gone, sprinting off across the dirt lot, as if they expected Leonidas to give chase.

He did watch as they departed, but not with any menace. A pained expression flickered through his eyes before disappearing, hidden behind a stoic mask.

"Well, I guess we know who's not good with kids," Beck said dryly and started walking, his back to Leonidas.

Alisa almost said that Leonidas hadn't done anything one way or another and could hardly be blamed for their reaction, but he, too, started walking, his pace brisk. She hurried to catch up since she was supposed to be the one leading.

They walked in silence until she rounded a corner and found herself on her old street. She slowed down as the empty lot where her apartment complex had stood came into view. Where once a fifteen-story structure had risen on a busy street full of other such buildings, there was now nothing more than a gaping hole in the earth. A few pieces of rubble remained here and there, but most of it had been cleared. Bulldozers and cranes rested at one corner of the lot, though nobody was working in the area today.

Her feet rooted to what had once been a moving sidewalk. She stared at the hole, dumbfounded by the destruction. Even though her sister-in-law had described it, and Alisa had looked at news photos during her rehabilitation, it hadn't truly been real until now. The bodies had been moved along with the rubble, and for that she was thankful, but it didn't keep her from realizing that hundreds of people had died here. Her neighbors. Her husband.

"Desolate part of town," Beck said, giving her a curious look. Wondering why they had stopped?

"Yeah," was all Alisa said, not wanting to discuss it.

She spotted a warped deck chair lying crumpled at the corner of the lot. It had somehow survived the blast and avoided the bulldozers. A deflated ball was smashed into the earth beside it. A toy that might have belonged to Jelena or any of the other children who had lived here. Alisa remembered playing volleyball on the rooftop court with her daughter, trying to teach her that the ball was supposed to go *over* the net, not be bounced into it so it would rebound and could be hit repeatedly.

Moisture burned her eyes, but she blinked it away. She would not cry with an audience looking on. Besides, Jelena had not been home when this had happened, so she survived. That was something. It was enough. It had to be.

Alisa turned, intending to head to her sister-in-law's apartment, but she bumped into Leonidas. He was gazing at the flattened lots, his jaw tight, irritation in his eyes. He looked down at her, his expression scathing.

"Sorry," she muttered, though she doubted he was angry because she'd run into him.

"You did this," he said, flicking his hand toward the empty lots. "There was no reason to bomb civilian structures."

"I wasn't anywhere near Perun when this happened," Alisa said, stung. Even though she knew he meant the Alliance and not her specifically, it felt like a direct accusation. "I'm sure they were targeting imperial ships. If your people were flying over the city, inviting fire, then that's hardly our fault."

"As if your Alliance ever targeted military ships. They attacked things that weren't defended, bombed what they could, then slunk away in the night."

"There were plenty of all-out-battles with military ships fighting military ships. I know. I was a part of that. War is horrible either way. You think I'm not aware of how shitty a situation this is? This was my *home.*" Her voice cracked on the last word as she flung her hand toward the smashed ball, the warped chair.

"Yet you chose to join the Alliance, knowing you would cause death and destruction." He shook his head and walked away.

Beck shifted his weight, but said nothing. He probably didn't know why Leonidas had blown up. In truth, Alisa didn't, either. Oh, she had roused his anger before over this very topic, but it had taken some poking and prodding. What had he seen in this empty lot? Something similar to what she saw?

She probably should have left him to steam on his own, but she jogged to catch up. A seagull soared overhead, not caring that the harbor was miles away and that fish wasn't likely to be found here.

"Did you lose someone too?" Alisa asked Leonidas. "Is that why you're angry?"

"I'm angry because your war was pointless and made the universe a worse place rather than a better place."

"That's not true. People have freedoms now that they never had under the empire."

"Freedoms don't feed them or keep them safe. You'll see when you've been out in the system more." His tone was more reasonable now, though his shoulders were still tense. He swept his gaze back over the empty lots before they headed down another street, and she had a feeling he was seeing more than the dirt and the cranes. "You'll see," he added softly.

Alisa wanted to refute him, but since the war ended, she hadn't been many places except for Dustor, which hadn't exactly been a paradise even before the fighting began. Her freedom-loving soul appreciated that there were fewer spy boxes floating through the skies here, but she admitted that the boys' talk of hits was alarming. Such a thing never should have happened in a policed city on an advanced planet. Still, she would wait until she had seen more of the system for herself to consider Leonidas's words more fully. He was clearly biased, having *liked* the suffocating imperial system. Of course those who had thrived in it had liked it.

They entered an area where the buildings still stood, an area Alisa had walked through often before on her way to the university and later to her job at DropEx. The streets were quiet, but people still went about their business, and the moving sidewalks worked here.

Nerves returned to her stomach as she stepped onto the one that would take them to her sister-in-law's place. It occurred to her that she hadn't commed ahead to warn Sylvia that she was coming. She had been thinking about the need to do so as they approached the planet, but then they had been attacked, and she'd forgotten. As an artist, Sylvia worked from home, but that was no guarantee that she would be there now. Alisa almost reached for her comm to make the call, but the idea of knocking on the door and surprising her and Jelena made her stay her hand. If Sylvia wasn't home, Alisa would comm and arrange a meeting time.

She stepped off the sidewalk in front of a centuries-old brick building with Old Earth lions roaring down from the edge of the rooftop. A mix of tall windows and roll-up garage doors dotted the front of the structure. A place for an artist. Alisa walked up a set of stone stairs to the door where a comm system waited.

"I have someone to meet," she said, realizing Beck was right behind her, as if he expected to be invited in for tea. "Will you wait here?"

Alisa did not want Jelena to be scared by a man looming in combat armor or another man wearing a cyborg military jacket. At eight, she was probably old enough to recognize an imperial soldier; after living through the war, she might know the significance of the patch too. Not that Leonidas had followed her. He had stopped beside a lamppost, his mouth moving as he talked quietly into his earstar comm.

"Sure," Beck said, giving her a salute.

She pressed the button for her sister-in-law's apartment, one of only ten loft residences in the building. Unlike most of the struggling artists Alisa had run into on campus, Sylvia had always done well for herself with her paintings and sculpture.

A long minute passed, and disappointment grew within her. She should have commed ahead.

Then a distracted, "Yes?" came over the speaker, and a flash of excitement filled her. It had been years, but she recognized that voice.

"Sylvia? It's Alisa."

"Alisa?" Sylvia sounded puzzled.

"Yes, I'm through with my obligations to the army now. I'm here to see Jelena, to take her with me, if that's not a problem." Alisa doubted it would be. Sylvia would have been caring for her for about six months, but she would surely agree with Alisa's right to take her. She might agree less with the idea of her niece being taken off to run freight for the rest of her childhood, especially if she was in a stable environment here. Sylvia wouldn't make a fuss, would she? Alisa dreaded the idea of a legal battle, especially here on Perun, where her position in the war could and would be used against her.

"It's good to see you, Alisa," Sylvia said slowly, and the video display above the buttons came on. A woman of forty, Sylvia had gray mixed in with her dark hair, a lean face, and a smear of yellow paint on her cheekbone. "Did you get my letters?"

She didn't sound that excited to see Alisa. There was wariness in her face that filled Alisa's belly with unease.

"*Letters?*" she asked. "Plural? I got one, just a couple of months ago when I was released from the hospital on Dustor."

"The one about Jonah?"

Alisa nodded.

"But not the one I sent three months ago? About Jelena?"

Alisa's feeling of unease increased to one of dread. "It might not have had time to reach me. What happened?" she asked, her mouth suddenly dry.

Sylvia sighed. "You better come in."

A soft buzz sounded, and the door lock released. Feeling numb, Alisa might not have opened it in time, but Beck grabbed the handle for her. His face was somber behind the faceplate of his armor. She hadn't told him about Jelena, but he was clearly catching the gist of the conversation.

Alisa stumbled over the raised threshold as she entered and had to catch herself on the wall. She found her way through the wide hallway, not seeing the polished wood floors or architectural details now. The door at the end opened, and Sylvia stood there, her face even graver than it had been seconds before.

"What happened?" Alisa repeated, searching her eyes as if the answer was within them, as if she could tear out the information with telepathy instead of waiting for an explanation.

"They came," Sylvia said. "Three months after the war ended, when we all thought we were safe, when we were rebuilding…I was here with her. But they came, and I couldn't stop them. They took her."

CHAPTER FOUR

Sylvia kept gesturing to chairs, but Alisa couldn't sit.

"What do you mean they took her?" she asked. "*Who* took her? The empire?"

Why would the empire want her daughter? Wasn't it enough that she had lost her husband? There was nothing special about her family, no dynasty or money for anyone to inherit. It didn't make sense.

"Men in black robes. There were four of them." Sylvia perched on the edge of the sofa. "I tried to stop them, but they easily got past me. One waved his hand and made it seem…I don't know. For a few minutes there, while they were invading my home, I thought it wasn't such a bad thing. I'm sure this wasn't my own thought."

"Not your own thought?" Alisa gaped at her, her mind refusing to put together the puzzle pieces, even though the robe alone would have suggested the identities of the kidnappers.

"I believe they were Starseers." Sylvia reached for a computer console built into the coffee table, the modern black interface looking strange set into the solid wood, the legs artistically turned, the surface elegantly engraved. "I can show you the video from the hallway. I got security to give it to me. I was trying to catch faces, to try and get enough to identify them."

Alisa rubbed the back of her neck, but nodded. She wanted to see for herself, to try and understand. Maybe it had simply been people dressed up as Starseers. They could have counted on Sylvia being too daunted by their presumed identity to chase after them. After all, she was alone. But now that Alisa was back, it would be a different story. She *would* chase them. But if this had happened three months ago, where could she start? Tears threatened for the second time that afternoon, but they were tears of tension and frustration this time, not of sorrow.

"Here it is," Sylvia said, and a video of the hallway near the front door began to play above the table. "I've shown the police. They put out a missing person report, and *I* added a reward to it for her safe return."

"Thank you," Alisa made herself mutter, though gratitude wasn't the emotion at the surface of her mind. She wanted to blame Sylvia for allowing this to happen. How could she have let strangers in to steal her little girl?

Alisa managed to keep the accusations from tumbling from her lips. Sylvia had been kind enough to take Jelena in; to throw that in her face would be unacceptable. No matter how much Alisa wanted to lash out at someone. She found herself wishing Leonidas had come in, if only so she could pick a fight with him and let out her anger.

"Unfortunately, they haven't had any leads other than the name I gave them along with the video," Sylvia said as the footage played. At first, the hallway stood empty, with nothing but four apartment doors and the front door visible, with the darkness of night pressing against a tall window next to it. "I heard some of them refer to the one who appeared to be the leader as Durant—I'm not sure if it was a first or last name. Durant. It's not common, but it's not uncommon, either. I checked the imperial and Alliance databases. There are tens of thousands of them out there. I've called the police every few days, but if the Starseers truly took Jelena, they have the power to disappear well and fully."

"That doesn't make any sense at all," Alisa said. "There are hardly any Starseers left in the galaxy, and there's nothing about Jelena that would make them want her."

Sure, her daughter had scored well on intelligence tests, thanks more to her bright father than her mother, Alisa was sure, but she had not been an exceptional genius. It wasn't as if she had been floating dishes around the kitchen or whatever it was Starseer children did before they formally started studying to control their powers.

At least, that was what Alisa thought. The strangest look came over Sylvia's face, and she opened her mouth and closed it twice without saying anything.

Before Alisa could question her, movement in the video caught her eye, and she shifted her attention to it. The front door had opened and four figures in black robes filed in, one after the other. Large heavy hoods drooped low, creating shadows that hid their features, even in the well-lit hallway. Alisa leaned down, peering in close, hoping to glimpse a face. Even if one only appeared for an instant, it ought to be enough to run it through the police databases and hope for a match. But the men either knew about the cameras or just knew that they had to keep their hoods low to remain hidden. They walked slowly, their faces turned downward, their hands in their sleeves, not revealing so much as a wedding ring that might be used for identification. All four of them wore pendants that reminded Alisa of Alejandro's, but his was the three-sun symbol of the Sun Trinity. These were the red moon and silver star symbol of The Order, the special Starseer religion about which she knew very little.

The figures disappeared from the lobby camera's field of view. Sylvia's door was at the opposite end of the hall from the front entrance, and it wasn't visible. Alisa shifted from foot to foot, waiting for them to come back into view. It only took a minute. The leader walked back toward the front door, a familiar girl with him. Her rowdy hair was tamed into two brown pigtails, there was a mole on the side of her face below her ear, and she had a cute, pert nose. Jelena.

She was older and taller than the last time Alisa had seen her, but there was no mistaking her. And there was no mistaking that she was walking side by side with the man as he held her hand and led her to the door, almost as if she knew him. How could that be?

Two more robed figures walked into view, heading for the entrance, but the last one stopped, turning back toward the apartment. Sylvia charged into view, pushed past him, and ran toward Jelena. The camera had not recorded sound, but from the contorted way Sylvia's mouth opened, it was clear that she was yelling. Jelena paused and turned, wearing an oddly vacant expression. Her young face crinkled as Sylvia yelled, as if she was trying to remember something. The man tugged at her hand, but she turned in the other direction, almost tripping as she stepped back toward Sylvia, who had almost reached her.

The figure behind the man leading Jelena away lifted a hand toward Sylvia. Alisa thought he would halt her physically, but Sylvia jerked to a stop before she reached him. She froze like a ship caught in a grab beam.

The man leading Jelena touched her shoulder, and she turned around to follow him out the door, but not before Alisa saw that vacant expression reaffix itself on her face. It was chilling, all trace of her daughter's playful spirit—all trace of her personality and who she was—gone.

As the men filed through the exit, Sylvia remained frozen in place. The door closed, the hallway empty except for her.

"Not my finest moment," Sylvia murmured from the sofa, wincing as long seconds passed.

Finally, the Sylvia in the video stirred. She looked behind her and forward, confusion stamping her face. Then she ran to the entrance, disappearing out the front door.

On the sofa, Sylvia leaned forward and stopped the video, leaving the image hovering above the table. "I ran up and down the block after that, looking for sign of them," she said. "They just disappeared. I asked the neighbors if anyone had seen them. There were people on the street coming home from work. Nobody remembered seeing them or Jelena." She swallowed and met Alisa's eyes. "Alisa, I'm so sorry."

"I don't understand," Alisa said, losing her earlier certainty that posers pretending to be Starseers had kidnapped her daughter. "You'd never seen them before? There was no previous contact?"

"Not with me, no."

Alisa frowned. "What does that mean? I'm sure *Jelena* didn't comm them to come get her."

"No, I doubt that." Sylvia's brow crinkled, as if she hadn't considered the possibility but now was. That was ludicrous. How would an eight-year-old know who to comm even if she was unhappy and wanted to leave? *Had* she been unhappy? With her father dead and her mother billions of miles away?

Alisa opened her mouth to ask, but Sylvia spoke again first.

"I was thinking that Jonah might have had some contact with one of their temples before his death."

"Why?" Alisa rubbed her head. "She wasn't…" It seemed a ridiculous thing to ask, but she made herself say, "She wasn't showing any Starseer tendencies, was she?"

She didn't see how that could be when everyone knew those abilities were hereditary, something that the colonists who had originally settled Kir had developed during the centuries they had lived there in isolation. These days, with Kir long since rendered uninhabitable during the Order Wars, fewer and fewer Starseers were born each generation, and not everyone with the genes inherited the abilities. Alisa certainly couldn't move objects around with her mind—or daze and kidnap defenseless children. Nor had Jonah ever done anything like that, at least not when she had been observing. Besides, children born on the core worlds in imperial hospitals were tested at birth for the gene mutations that signaled the potential to gain those abilities. Nothing unusual had come up on Jelena's tests.

"She is about the age when those things start to come out," Sylvia said carefully. "I know Jonah was always careful to keep his talents a secret, but I'm surprised…He never told you?"

Suddenly, the apartment seemed very still, very quiet. Alisa grew aware of a mechanical clock ticking in a distant corner of the loft.

"No," she whispered.

"I never manifested the abilities. As you can clearly see." Sylvia grimaced as she waved to the frozen video. "But Jonah used to play with his talents on the farm as a boy. We were lucky we were in such a rural area and that he wasn't born in an imperial hospital."

"But Jelena was born here, tested here…" Alisa spoke slowly, trying to wrap her mind around the idea that Jonah had kept secrets from her. *Big* secrets. He had been so open, always laughing, always friendly. Surely, those were not the traits of a member of a sinister and secretive order.

A teakettle whistled in the kitchen. Sylvia got up, held up a finger, and walked to attend to it. Alisa wanted to leap on her back and strangle the answers out of her. An interminable amount of time seemed to pass before she returned with two cups in her hand. She offered one to Alisa, who only shook her head. She wanted answers, not tea. Jelena *had* been tested. She remembered the doctors doing a cheek swab.

Sylvia sat back down and sipped from her own cup. "A few days before you went to the hospital to deliver her, Jonah came to me. As a scholar, he didn't have much money then. As I'm sure you remember."

Alisa nodded tersely, barely keeping from growling a, *Get to the point.*

"He asked to borrow some from me. He was nervous and wanted physical coins, nothing traceable by the banking system. I had an inkling as to what it was about, though he wouldn't speak of it or say who it was meant for."

"You gave him the loan?"

"Yes. I suspect he was paying someone off at the hospital, either arranging for those tests to disappear or perhaps for there to be a mix-up. Another baby would have been retested if she came up positive." Sylvia lifted her shoulders. "Jonah wouldn't have done anything to harm anyone, but you understand the dangers, the chance that he—both of you—would have lost your daughter if she had tested positive. Even though there were Starseers in the imperial line, the government has always been fearful of those with the powers."

"With good reason," Alisa blurted out before realizing that she wasn't just talking to her sister-in-law anymore, but with someone whose ancestors had apparently come from Kir. It was as if the woman she and Jonah had shared coffee with on a weekly basis was a stranger now. "I mean, I wouldn't have wanted to risk our daughter being taken away, either. Is that what always happens? Happened?" She reminded herself that the empire wasn't in charge anymore, and she had no idea what kind of policy her own people were establishing.

"The children were often taken away to special orphanages, yes. If the parents weren't aware of the risk beforehand and didn't find a way to hide them. Sometimes the parents had no idea. In our case, several generations had passed since anyone in the family had shown any talents. From my limited understanding of the science, the genes are dominant, so they're passed on easily, but the Starseer abilities themselves rely upon epigenetic triggers to manifest, and despite much speculation and a couple of studies involving those in the imperial bloodline, nobody's quite sure what exactly those triggers are. Stress is believed to be a component, a major stressor undergone at the appropriate age."

"Such as the stress of having your home bombed and your father killed?" Alisa asked bleakly.

"Perhaps. I remember Jonah first displayed talent after recovering from a bout with pneumonia. But there's much that even modern science does not know. The Starseers themselves are very secretive, and few outside of the imperial bloodline have come forth over the centuries to volunteer themselves for studies."

"What did the empire do with those it took and sent to orphanages?"

"From what I've heard, they wanted to use those with Starseer potential to their own advantage and raised them with the idea of indoctrinating them to be loyal subjects, but since so many children never developed abilities, the empire most likely ended up with a bunch of normal children who grew up bitter that they had been taken from their parents." Sylvia lowered her voice. "Some speculate that they just got rid of the babies." Her grip tightened on the teacup. "Jonah didn't want to risk that."

"No. Hells, no. I understand that, but why didn't he ever tell me?"

Sylvia smiled slightly. "You used to tease him for being overly bookish when you two first met."

"I tease everybody. Myself included. It's part of my charm."

Sylvia snorted. "Indeed. But Jonah was sensitive. We studious, artistic types often are." She waved her hand toward an easel set up in the corner. Alisa had been too distracted to look at what she was working on and did not notice now, either.

"So?"

"You already thought him a tad odd, and he had a huge crush on you as soon as you sat together in Professor Lingenbottom's class. He worried that if you found out about his heritage, you would think him tainted. Besides, our family has been here, growing wheat and corn out in the hinterlands for generations. It's not as if anyone remembers that we originally came to Perun as refugees from Kir after the Order Wars. Also, Jonah had very little interest in learning about his heritage. I still remember when we were children and a Starseer came to visit after Jonah first started demonstrating his powers. I'm not sure what the gist of the private conversation they had was, but Jonah ran screaming out to the corncrib and wouldn't climb down until the man left."

"The Starseers don't have reputations for benevolence and kindness." Alisa shuddered, horrified to know her daughter had been taken by them. They operated off the grid, hiding from the empire and everyone else most of the time. Even if a face *had* shown up on that video, it probably wouldn't have been in the Perun police database. How could Alisa ever find the people who had taken Jelena if they didn't want to be found? The name Durant wasn't much to go on.

"No, our first contact with them, after centuries of isolation, was when they regained spaceflight, left their planet, and tried to take over the rest of the system," Sylvia said dryly.

"What do you think they want with Jelena?"

"I would guess to raise her as one of their own."

Alisa slapped her palms against her thighs, then stalked around the room, distress and horror giving way to fury. "Well, they don't get to," she said. "Presumptuous bastards. She's my daughter, and *I'm* going to raise her. I already gave up too much for the Alliance, four years of my life and hers. They promised it would only be for a year, Sylvia. And it was four. *Four.* If I hadn't been gone so long, this never would have happened. Jonah—"

"Would probably still be dead," Sylvia said with a sad sigh. "And if you had been in the apartment when the bomb went off, you would be dead too."

Alisa pushed her hands through her hair, almost tearing off a chunk. "Logically, I know that, but I can't help but wonder if—fear—I did the wrong thing, made the wrong choice. The Alliance would have won without me. I shot down a few ships, flew some people around, but that's it."

Sylvia spread her hand, palm up. She wasn't going to deny Alisa's self-recriminations. Maybe she agreed with them.

Alisa's comm beeped. She ignored it and stalked over to the window, scowling out at the building behind this one, the hint of blue sky visible above it. Earlier, she had been admiring that blue sky, but now, its cheery brightness seemed to mock her. Stormy gray clouds would have been better. She felt so lost. Where could she start looking for her daughter? Was Jelena even on the *planet*? Three months had passed, and Alisa had no leads. Nothing.

The comm beeped again.

Alisa snatched it off her belt clip and roared, "*What?*"

"Uhh, got a problem, Captain," Beck said.

"If you have to take a piss, just come inside and do it."

"No…the combat armor takes care of that."

"Ew." She scowled at her unit, still irritated. She forced herself to take a deep breath. "What's the problem?"

"Someone's spying on us."

"Are you and Leonidas looking suspicious and intriguing?"

"I'm definitely not. The mech…he always looks suspicious. He's been chatting up old girlfriends since you left."

Alisa blinked, the image so startling that she forgot about her own problems momentarily. "Really?"

"Nah, I don't think so. I did hear a woman's voice come from his earstar, but not much more than that. He's been whispering and keeping his back to me. I caught him agreeing to meet someone at a certain time, but that's it."

"Who's doing the spying?" Alisa asked.

"One of the kids from the field."

"I was imagining mafia thugs."

"Don't underestimate kids, Captain. They make good lookouts since nobody pays attention to them. They work cheaply too."

"It's probably just the one that was intrigued by your armor. Maybe he wanted to look more closely."

"I had that thought," Beck said, "but *I'm* not the one the kid was staring at."

"Leonidas?"

"Leonidas. I'm not sure if he ever saw his spy—or if he's paying attention to me now. The kid was quick and stayed out of sight, but I glimpsed him looking at the mech and comming somebody. I think he might have taken a picture too. If I hadn't been wearing my helmet with the built-in cameras, I wouldn't have spotted him behind me."

"It must not have been the boy who knew your specs so well."

"It wasn't. It was one of the older ones. I turned around to look, and he darted out of sight. I ran back to the alley I think he went into, but he had disappeared. I'm sure he knows this neighborhood a lot better than I do."

Alisa grumbled under her breath. She didn't particularly care if people were spying on Leonidas, not now. But she didn't know what else could be gained by staying here, either. She had already learned far more than she expected. More than she wanted. The idea of her sweet Jelena having Starseer powers was creepy, but it probably made it more important than ever that she was raised by someone who loved her, someone who cared.

"Me, damn it," she muttered.

"Pardon?" Beck asked.

"Nothing. I'm coming out." Alisa turned to Sylvia. "I need to go."

Sylvia rose to her feet. "Can I do anything to help?"

"Not now." Alisa didn't even know what could be done yet. She closed the comm channel and lowered the device. "Before I go…I've wondered. Can you tell me, is there any possible way that everyone was mistaken and that Jonah wasn't home when the apartment building was bombed?" The idea of searching for her daughter alone daunted her. By all the gods in all the galaxies, she wished Jonah were alive to help her. More than that, she wished he were alive, period. "Is there any way he might have made it?"

Sylvia was shaking her head before Alisa finished. "No. I was called in when they scanned the remains." She turned toward a window, blinking a few times as her eyes grew damp. "I saw them, watched them do the test, and verified that the genes matched up. He's gone."

Alisa's legs grew weak, and she groped for the back of the sofa for support. She had not expected anything else, and yet, a silly part of her had hoped that she would not only find Jelena when she arrived on Perun, but that somehow, Jonah would be there, too, that it all would have been a mistake.

She brushed the back of her hand across her eyes. This was as much Sylvia's pain as hers, and she managed to utter a soft, "I'm sorry."

"So am I." Sylvia came around the sofa and hugged her.

Alisa had never been that comforted by human contact, but she returned the hug.

"Do you need any money?" Sylvia asked. "A lot of the banks crashed in the last months of the war, and nobody has much—we've been clinging to physical assets and coin. You've probably noticed the imperial morat tanked and is barely worth anything in the rest of the system."

LINDSAY BUROKER

"I'm fine," Alisa said, even if she wasn't, not in any sense of the word. But she didn't want to take money from her sister-in-law, especially if she was struggling too. Money seemed so unimportant now, anyway. She stepped back, wiped her eyes again, and forced a smile. "Thank you."

With her legs feeling numb, she walked back out to the front of the building.

As Beck had implied, Leonidas was on the comm, but they weren't separated. They were both by the lamppost now, their heads tilted together. Leonidas had taken off his earstar and held it so they could both listen.

"What is it?" Alisa asked when the men turned in her direction, Leonidas reaffixing the earstar.

"Dr. Dominguez needs my help," Leonidas said. "He's run into trouble at the library. Someone is stalking him."

"Someone more ominous than a twelve-year-old boy?" Alisa glanced at Beck.

"Apparently."

"Are you going to help?" She remembered that Leonidas had asked Alejandro for help, something related to studying cybernetic implants and performing a surgery on him. Alejandro had refused, saying that he did not have the necessary knowledge, though it had sounded as if he did not *want* the knowledge. She did not bring this up, since she'd been eavesdropping and was not supposed to have heard the conversation.

"Yes," Leonidas said without hesitating. He gave her an assessing look that she wasn't sure how to read. "Come with me." He waved for her to follow and started back toward the train station.

"Uh, I don't respond well to commands," she said, making him pause. "Unless that was your way of asking me out on a date. But if that was your intent, I would expect flowers and chocolate. Definitely chocolate." Three suns, she could use some chocolate about now. "Oh, and perhaps use a more diffident tone."

Beck smirked. Leonidas simply looked exasperated.

"You'll be safer with me if Beck's spy turns into something more dangerous," Leonidas said, wriggling his fingers again, an order to follow.

50

"*My* spy?" Beck protested. "That kid was snapping pictures of you, buddy. And I can take care of the captain just fine. We've got chicken feed to buy."

Leonidas's eyes closed to slits. "You will not come to assist Dr. Dominguez?"

"What do you think we can do that you can't, mech?"

Alisa agreed with the sentiment—all she had was her old Etcher in her holster, and her fighting skills were meager without the cockpit of a combat ship around her. But Leonidas's question made her wince, feeling guilty. Even though Alejandro and his orb weren't on her radar now, as far as problems went, he *had* patched her up after they escaped the pirate ship, and she felt a degree of debt toward him for that. His solicitude was one of the reasons she hadn't seriously contemplated sending word about him and his orb off to Alliance headquarters.

"Stay then," Leonidas said coolly and resumed walking.

"We better help," Alisa said with a sigh. "Though you're probably right in that there's not much *we* can do that he can't. Especially me." She rapped a knuckle on Beck's armored shoulder and started after Leonidas.

"After a few good jobs, when you're flush with cash, you can get some combat armor, too, Captain."

"I suppose being able to pee wherever you're standing would be useful."

Beck snorted. "That's really only for emergencies."

"Like when you're in battle and get so scared that you lose control of bodily functions?"

"Basically. Or when an overly muscled mech stalks up to you, disarms you, and breaks your favorite gun."

"You weren't in your armor then."

"No, but I wished I was. You get what you needed in that building?" Beck pointed his thumb over his shoulder as they followed Leonidas away from Sylvia's apartment.

Alisa's humor drained away. "No."

"Maybe you'll find what you need at the library."

It was possible. Assuming that whatever was vexing Alejandro didn't turn out to be that serious, she could make time for some research there.

Alisa doubted any imperial subjects could help her locate the men who had taken her daughter, so there was little use in talking to the authorities here—as Sylvia had already found. From everything that Alisa had heard, the Starseers operated outside of governments, answered to nobody, and had ties to few who weren't in the Order. That meant she would have to find a Starseer to get information on Starseers. There had to be at least a few here on Perun. Maybe the library would have data about a monastery or group residence or whatever they called their homes.

"Maybe I will," she replied, nodding to herself.

Of course, even if she found a Starseer, there was no guarantee the person would talk to her, and it wasn't as if she could coerce someone with prodigious mental powers into answering her questions. Maybe Leonidas could. After all, the imperial army had originally created their cyborg soldiers as an answer to the Starseer warriors, pitting physicality, endurance, and the ability to take a lot of damage against the mental powers of the Order.

"Beck, next time you hear me making sarcastic comments to Leonidas, stop me, will you?" She should dull the edge on her sharp tongue if she wanted his help. Of course, that might be moot until she actually located a Starseer. Still, she probably shouldn't be so sarcastic with him. He had a knack for making her feel silly and immature about her comments.

"Stop you? I'm usually cheering for you. When that bastard orders you around, you should definitely tell him to balls off." Beck quirked his eyebrows at her. "Or to bring you chocolate."

"Chocolate *is* the way to my heart. And also to my compliance. Especially the good dark stuff. None of that wimpy cow or jakloff milk diluting the flavor."

"Well, I'm not telling *him* that. Nobody wants you complying with the mech, Captain."

"I'll keep that in mind."

CHAPTER FIVE

To Alisa's surprise, nobody rushed out to stop Beck from walking onto the open tree-filled campus of Morgan Firth University in full combat armor. Students in sandals and sarongs, strolling from class to class and enjoying the warm day, did give their group strange looks. Most of them veered away. A few glimpsed Leonidas's jacket and veered *far* away. The reactions here—and of those boys in her old neighborhood—surprised Alisa. Even though she supposed she'd never wanted anything to do with cyborgs, even before the war started and they officially turned into enemies, she had not considered that the imperial subjects—Leonidas's own people—would ostracize him.

Their luck ran out at the Staton Hall Library, its two intertwining towers spiraling up to great heights from the rounded base of the main building. As they walked up the wide marble stairs leading to the open double doors, an armed man in the blues of campus security stepped onto the center of the landing to block their way.

"No weapons allowed in the library," he said, frowning at all of them and especially Beck, as he tapped a perky teal earstar hooked over his ear. Opening a comm? Or starting a video recording? "Or on campus at *all.*"

"We're here to assist a colleague who's in trouble inside," Leonidas said.

"What kind of trouble could someone be in in the library?" the security guard asked. "They don't shoot you if you don't pay your late fees."

"Unknown, but he was adamant." Leonidas walked toward the door, making it clear he would go around the guard.

Beck followed, but the guard pulled out a stun gun and leveled it at his chest. "Stop or I *will* call for police robots."

The stunner probably wouldn't have affected Beck through his armor, especially since he still wore his helmet, but he did stop, looking to Alisa for orders.

"You are an alarming figure in all that armor," she told him. "Why don't you wait out here and chat up the security officer until we're done?"

Beck scowled fiercely.

Leonidas, perhaps noticing that the guard was more focused on Beck, continued toward the open doors.

"Wait," the man blurted. "Are you armed?"

He glanced toward the hip where Leonidas kept his destroyer and toward a similar spot on Alisa. She was about to ask if she could turn her weapon in to the front desk person to hold, but Leonidas glared at the guard and said, "Yes."

"Then you can't—"

Leonidas turned his back on him and strode inside. The guard's stunner twitched, but he opted to keep it aimed at Beck's chest. An alarm at the door beeped with indignation as Leonidas passed through. Whether it was reading his gun or all of his cybernetic parts, Alisa didn't know.

"I'm with him," she said and walked after Leonidas, giving Beck a wait-here signal, and hoped the guard would not stun her, either.

"I'm calling headquarters," the guard growled and turned toward Alisa, his stunner leaving Beck's chest.

She was watching over her shoulder and tensed, expecting to have to dive to the side if she didn't want to be hit. But Beck's hand darted out, and he caught the man's wrist. With the servo-enhanced strength of the armor, the guard did not have a chance of escaping that grip.

"That's not necessary," Beck said, nodding after Alisa. "Why don't we chat about it?"

Alisa worried that the campus police truck would be waiting for them when she and Leonidas came out of the library, but she hustled to catch up with him, hoping they would have time to find Alejandro and also hoping that she could do her research. Maybe security would be more likely to remember and hunt down the men, and she could slip unnoticed into the stacks.

Leonidas paused on the sprawling marble tile floor of the grand foyer and tapped his earstar, murmuring something. A few students using the physical materials check-out stations glanced at him, but unless one noticed his military jacket and Corps patch, he was not as strange of a sight as Beck in his armor.

"Which floor?" Leonidas was asking as Alisa joined him.

She glanced back toward the entrance. She had set off the door alarm, too, and doubted it was a good idea to linger so close.

"Basement Three," came a hushed whisper that she could barely hear. "Two of them are blocking the door, so I can't get back to the elevator. There are at least two more looking for me in here."

"On my way."

Leonidas did not immediately start walking, so Alisa assumed he had not been here before and needed to call up a map.

Glad to be semi-useful, she said, "This way," and headed around the corner to where the closest elevators waited.

Several students were already waiting. When the chime dinged and the doors opened, Leonidas glared at them and strode inside. A couple of boys started after him, but he hardened his glare and flexed his muscles to make his looming stance even more intimidating than usual.

"We'll get the next one," one of the boys said, both of them scurrying back.

Leonidas looked at Alisa and pointed at the floor next to him.

She walked inside, but to be contrary, she stood on the opposite side of him from where he had pointed. Silent rebellion. He hit the button for the appropriate basement level and drew his destroyer.

Alisa eyed the big handgun, imagining the charges that would be brought against them if they shot up the library, not to mention leaving bodies on the carpet. "You think that will be necessary?"

She expected him to glare and tell her to leave the combat to him, but he looked down at the weapon and seemed to reconsider. He holstered it.

"Perhaps not. I don't know who exactly is targeting the doctor." As the elevator neared the basement level, he added, "Stay behind me."

"Yes, *sir*," she said, giving him a perky and completely insincere salute.

He glared at her. "Did the Alliance *truly* promote you to captain?"

"War makes for desperate times."

He grunted. "I see."

Leonidas stood to the side of the elevator doors as they dinged and opened, waving for her to stand against the wall behind him. She did so. She might be insouciant, but she wasn't willfully stupid. Or at least, she tried not to be willfully stupid.

The lights were out. They shouldn't have been. There were lots of archives in the basement, and the rooms weren't as populated as the upper levels of the library, but Alisa had retrieved materials down here as a student and remembered lights.

After looking and listening for a few seconds, Leonidas eased out of the elevator. Alisa did not hear a thing, but he burst into motion and disappeared from her view. She rested her hand on her Etcher and held the door open, but did not step out. The area around the elevator lay open for several meters in all directions before the rows of desks and towering bookcases started up. She didn't want to be exposed, especially when all she could glimpse were shadows and the vague outlines of the furniture. Dots of red emergency lighting lined a walkway on the floor, but nothing brighter came on.

Thumps, grunts, and a short broken cry of pain came from her right. The noises did not last for more than three seconds, and then it grew utterly quiet again.

Trusting that Leonidas had been the one inflicting the damage rather than the one receiving it, Alisa eased out of the elevator. He stood in the shadows to the side, two unmoving men in unremarkable clothing lying at his feet. Alisa assumed they were not dead, but she didn't ask, not positive she wanted to know the answer.

The doors closed behind Alisa, the elevator being called up to another level. She found the basement room unsettling without the lights on, but told herself Leonidas could handle any trouble they came upon. She joined him, stepping over someone's legs to do so. It was too dark to see much of the man's face, but she doubted she would recognize him even if she pulled out the flashlight on her multitool.

After listening intently for a few seconds, Leonidas waved two fingers at her, gesturing for her to follow. This time, she didn't salute him or make any snarky comments about his propensity for taking command and giving orders. She doubted they were alone down here, so she stayed quiet.

He followed the wall away from the elevators, around a corner, and past dark aisles of old books, the air having a musty and dusty smell, even though Alisa knew that robotic cleaners kept all of the library's floors tidy. One couldn't tidy up age. She had been told that some of the original books brought from Earth on the first colony ships were in Staton Hall, preserved and protected throughout the centuries. She was glad her people hadn't bombed *this* building.

Something stirred down one of the dark aisles they passed, and Alisa jumped, reaching for her Etcher. Leonidas caught her wrist before she could draw it, his calloused hand rough against her skin, though his grip was not tight. He held up his other hand to his lips.

A soft beeping came from down the aisle, and two beady red lights swiveled into view a foot off the floor. Alisa let go of the hilt of her gun. It was one of the floor cleaning robots she had just been thinking about—she would have felt like an idiot for shooting it.

A thud came from deeper within the library, like a book falling to the floor.

Leonidas released Alisa and veered down the next aisle, heading in the direction of that noise. Alisa followed more slowly, careful to tread softly. As large as Leonidas was, he was good at running without letting his combat boots make a sound.

He turned at an intersection created by rows of bookcases, and Alisa lost sight of him. Though she didn't want to make noise, she picked up her pace, having no doubt there were things more inimical than floor-polishing robots down here.

More thuds sounded, then something akin to a crash.

"Got you," a man with a deep voice blurted.

Another crash came from the back of the room, and someone gasped in pain. Alisa hurried, trying to pick her way through the aisles toward the source. That had sounded like Alejandro.

She turned down an aisle, no longer trying to follow Leonidas since she did not know where he'd gone, and flashlight beams came into view, streaking about, cutting through the darkness. Someone was standing at the end of the aisle she had picked, his broad back silhouetted against the lights in front of him. Whoever he was, he wasn't wearing a robe or a military jacket, and the way he crouched back from the mouth of the aisle made him look like a spy, or someone skulking and preparing a surprise attack. Alisa hesitated, not sure whether to backtrack and go down another aisle, or to rush forward and try to surprise *him*.

More thumps came from somewhere ahead of the man. Alisa could see something in his hand, but she wasn't sure what it was. A weapon? Maybe a flashlight that wasn't turned on? He switched it from his right hand to his left so he could reach for something at his belt. A blazer pistol.

Alisa crept forward as quickly and quietly as she could. The man slid his weapon out of his holster, lifting it to aim at someone.

She gave up on silence and sprinted the last five meters, tugging out her Etcher as she ran. As the man stepped forward, about to fire, Alisa clubbed him in the back of the head with the hilt of her weapon. Unfortunately, he did not conveniently crumple into an unconscious pile.

He grunted and whirled toward her, his blazer still in his hand. She knocked his arm aside before he could aim it at her, then lashed out with a straight kick. The toe of her boot cracked him in the knee hard enough that it buckled. He snarled and tried to grab her as he went down, but she leaped back, adrenaline giving her speed she had rarely claimed in the army unarmed combat practices. As soon as her feet touched down, she launched another kick, this one taking him in the chin. His head snapped back, and he pitched to the floor. This time, he did not move again.

A second dark figure loomed into view at the end of the aisle. Alisa started to bring her Etcher up again, leaping back to give herself more room to fire.

"It's me," Leonidas said, crouching to spring away in case she shot.

Alisa lowered her gun and took a deep breath, trying to calm herself in the aftermath of the skirmish. Funny how she could maintain her cool easily while weaving among enemies and fighting for her life in the cockpit of a combat ship, but turn into a nervous mess during a flesh-on-flesh fight.

"Thanks for taking care of him," Leonidas said, waving toward the unconscious man.

HONOR'S FLIGHT

"It seemed like the thing to do." Alisa crept past her victim, not wanting to be anywhere nearby when he woke up.

Leonidas removed the fallen man's gun and searched him before following her out into a wider aisle that bisected the rows of bookcases. Alejandro leaned against a table nearby, his graying hair damp with sweat. Someone's earstar rested on the table next to him, the tiny embedded light shining brightly enough to reveal a contusion on the side of his face and a swollen lip. Six men lay sprawled on the floor between Alejandro and Alisa. She allowed herself to think that Leonidas had needed her help and might have been shot if not for her distracting the seventh man, but she doubted that was true.

Alejandro pushed away from the table, looking shaky. Alisa couldn't blame him. He had proven himself an able doctor when helping her and many others after the pirate ship incident, but he was no warrior. He seemed like someone who had gone through his whole life without anyone throwing a punch at him—or drawing a weapon on him. Until recently.

He stepped over two fallen men, one still groaning and clutching his belly, and stopped at a third. The downed figure wore a familiar satchel slung over his shoulder, Alejandro's satchel. Alejandro did not hesitate to pry it off and return it to his own shoulder after peeking inside.

"A lot of people are interested in that orb," Alisa observed.

"Yes." His lips flattened into a line. "I'm not sure how so many have learned about its existence and that I have it." He looked at her, his eyes closing to slits, his lips still pressed together in irritation.

"*I* didn't tell anyone," Alisa said, reading an accusation in that gaze. It was true that she had considered sending a message to someone in the Alliance government, but she hadn't. Not yet.

Alejandro continued to hold her gaze, not breaking it until Leonidas finished removing the fallen men's weapons and joined them.

He held out a blazer. "Doctor?"

"No, thank you." Alejandro lifted a hand, refusing it. "I wouldn't know how to shoot it even if I could stomach the idea of firing at people."

Leonidas opened his mouth, but a soft ding sounded in the distance, and he did not speak, instead holding up a hand and cocking an ear toward the noise. Alisa was fairly certain that had been the sound of the

59

elevator arriving. Had one of Alejandro's assailants escaped and called down reinforcements?

She did not hear anything else, but Leonidas's expression grew grimmer. He pointed at the flashlights. Alisa did not know what he wanted at first, but when he started turning them off, she got the gist. She called up the holo-display on the earstar on the table, intending to turn off its beam. It asked for a passcode. She dropped it on the floor and ground it under the heel of her boot. The light went out.

Leonidas frowned at her, or perhaps the noise she had made.

"Just giving it my passcode," she whispered.

Alejandro flicked off the last flashlight, and darkness returned to the area.

A touch came at her shoulder. Leonidas. He took her arm, linked it to Alejandro's, then led both of them toward the back wall of the library, far from the elevators.

Alisa had not heard anything since the ding, nothing to suggest that someone had come onto the floor instead of leaving, but she had learned to trust Leonidas's superior hearing, so she was confident that he had detected something ominous. She was, however, surprised that he did not tell them to wait there and go confront whoever it was. Her own meager martial contributions notwithstanding, he could clearly handle whoever these thugs were.

Yet he led them deeper into the library, through two more aisles of bookcases and to the back wall. The tiny red emergency lights lined the floor along a perimeter walkway, and Alisa could see him when he stopped to look both ways. He pointed toward a door lit with an exit sign that glowed a soft green in the darkness.

Alejandro walked that way without objecting, his hand clutched possessively over his satchel. Leonidas paused before following, tugging a small device out of his pocket. He tapped a couple of buttons, twisted something, then tossed it into the air. The tiny device flew off of its own accord. An aerial camera?

Alisa started to ask what he was doing, but he pressed a finger to his lips before she could speak. The presumptuousness would have irked her, but his face was grave in the faint red light illuminating it from below. He touched his ear and pointed again toward the door.

Silently, Alisa crept after Alejandro. He opened the door, and it creaked faintly. Alisa glanced over her shoulder, wondering if that had been too much noise. Who did Leonidas think was following them?

He shook his head grimly and waved for her to go through. The landing outside was just as dark as the library. Leonidas followed them out, closing the door softly behind them.

"We have a problem," Alejandro whispered, turning his flashlight on.

"Silence," Leonidas breathed. "He'll hear."

"Who?" Alisa mouthed.

His back to Leonidas, Alejandro directed his flashlight upward. This was an emergency exit, and there should have been stairs leading back up to the above-ground levels, but they were missing. A sign strung across the empty space read: *Please use the west exit. East exit basement levels 0-2 closed for repairs.* They were *very* closed. The doors were there, higher up in the dark well, but the metal stairs and landings had been removed for several levels. Alejandro's flashlight beam bounced off the bottom of the landing three floors above. Thanks to the library's high ceilings, it had to be close to forty feet. The stairs leading *downward* were intact, but Alisa had little interest in traveling deeper into the bowels of the library. Unfortunately, she doubted they could reach the west exit right now.

A holodisplay popped into the air at her shoulder, surprising her. Leonidas had his netdisc out, and it was projecting the view of a moving camera displaying the room they had left. Familiar dark aisles swept past, the view from above the bookcases. Alisa would not have guessed that Leonidas had spy equipment with him. Maybe he had intended to use it with whoever he had been making plans to meet later.

The camera slowed down as it neared people, a group moving away from the elevator, following one of the red-lit walkways. There was just enough illumination to make out military uniforms, not the plain black of the imperial army, but black highlighted with crimson. Alisa sucked in a breath. She hadn't seen those uniforms often during her time in the military, but she knew them well. They belonged to—or had belonged to—the emperor, specifically, his imperial guard, bodyguards as well as a battalion of soldiers that worked closely with him, doing his work. Their reputation wasn't quite as forbidding as that of the Cyborg Corps, but they were known to be very good at their jobs. These men all carried assault rifles on their backs and blazers in belt holsters. Apparently, the security guard hadn't had any success keeping them out of the library, either.

A single man not in a uniform walked beside the group, his neck thick and muscular, his dark hair cut short. Though most of his clothing was plain, he wore a jacket similar to the one Leonidas always had on. Alisa could not make out what the patches were, but his look alone was enough to make her whisper, "Cyborg?"

He nodded once.

"Someone you know?"

The cyborg in the video halted, raising a hand to stop the soldiers. He tilted his head, as if he had heard something. Them? Could he hear her whispers even across the library and through the thick metal exit door?

"No," Leonidas breathed. "He's young, probably a first- or second-year recruit. Nobody who served in my unit of veterans."

"Does that mean he'll be inexperienced?"

"It means he'll have all of the latest technology, the best and most modern cybernetic implants," Leonidas whispered, that grim expression on his face again.

"Oh. Does that mean he would win if you two fought?"

His chin came up, his eyes hard. "It does not."

In the video, the cyborg turned toward the camera and looked up at it. He had hard, dark eyes. The flying spy device had stopped, as if sensing possible discovery, and probably was not making any noise as it lurked near the ceiling. That did not keep the cyborg from lifting his rifle and blasting it. The holodisplay above Leonidas's netdisc turned black.

Leonidas stuffed his computer back into his pocket. "We have to get out of here." He glanced upward—Alejandro had turned his flashlight toward the steps leading down, but Leonidas could probably see all the details of the missing stairs. His eyes were supposed to be as enhanced as his ears. "I can make that jump."

"Congratulations," Alisa whispered. "We can't."

"I have no rope." Alejandro patted his satchel.

"What kind of researcher doesn't bring rope to the library?" Alisa asked.

He gave her a dry look.

"I could boost you up," Leonidas said, still considering the landing above. *Far* above.

"You are *not* hurtling us forty feet in the air," Alisa whispered.

She was sure he imagined them easily grabbing on after being tossed up there like a ball, but *she* imagined getting conked in the head by the metal floor and passing out. And Alejandro seemed even less athletic and agile than she.

"I—" Leonidas pressed his ear against the door, then backed away and shook his head. "They're coming. We go down. Our only choice."

Alejandro hurried down the steps, not hesitating. Alisa suspected he knew far more about who had sent those people than she did. She hustled after him, with Leonidas following more slowly, guarding their rear as they descended. How had she gotten herself into this? She had just wanted to come to the library to do some research. Her battle was with the Starseers, not whoever had taken charge of the remnants of the empire.

"We'll go down a couple more levels," Alejandro said, as he continued past the landing on the floor below, "then cut through to the elevator, try to go back up without them noticing us."

"Assuming they don't have people posted in the elevators," Alisa said.

"There's no other choice, unless you know a way out. We're fifty feet under the ground now." He glanced at a sign by the next doorway they passed, denoting this was B5. "Maybe more."

Leonidas did not override his suggestion, and Alejandro continued to B6 before trying a door. It was locked.

"Of course," he said.

A clang came from above them. The door on B3 opening.

Wordlessly, Alejandro continued down. At first, he walked softly, keeping his shoes from ringing on the metal steps, but the thunder of boots pounding on the stairs above echoed down the well. Alejandro hurried, no longer worried about sound. It probably did not matter. Their footfalls would be lost in the cacophony in the stairwell now. Flashlight beams slashed down through the passage, seeking targets. Alejandro tried a door on B7, but it, too, was locked.

"Leonidas?" he whispered, pointing at it. "Can you open it?"

"Down one more," Leonidas barked, passing them and pointing at a sign. It claimed that an environmental room was on the next level, probably the last level in the basement. Alisa did not know. She had never been down this far. "There'll be machinery making noise," he added. "Easier to hide."

The stairs ended on a cement pad, a door the same as the others the only way to continue on. Leonidas tugged at it. Like the others, it was locked. He braced one hand against the wall, then tugged harder, one swift motion. Metal snapped, and the door opened.

Movement came from the landing above. Someone leaned over a railing and shouted. Leonidas waved Alejandro and Alisa through. She had no sooner than crossed the threshold when a blazer sounded, a beam of red brightening the air behind them.

"They're shooting to kill," Alejandro blurted as overhead lights flickered on in the vast environmental control room.

Leonidas lunged inside, shutting the door behind him. Since he had broken the mechanism, there was no way to lock it. Not that locking it would help if the soldiers had a cyborg like him with them.

A large cylindrical piece of machinery was bolted to the wall next to the door. Alisa had no idea what it was, but it looked to weigh a ton. Leonidas grabbed one of its legs and pulled upward, his broad shoulders and back flexing. The sound of warping metal filled the cavernous room, drowning out the hums and beeps of machinery. Rivets snapped. He went to the other side, pulled up the other leg, and shoved the massive cylinder sideways. It toppled as someone tried to open the door.

Bangs came from the stairwell. Someone shouted an order, and it grew silent on the other side of the door. In a second, the cyborg would probably be there, doing his best to move the blockage.

"Go," Leonidas barked, waving Alejandro and Alisa toward the far side of the room.

Machinery filled the space, towering pumping stations, water heaters, snarls of pipes, and other items she could not identify. Alisa could not see the elevators through it all, but she ran in the direction where they should be. There was no way she was going to let herself get killed over Alejandro's orb.

As she ran, loud clangs and clanks and thumps sounded from the door. She had not yet heard the screech of that big piece of machinery sliding across the floor. Maybe Leonidas had found a way to wedge it against something so that the other cyborg could not easily push it. Easily. She snorted, finding it crazy to attribute that word to something that weighed hundreds of pounds or more.

She and Alejandro, who was sticking close behind her, ran through an open area in the center of the room. Even though the lights were on in the control room, they weren't strong lights, and deep shadows lurked all around the towering machinery. She glanced toward a large square drain in the center of the floor. A couple of pipes came through from the ceiling, plunging into the cement floor near it. Sewage.

She wrinkled her nose and ran on, being careful not to get lost in the maze of equipment. The elevator doors came into view, and the sounds of banging faded behind her. She ran and hit the button, relief washing over her. They were going to make it.

The button flashed at her, and a holodisplay appeared in front of the wall, a simple map showing the status of the cars. Only one descended all the way to the bottom level of the basement, a cargo elevator instead of the normal passenger ones, and the level it was currently on throbbed. B3.

"They've held up the elevator," Alejandro said as Leonidas joined them. "Unless we can climb the shaft, we're stuck."

Leonidas shook his head. "We would be blocked by the car even if we could go that way."

He did not point out the slim likelihood of Alisa and Alejandro being able to climb up an elevator shaft, but Alisa certainly thought of it.

"We're trapped then." Alejandro's shoulders slumped.

"The sewer," Alisa blurted, even as she cringed at the idea of trying to escape into the waste stream for the entire library.

"We can try," Leonidas said, turning back the way he had come.

A thunderous bang came from the far side of the control room, the screeching of metal along the floor accompanying it. Leonidas's run turned into a sprint. Alisa raced after him, even as she felt crazy for doing so—the soldiers and the cyborg had made it out of the stairwell, and she was running back in their direction.

By the time the grate came into sight again, Leonidas knelt beside it, gripping the crisscrossing bars. He probably could have torn it from its hinges easily, but he took his time, focusing on the lock.

"This way," someone called as footfalls pounded across the cement floor.

Alisa dropped down next to Leonidas. "Problem?" she whispered.

She had drawn her Etcher, but the last thing she wanted was to get in a firefight with someone who was Leonidas's equivalent—or *more* than his equivalent. Besides, if she fired at imperial soldiers on the imperial home world, she had no doubt that she would be arrested and never let off the planet again. Or maybe they would simply kill her outright.

"Trying not to make it obvious," Leonidas said.

He tugged once, the gesture short and effective. The lock popped.

He lifted the grate enough for them to squirm through. Alejandro did not hesitate. He slithered through and dropped, even though they could not see what awaited them in the darkness below. Alisa went after him, nearly kicking him as she fell. She realized he was bracing himself against the sides, his feet and hands planted. As she dropped past him, her heart leaping into her throat, she stuck her legs and arms out, trying to do the same thing. His caution was understandable. Who knew how far this dropped?

But her hands wouldn't reach. She plunged into darkness, unable to stop herself.

CHAPTER SIX

Alisa wasn't sure how far she fell, but the square of light up above grew small before she splashed down. Cold water enveloped her and washed over her face. Only the memory that people were hunting for them kept her from sputtering and cursing. Judging by the smell—or lack of smell—she had landed in water and nothing more, but she rushed to find her feet and get her head out. It came up to her chest.

Someone splashed down beside her, making less noise than she would have expected. She was sure she had struck on her back, slapping water all over the place. She reached out and found a shoulder that was too broad to belong to Alejandro.

"Leonidas?" she whispered.

"They didn't see me," he whispered back, his voice barely audible over the flowing water. Pipes somewhere to the side emptied into this area, and the current tugged at Alisa's waist. "I closed the grate before I let go. It may take them a moment to figure out where we went."

Alejandro, who had made his descent in a more controlled manner, walking his hands and feet down the walls, slid into the water next to them.

"This way," Leonidas said, striding away from the drainage chute—and the only source of light.

"You know where you're going?" Alisa asked, surprised. He hadn't even known where the elevators were when they had entered the first floor.

"Away from them." He found her back with his arm and pulled her along faster than she could have walked in the deep water. She might have objected, but she sensed he was doing the same thing with Alejandro on his other side. "I don't want to shoot imperial soldiers."

"I don't want to be *shot* by imperial soldiers," Alisa said.

"Then leaving is a good idea."

"I'll agree with that," Alejandro muttered.

They followed the current deeper into the darkness, Leonidas striding forward fearlessly. Alisa wanted to pull out her flashlight to get a better feel for their surroundings. She could imagine inimical things down here. White alligators, fang fish, poisonous water snakes...

"Can you see?" she asked Leonidas.

"Not much. We've gotten too far from the light."

"So, you can't see in complete darkness? You're like a cat?"

"I'm a human with eye implants," he said, his tone taking on that faintly miffed quality it had whenever someone implied he wasn't entirely human.

"Too bad. I was going to offer to rub your ears later if you were like a cat."

That did not earn her a response, and she had no idea if he was shooting her a scathing look. Probably.

The sound of rushing water increased up ahead, making Alisa wish he had said he *could* see. There were supposed to be centuries' worth of old channels for storm water and sewage that snaked around under the city, and she remembered stories of people living down here, too, in abandoned transportation tunnels that were deeper than the existing lines, that came from a time before the capital had been built up, newer levels atop older.

Something brushed past Alisa's shoulder, bouncing off before flowing along with the current. Maybe it was good that none of them could see. The odor grew fouler as they continued on, and she feared the water dumping into their channel from the nearby pipes was true sewer water.

"I'm sorry you're involved in this, Captain," Alejandro said, sounding weary as he slogged along with Leonidas's help. "I didn't expect Leonidas to bring you."

"He said I would be safer with him than staying behind with Beck," Alisa said, aware of Leonidas's muscled arm wrapped around her back. One could easily feel safe in his arms, but their current situation was too bizarre for her to feel much more than discomfort, especially when something slithered past her leg. She jerked her foot away, thoughts of snakes returning.

"It's possible he has an inordinately high opinion of himself," Alejandro said.

"I just assumed he had an inordinately low opinion of Beck."

"That is also possible."

"Usually," Leonidas said, "people talk about me behind my back, and I'm forced to use my enhanced auditory faculty to hear what disreputable things they're saying about me."

"We didn't want you to strain yourself," Alisa said.

His arm tightened around her briefly, and she wasn't sure if it was a fond squeeze of acknowledgment—he sounded more amused than irritated by their commentary—or a reminder that he could break her in half with his pinky.

"If they catch up with us," Alejandro said, "you should veer off in another direction if possible, Captain. This isn't your fight."

Water full of clumps of questionable material flowed in from a pipe, splatting onto Alisa's shoulder, and it was a moment before she could respond. Her last meal was too busy trying to come up.

"You're not going to make a similar suggestion to me?" Leonidas asked, turning them around a bend that Alisa had not seen in the darkness. The dreadful aroma was getting stronger, threatening to sear the nose hairs out of her nostrils. "I know nothing about your secret treasure," he added.

"I know, but you're...we're...on the same side."

"The war is over, Doctor," Leonidas said. "The empire has fallen."

Alisa punctuated this somber statement with gagging sounds. Rebusde's river of decay, she was going to end up puking all over Leonidas. What would his enhanced cyborg senses think about that? She took deeper breaths, trying to calm her queasy belly, doing her best not to breathe through her nose.

A distant clang sounded.

"Any chance that's not related to us?" Alejandro asked. He didn't seem affected by the stench. Maybe doctors were used to all manner of human excrement and grossness.

"They found the grate," Leonidas said.

Wonderful. *Their* cyborg probably wouldn't be slowed down by shepherding two civilians along.

"Any chance you know where we're going and that we'll be out soon?" Alisa asked, sucking in gulps of air between the words. It did not help. Her belly roiled with discontent.

"I know the direction to the harbor," Leonidas said. "There should be a sewage treatment plant there, perhaps a way to climb out."

"The harbor is *miles* from the library," Alejandro said.

"I know."

Alisa lost it. Maybe it was the suggestion that they had to travel miles in this, with sewer sludge flowing all the way to their chests, or maybe she was just succumbing to the inevitable. Either way, she turned to the side and threw up. Her only consolation was that the water was flowing in that direction, so it would not come back and hit them. A small consolation. There were worse things than vomit in the channel.

Leonidas continued to carry her along. Apparently, they couldn't risk slowing down for regurgitation breaks.

"I'm sorry, Captain," Alejandro said again when she was done.

He sounded miserable. At least she wasn't the only one.

"I think there's a tunnel ahead without water in it," Leonidas said. "It may tilt upward, an old subway passage perhaps."

"It's pitch black in here," Alejandro said. "You can't possibly see anything."

"I can hear auditory changes, get a sense of the layout based on the echoes."

"Like a bat?" Alisa managed to rasp, not trusting her voice.

At first, Leonidas did not answer, and she thought he would ignore her, but then he said, "I think I preferred it when you compared me to a cat."

"Perhaps he was intrigued by the proffer of an ear rub," Alejandro said.

"Yeah," Alisa said. "I'm sure the idea of being rubbed by someone who just puked on him gets him excited."

"One hopes you would shower first."

"Shower? I'm going to need the top layer of my skin cells lasered off to feel sanitary again."

Another clang sounded in the distance. They all fell silent. Alisa had the uneasy feeling that their pursuers knew exactly which way they were going and were catching up.

Her foot scuffed the bottom of the channel. As Leonidas turned them to the side, the ground rose, slick with slimy growth under her boots. She stuck her hands out in front of her and found the rough stone of a crumbling wall. By feel, they climbed into a higher passage that connected to the main one. Leonidas let go of her as she pulled herself out of the water. The scent had not lessened any, but she felt better being out of the grimy sludge.

"Hurry," Leonidas urged as Alisa clambered to her feet, leaning against the wall for support.

Now, voices were audible in the distance. She did not know how the soldiers were tracking them, but they seemed to know exactly where they were.

Alisa forced her legs into motion, first walking and then, at Leonidas's light touch on her back, running. She kept her hands outstretched, one in front of her and one using the wall to the side for guidance. She did not want to smack into another wall with her nose. Leonidas ran soundlessly at her side, clearly pacing himself so that he would not leave her and Alejandro behind. She could hear Alejandro both by the sound of his breathing and by the thump of his satchel against his side as he ran.

The tunnel curved, then connected with another in what she guessed, by the sudden disappearance of her wall, was a cross-shaped intersection. Leonidas kept going straight. Alisa was completely lost and had no idea which way the harbor was or even if she could have found her way back to the library. She wondered if Leonidas had truly kept his bearings or if he was just guessing.

They had run for about five minutes, with their passage widening, when two pinpricks of light appeared up ahead. Alisa's first reaction was one of relief as she believed they had reached the surface, but as the lights grew larger and brighter, she realized that they hadn't traveled upward enough to be anywhere near the surface. A faint rasping came from the direction of those lights.

"Run faster," Leonidas said, touching Alisa's back again to urge greater speed.

"What is that up there?" Alejandro asked, panting from his exertions.

"An automatic sewer cleaner," Leonidas said.

Normally, that would not have sounded ominous, but it was coming straight toward them.

"Will we…be able to…get around it?" Alisa asked, her legs burning.

"There's an intersection between us and it," Leonidas said, not even slightly winded. "If we make it in time, we can turn off and avoid it."

"That…sounded like…a no," Alisa said.

"Just keep running," Leonidas said.

She did not try to speak again after that, siphoning all of her energy into her legs. The lights grew larger, appearing to be several feet off the ground, giving her a sense of the size of the cleaning machine. It might fill the entire tunnel.

It rasped and ground as it continued toward them, and Alisa realized it was coming at a good speed. Images of being flattened under huge wheels and spinning brushes filled her head, and she ran faster, looking for the intersection Leonidas had promised. She could make out the gore-covered gray walls now, the light of the cleaner stealing some of the darkness of the tunnels.

A grunt sounded behind her. Alejandro had fallen behind, his robes heavy with water and pulling at his legs. Leonidas threw him over his shoulder, then easily caught up with Alisa. He did not offer to pick her up, merely pointing ahead of them.

"There."

Alisa could barely see the spot. She was squinting now, half-blinded by the bright lamps of the cleaner. Leonidas ran ahead of her, then disappeared from the light, jumping into a side tunnel. She sprinted toward it on leaden legs, the towering body of the cleaner filling her vision, giant brushes and whirring circular blades that cut away the grime on the walls to either side of it. There was no way someone could run past it, and its huge body would be capable of crushing anything in its path.

She made it to the intersection and leaped after Leonidas, her ears full of the rasping and grinding. Thinking they were safe now, she paused, leaning forward and gripping her knees as she gasped for air. But Leonidas grabbed her.

"Keep going," he ordered.

"What?" she blurted, feeling betrayed.

The headlight beams swung into their dark passage, driving away the shadows. The cleaner was turning here too.

CHAPTER SEVEN

"Climb," Leonidas barked as the light beams of the massive tunnel cleaner flared, nearly blinding Alisa.

"Climb what?" she demanded, scrambling backward, away from the machine. Not that it would matter. It was turning slowly around the corner, but it would pick up speed soon—it must have been zipping along at twenty-five miles per hour in the other tunnel. Leonidas might be able to outrun it, but Alisa and Alejandro never could.

"The side of the tunnel." Leonidas gripped her and lifted her from her feet, thrusting her at the wall.

The ancient stones were jagged and uneven, but she would hardly consider them a ladder. But she did not argue. She did her best to find a grip. Would it be enough? The cleaner rolled toward them, nearly touching the ceiling with its bulky automatic control cab. Brushes and blades whirred, sweeping and chipping away the accumulated sediment and organic matter. With the ominous grinding in her ears, Alisa scrambled up the rough wall, her toes wedging into gaps between the stones where mortar had cracked and fallen away in pieces.

The cleaner rumbled toward her, picking up speed as it moved away from the corner. She slipped, cursed, and recovered, nails breaking painfully as she dug them into the crumbling mortar.

"Isn't there an override or command to turn that thing off?" Alisa asked in frustration. "Surely even the empire doesn't want its city sewer workers getting eaten by the machinery."

"If you were a legitimate worker down here, you would have a remote control to deactivate the automatons," Alejandro said from the wall beside her. He was slipping even more than she, struggling to find hand and toeholds.

Alisa glanced behind her. Leonidas stood in the center of the tunnel, facing the oncoming mechanical beast.

"What are you doing?" she blurted as she climbed higher, imagining him being smashed beneath the massive construct. Even with his enhanced cyborg bones, he surely could not withstand being run over by a five-ton machine.

"Go," he ordered, almost yelling to be heard over the noise. "To the ceiling, to where the arch starts."

"Arch?" Alisa glanced up.

She was close to the top of the wall now. It did arch in the middle, rising a few feet higher there than at the sides of the tunnel. Maybe there would be room if she reached that gap and could somehow hang upside down as the cleaner swept past below. All she needed was to turn into a spider to manage the feat...

Cursing, she climbed as high as she could, to the point where she could see over the cab of the cleaning vehicle. With the headlights blinding her and utter darkness behind it, she couldn't see much else, but thought the machine dipped down in the back. Maybe there was a cargo area?

Bits of mildew and slime sheered from the walls and smacked her face as the huge swirling brushes approached. She tried to climb higher, but her foot slipped, and she almost fell off the wall. With terror surging through her limbs, she found the strength to hang on.

As the top of the cab drew closer, she sucked everything in, hugging the wall. She prayed it would rumble by below her instead of knocking her from her perch.

The lights passed first, and Alisa thought she might be safe. Then the corner of the cab hammered her in the back. She tried to hang on, ignoring the pain of the blow, but gravity fought against her. She tumbled backward, horror coursing through her body as she imagined the blades and brushes sweeping her under the machine where she would be crushed. If she died down in this nameless hell, her daughter would never know what had happened to her.

But she only fell inches, onto the top of the cab, then bounced off something protruding from it, some vent pipe. She tumbled away and fell, not down in front of it and into the sweepers but down behind it. She landed on a flat metal surface.

She held her breath, expecting some giant cleaning appendage to smash into her. Bits of slime and shards of mineral deposits struck her, plastering her face, but nothing larger came near her. Corrugated metal vibrated beneath her back. She *was* in a cargo bed.

A grunt of pain came from above her, followed by someone tumbling down from the arched ceiling, almost landing on top of her. Alejandro. He slammed into the bed next to her, his foot clobbering her leg. Given that she had thought she would be pulverized under a machine a moment earlier, it was a small pain to endure.

"Apologies," Alejandro said.

"You're forgiven."

A soft clank sounded, something landing on top of the cab.

"Leonidas?" Alisa asked.

She spotted him crouching up there. He must have jumped and landed on top of the cleaner. He slid around the vent pipe and joined them in the cargo bed.

Gradually, Alisa's hammering heart slowed as she realized that none of them were going to be smashed. More than that, they were getting a ride.

She scooted out of the middle of the bed and put her back to the cab so she could see behind them—not that she could glimpse anything in the blackness back there. A soft breeze tugged at her wet hair and clothes, created by the cleaner. It had returned to full speed and was cruising down the tunnel. Alisa had no idea where it would take them, but she would settle for anywhere away from the people trying to catch them.

No, not *catch* them. The soldiers had been *shooting* at them in that stairwell.

One of the men scooted over to sit beside her, his back also to the cab. Alisa wrinkled her nose. They might be in a dry tunnel for the moment, but the stench of the sewer clung to them all.

"To think," she said, "I was feeling bad for Beck because he got left outside of the library. Now I think he was the smart one, deliberately getting himself in trouble with security so he could avoid this."

"Better than getting in trouble with the imperial army," Leonidas said dryly. He was the one who was sitting beside her.

Alejandro grumbled something from the other end of the cargo bed, though she couldn't make it out over the continuous grinding of the machine.

"I believe he's thanking us for coming to help," Alisa said, offering a possible translation.

"Actually, he was cursing," Leonidas said.

"Cursing us?"

"No, cursing in general."

"I didn't think holy men were allowed to do that," Alisa said.

"I wasn't thanking you," Alejandro said, "but you're right that I should have been. You both risked your lives to help me. I appreciate that. I'm just frustrated that I'd barely started to use the library when those men showed up, following me around. It was alarming enough when it was plainclothes people. But having soldiers after me is worse. And somewhat perplexing. Although, now that I think about it, perhaps it isn't."

"Care to explain?" Leonidas asked.

"This…mission of mine, it's not anything I would have chosen for myself. It was someone's dying request. I am, quite frankly, a poor candidate for it, given my background. I thought that at the time, and I believe it even more now that so many people know about it and are after me."

Alisa shifted her weight uneasily, hoping he wouldn't imply again that *she* was the reason people knew about him and his orb.

"He knew it, too, I think," Alejandro continued. "That I was a less than ideal candidate. But I was the doctor with him there at the end, and he had few options."

"Who?" Alisa asked.

Maybe she should have kept her mouth shut so Alejandro might have forgotten she was there. Even though they had been through numerous binds now, he always seemed to remember that she was Alliance, through and through. Not someone to be trusted with secrets.

Leonidas surprised her by repeating the question. "Yes, who?" he asked. Alejandro hesitated. "Do you truly need to know? Here?"

Here was probably code for: with the former Alliance officer listening.

"They may still be after us," Leonidas said. "If we get into a shoot-out...Those are my former colleagues, Doctor. I don't want to shoot them, not for something I don't understand. I've trusted you to a degree thus far because I know you worked for the emperor's family once, but if you're on some quest for personal gain..."

Alisa blinked. Alejandro had been the personal physician to the emperor's family? Had Leonidas known that all along? Or had Alejandro admitted it to him somewhere along the journey?

"I'm not. As I said, it was a dying man's wish." Alejandro sighed. "It was the *emperor's* dying wish."

Leonidas did not respond right away, and only the sound of the perpetual grinding of the sewer cleaner filled the air.

"I suspect we had similar reasons for ending up on Dustor," Alejandro went on. "Were you not also fulfilling a final order before the war ended?"

"I cannot speak of that," Leonidas said.

"As I cannot speak of my mission." Alejandro glanced at Alisa, his face just visible in the light that reflected from the tunnel walls.

"Not with me here, eh?" Alisa asked. "Want me to put my fingers in my ears so you two can talk?"

Alejandro did not smile. "I was sworn to keep the mission a secret until I completed it and could hand the result over to the proper person." He spoke vaguely, but now he met and held Leonidas's eyes. Leonidas nodded back once, solemnly, and Alisa suspected the words hadn't been quite so vague to him. "You have my word," Alejandro continued, "that none of this is for personal gain. I own a lovely house by the seashore in Farmington, and there's physical gold and diamonds there, enough that I can retire and needn't worry about exchange rates or the fate of the imperial morat. My wife had me set everything up, back when I was making good money as a surgeon."

"You're still married?" Alisa asked, eyeing his sodden robe. Weren't Sun Trinity monks supposed to be celibate? Or was that robe just a disguise? Maybe he had chosen it in the hope that people wouldn't suspect him of being on some clandestine mission.

"No. It's been over for ten years. My wife did not appreciate my long hours and my dedication to my work."

Silence fell, Leonidas not asking any more questions. Had Alejandro given him enough? He seemed so loyal to the empire that Alisa would not be surprised if he would give his life to help Alejandro with his quest, even when Alejandro had refused to help him with *his* quest, whatever it was. Leonidas was a good man. The fact that he was loyal to the other side didn't change that. She wondered what it would be like to have someone like that loyal to her. Or at least working for her for a fair amount of pay.

A silly thought perhaps. He would probably leave soon, perhaps going with Alejandro to help him with his orb quest, even though he knew nothing about it. And what would she do once they left? Report everything she had seen and heard to her own government? It seemed disloyal, since she was starting to think of these men, especially Leonidas, as friends. But what if Alejandro's mission could help the empire regain control? What if he sought some ancient Starseer artifact with great power? There were legends of such things, though they hadn't been seen for centuries and might not exist at all.

"Who do the soldiers belong to now?" Leonidas asked. "The emperor and his son are dead. I've been off world for too long and haven't had a chance to read up on the news. Who's in power on Perun?"

"Is he dead?" Alejandro asked. "The son? I've wondered that."

Leonidas's shoulder moved next to Alisa as he shrugged. "They say he didn't get out when the palace was bombed. Even if he did, he's ten. Far too young to rally troops around him and try to take back some of the stolen planets."

Stolen? *Liberated* was more like it.

Alisa managed to keep her mouth shut, hoping the men would forget her allegiance and speak freely, but barely.

"No, if he was still alive and safe, he would need a regent to advise him," Alejandro said, "and I don't know who that would be. The corporations all had their hooks in the emperor, their smooth-talking representatives insinuating themselves as advisors. There was nobody Markus could have trusted, which I think he knew, in the end. Perhaps that's why he didn't name a regent. Or maybe he just never expected to die." Alejandro lifted an arm, a resigned gesture. "To answer your question, Senator Bondarenko is in charge of Perun and commands those troops now. He toyed with naming himself emperor, but I don't think he could get the support. A lot of the factions are holding out, thinking the prince might be found and that a new government could be formed around him."

"And Bondarenko would be against that happening," Leonidas said.

"Oh, I'd say so. The rumors suggest that he had a hand in betraying the emperor, in handing the location of the off-world hidden palace to the Alliance so they could launch a surprise strike at him." Alejandro looked toward Alisa.

"Don't look at me. I was just a pilot. I wasn't a part of that attack." Granted, she had heard about it and had been a part of the epic assault on the chain bases that had distracted all of the imperial forces, drawing them away from defending the emperor.

"Bondarenko knows about the orb then," Leonidas said.

"Apparently."

"And he wants it for himself."

"Apparently," Alejandro repeated.

Alisa thought Leonidas might press him again, trying to find out what the orb was for, but he did not. No, he was a good soldier, probably used to obeying orders and being a pawn of the higher-ups. Even though none of this had anything to do with her, it irked her that Alejandro wouldn't tell Leonidas the whole story when he had proven his loyalty to the emperor and even to him, coming to help Alejandro simply as a favor.

She leaned against Leonidas's shoulder, in part because she was tired, and it was easy to do so, but in part because she wanted him to know…she didn't know what exactly. That she supported him? *Could* she? So long as it didn't involve betraying her own government, perhaps she could.

He shifted, looking down at her. Maybe he would tell her to move, that he didn't want her support—or for some scruffy Alliance pilot to lean on his shoulder.

Instead, he said, "I apologize."

"What?" Alisa frowned up at him.

"For losing my temper with you back on the streets, when we were look-ing at the destroyed lots." He paused, gazing into the darkness behind the cleaner. "It reminded me of the early years of the war, of being a ground officer and walking through devastation left by the Alliance. There were many other places like that, places where the bodies hadn't yet been moved away, the rubble cleared. People were dead and dying, some soldiers but some civilians caught in the middle of the fighting."

"Oh," Alisa said, not sure what else to say.

He had apologized, but he also made her feel to blame, because her side would have been responsible for the horrors he had seen. She had seen atrocities perpetrated by *his* side, and knew the empire had been no less destructive, but she hadn't been a ground troop. She hadn't often seen buildings razed, people left to die in the ruins. She *had* seen destruction of ships in space, but distance had always made those deaths seem less real.

"I used to live in an apartment building on that empty lot," she said. "My husband was there when the bombs dropped. I didn't learn about his death until months later, from my sister-in-law."

She wasn't sure why she blurted the confession. So far, she had kept her losses to herself. Bitterly, she realized it had been more of a desire to one-up what he'd seen in the war than a need to tell him for the sake of telling. He shouldn't blame her, because she had lost more than he had, at least more than he was describing. Seeing strangers dead was horrible, but losing one's family was worse. He shouldn't be blaming her for anything, damn it. Not when worse had befallen her because of the war.

Alisa swallowed and looked away, wishing she could retract the confession. She didn't want sympathy or anything else from him. Her reason for sharing had been petty. It seemed to cheapen Jonah's death.

Leonidas shifted to put his arm around her. By the three gods, she hadn't been fishing for comfort. She hadn't even expected him to be someone who would offer it. She wiped her eyes, tears lurking there for all the wrong reasons.

"War is ugly," he said quietly. "Even if your side comes out on top, nobody wins."

"Yeah," she whispered, having nothing wiser to contribute.

She thought about pushing his arm away and saying she was fine, but after the day she'd had thus far, she found herself reluctant to do so. She doubted he truly cared, but it felt good to have someone offering an arm.

She probably should have sat in silence and appreciated it, but her inappropriate humor was piqued when more sewer gunk flew off the brushes to spatter them on their faces, and she imagined how disgusting the arm around her must be.

"This would be cozier if you didn't smell so bad," she said.

He grunted and withdrew his arm. "You smell just as bad."

"I know." Alisa bit her lip, regretting the comment. He was still sitting next to her, but the world felt lonelier with the arm retracted. "But I have grand plans to bathe soon," she said, hoping to salvage the situation or at least make him feel that she hadn't been rejecting him. "I hope you do, too, before you show up for your ear rub."

"My what?"

"I thought you sounded intrigued by the idea of an ear rub earlier. Didn't you say you would prefer to be treated like a cat rather than a bat?" Hm, that had sounded funnier in her head.

Leonidas did not seem to know how to answer the question. Or maybe he did not think it was worth answering. He eventually said, "You're an odd woman, Marchenko."

"I know."

Somehow, she had ended up being the one feeling rejected. Her and her big mouth.

Light flashed in the darkness behind them, and she stiffened. Leonidas bolted to his feet, jostling her.

"Another cleaning machine?" Alejandro asked, turning to look.

"No," Leonidas said. "It's their cyborg."

The light was far in the distance—it had been some time since the cleaner turned a corner—and it was moving. Alisa could not see anything around it, but from the way it jerked about, it seemed like someone might be running with a flashlight.

"You can see him?" she whispered.

"Yes, and he'll catch us soon."

Alisa pulled out her Etcher, hoping it would still fire after being doused in the sewer. A blazer weapon would have, but she had bullets with gunpowder inside them. Did it even matter? Would a bullet stop a cyborg?

She scrambled to her feet. She would at least try.

"Leonidas?" Alejandro asked, worry in his voice.

"You two stay here," Leonidas said, stepping toward the rear of the cargo bed. "I'll keep him busy so you can get away."

"No," Alisa said, surprising herself with her concern for him. He had said the young cyborg had newer implants than he did. And he might have denied that they would automatically mean he would lose in a fight, but she worried that would be the case, that youth and greater powers would win out against age and experience. "We can all fight him, shoot at him. There's nothing for him to hide behind, right?"

Alisa bit her lip, ragged and tired nerves flaring to life again. Even with the cleaning machine rolling along quickly in the tunnels, the flashlight was already twice as close as it had been when she first spotted it. Alejandro did not have a weapon, and hers might not fire until she got new bullets. What help could they truly be?

"There's nothing for either of us to hide behind," Leonidas said fiercely, and then he sprang away, leaping off the back of the cleaner and sprinting toward the light.

Alisa crouched at the rear of the cargo bed, staring back, frustrated that she could not do anything. It was too dark to risk shooting at their enemy. She would be just as likely to hit Leonidas. Besides, the cleaning machine kept rumbling along, quickly taking them away from where the men would collide.

Alejandro rose to his knees, also looking back. "I didn't mean for him to sacrifice himself," he whispered.

A blazer beam flashed crimson. Alisa thought Leonidas dropped into a roll to avoid the attack, but only because it continued past him. It was too dark to tell much more. A bang sounded, and smoke filled the tunnel, obscuring the flashlight beam.

The sounds of flesh striking flesh came from within the smoke, the cyborgs meeting in a flurry of blows. Alisa couldn't tell what was happening, other than that the soldier had stopped advancing. Then the cleaner came to an intersection and turned a corner. Leonidas and the battle completely disappeared from sight.

CHAPTER EIGHT

Alisa slogged through the salty night air with Alejandro, following a board-walk along the harbor, her head throbbing with each step. The headache was only one of her physical complaints. They had been denied access to the late-running trains and trolleys thanks to their stench, and she had a blister from walking in wet shoes. A moving sidewalk had carried them for a while, but even then, guards and off-duty soldiers had given them suspicious squints. Apparently, anyone smelling of the sewers was up to something fishy—or, more likely, did not belong in the nicer parts of the city.

As they passed a sign proclaiming that the space base lay a mile ahead, Alisa glanced back for the hundredth time. She and Alejandro had both lost their comm units in the sewers, so she couldn't check on Beck or Leonidas until she reached the *Nomad,* but she kept expecting to see Leonidas jogging up behind them, even though it had been several hours since they had parted ways. She and Alejandro had ridden the cleaner until it arrived at the sewage treatment plant near the harbor, and it had taken them some time to find a way up to the surface. They had covered more miles since then, and Alisa's battered body sagged with weariness. She wanted a long shower and her bunk, but she doubted she would sleep, worrying instead about Leonidas's fate and about how she would find her daughter. Somehow, she doubted she would be allowed in the library again tomorrow if she showed up at the door. The imperial soldiers would probably be watching the entrance, and she might been marked as a member of Alejandro's orb-carrying party.

"I shouldn't have told him," Alejandro said quietly, noticing her glance. His voice was weary, his shoulders slumped.

"What?"

"It was calculating to do so, and I knew exactly what would happen when I made the choice. But…I'm regretting it." He sounded like someone confessing to a priest rather than someone who carried the wisdom of a religious order with him at all times.

"You mean telling him about the emperor?" Alisa asked quietly, glancing around. It was late enough that few people were out, and most of those who were favored the public transportation options over walking. "That your mission had been assigned by him on his deathbed?"

"Yes. I knew that Leonidas, as a loyal former fleet officer, would feel duty-bound to help me if I told him. He'd worked for the emperor's staff before, if not directly for the emperor himself, and I know he received a few awards that the emperor personally pinned on his jacket. I needed his help, even though I didn't want to need it, if that makes sense."

"He's a powerful ally." Alisa thought of the way she had tried to hire him.

"Yes. And my odds for success go up a lot with his help, something that wasn't guaranteed until I told him about my mission. But I didn't mean for him to get killed."

"We don't know that's what happened." Alisa refused to believe that Leonidas was dead. It was too soon to start thinking that way. He could have simply lost track of the cleaning machine after dealing with the other cyborg and been forced to find his own way out of the sewers. "Besides, I think you're wrong."

"About what?"

"That you had to tell him that to gain his help. He seems like someone who would be loyal to his friends, even those recently made, as well as his old emperor." Alisa thought about pointing out that Leonidas had gone to the library to help Alejandro before he had known the rest of Alejandro's story.

"Yes, you're probably right. I do hope he's all right. I would not wish to carry his death on my conscience."

They finished their walk in silence. To Alisa's relief, nobody stopped them when they entered Karundula Space Base. The automated security scanner at the doorway recognized them as passengers and crew that left earlier in the day and had nothing to say about the dried sewage decorating their clothes. It was fortunate that Alisa's ship was docked in an exterior berth. They might have had more trouble walking into the main building where lights remained on and security guards patrolled the concourses.

When the *Star Nomad* came into view, Alisa was so relieved to be back that she nearly ran forward and hugged the hull. Her relief was short-lived because she soon remembered that when she had left, she'd thought she would return with her daughter at her side.

Swallowing a lump in her throat, she hit the button to open the hatch and lower the ramp. Since it had been dark for hours, she expected the others to be asleep, but Mica and Yumi sat cross-legged on the floor of the cargo hold, candles scattered about them and the overhead lights off. They were engaged in some kind of fast-breathing exercise—or maybe a séance.

"Job hunting going well?" Alisa asked as she walked in, Alejandro behind her.

She looked around, hoping to spot Beck lounging somewhere.

"We gave up on that a couple of hours ago," Mica said, crinkling her nose as Alisa drew closer. Yumi's eyes were closed, and she did not seem to notice that anyone had come in. "Given that the imperials are now cut off from the rest of the system, they have surprisingly good records of their former subjects who chose to become Alliance soldiers. A tip for you: that's not a selling point when applying for positions here."

"I'm surprised you were denied so quickly," Alisa said. "You'd expect applications to sit for days in a quagmire of a virtual queue somewhere."

"Robots. They reject you quickly. Some messages came in for you while you were gone." Mica waved in the direction of navigation.

"Thanks. Has Beck been back?" Alisa asked. "I lost my comm."

Mica shook her head. "I thought he left with you."

"He did. We were separated."

"Did it have something to do with the stench you're wearing like a dreadful perfume?"

"No, and Alejandro stinks too. You needn't look straight at me when you say such things."

"Were you two bonding in a sewer together somewhere?"

"You got the location right." Alisa considered Alejandro, his filthy robes and his usually clean-shaven chin dark with stubble. He looked like he had a headache too. "I don't know about the bonding. Do you feel bonded to me now, Doctor?"

Alejandro rested his palm against his stomach. "I feel like I may throw up."

"Apparently, we're not bonded, Mica."

"Unfortunate."

"The stench is far more dreadful in here, isn't it?" Alejandro asked. "I'm going to scrub myself in the sanibox. And perhaps burn my robe." He shambled toward the stairs, looking like he had been run over by the sewer cleaner. More than once.

"Rough night?" Mica asked.

"Very much so. You haven't heard from Leonidas, by chance, have you?"

Mica shook her head. "I haven't seen him since he left with you. You seem to be losing crew and passengers left and right."

"The mind is peaceful and calm," Yumi intoned. "The breath is the center, the core, the focus. The—" A round of coughing, or maybe that was gagging, interrupted her litany, and her eyes opened. "Captain, your fecal aroma is disturbing our meditation."

"I think our passenger is telling me to take a shower, Mica."

"An accurate interpretation, I believe."

The ship had a couple of heads, but only one sanibox. Alisa would have to wait for Alejandro to finish, but she supposed she could be polite and take her fecal aroma to another part of the ship. She dreaded the idea of smelling up NavCom or her cabin. Maybe she would wait outside of Alejandro's cabin. This night of misadventure had been his fault.

Mica's gaze shifted past Alisa's shoulder, toward the still-open hatch. Alisa turned, worried that the soldiers might have already figured out where Alejandro and his orb had fled. But a familiar figure limped up the ramp.

"Leonidas," Alisa blurted and rushed forward to help him.

She had never seen him limping or showing any sign of pain, even after his fight with the cyborg Malik. Now, blood saturated the shoulder of his jacket, cuts slashed his sleeve, contusions darkened his cheeks and jaw, and a cauterized gouge in the side of his neck marked a spot where he had been hit with a blazer—had that beam cut an inch to the right, it might have killed him.

He looked like he might collapse when he reached the top of the ramp, but he stood straight and lifted his chin as she rushed up. "He was *not* the superior fighter."

"Does that mean he looks even worse than you?" Alisa did not know if he would be too proud to accept help, but she slid her arm around him without asking and waved toward the stairs. "You can lean on me, if you want. Let's get you to sickbay. Alejandro owes you some bandages and a tube of QuickSkin for the help you gave him tonight."

At first, Leonidas merely gazed curiously down at her and did not move. Did he object to her offer of help? Or the implication that he needed it? Eventually, he stirred, walking at her side. He did not lean on her, but he didn't push her arm away, either.

"Perhaps it's selfish," Leonidas said, "but I'd like to think that I deserve more than bandages and tubes."

"Like what? Money? Medals?"

He paused at the base of the stairs, either to collect himself or to wonder why Mica and Yumi were sitting amid all those candles. "To be honest, I'd like some cookies right now."

Alisa almost laughed, though she supposed it made sense. It had been a long and arduous night, more so for him than for her and Alejandro, and he must be craving carbohydrates. With all those muscles of his, he probably burned through energy stores quickly.

"I have some chocolate in my cabin," she said.

"Oh? That might do."

Yumi sighed noisily and stood up. She wrinkled her nose, made a gagging sound again, and stooped to blow out and pick up her candles.

"Is our meditation session over?" Mica asked blandly.

"We cannot be expected to reach a state of higher consciousness with all of these distractions. We will try again when—" She made another gagging noise, abandoned the candles, and pushed past Alisa to sprint up the stairs. She tripped, then disappeared into the core of the ship, the gagging sounds continuing.

"I hope she makes it to the head," Alisa said. She didn't have any cleaning robots currently, thanks to everything of value having been taken from the ship during the years it had resided in a junkyard. "Especially since Beck is missing. He's the only one here who's volunteered to clean for me."

"He's the only one here that you actually pay," Mica said, picking up discarded candles.

"I'll gladly give you a salary if you agree to stay on board and officially take the position of ship's engineer."

Mica sighed at her.

"No, no, you needn't overwhelm me with displays of gratitude. Having you here is reward enough." Alisa tilted her head toward the stairs. "Ready, Leonidas?"

"Yes." He still would not lean on her, but he did lean on the railing as they climbed.

Alisa could have let go of him since there were railings all the way to sickbay, but he had been willing to sacrifice himself so that she and Alejandro could get away. She found herself reluctant to let go, as if it would be abandoning him. Even through his clothing, she could feel the hard muscles of his torso. It was almost as if he wore combat armor even when he didn't. Sleeping with him would be like sleeping with a particularly angular boulder. She smirked, imagining the poor wives of cyborgs waking up in the morning with bruises from having rolled over and bumped against those granite bulges.

"Are you experiencing inappropriate humor?" Leonidas asked, eyeing her smirk as they reached the top of the stairs.

"Yes, but I'm keeping it to myself." She turned him up the walkway, toward the interior of the ship. "I thought you would approve."

He grunted.

"Do many cyborg soldiers get married?" she asked.

"No."

Alisa kept herself from asking if it was because of bruises suffered in bed. She doubted she could ask the question in such a way that wouldn't be misinterpreted as being insulting. Actually, it was probably insulting even if interpreted correctly.

"Too busy blowing people up to have time to seek love?" she asked.

"The empire was a demanding employer."

"If you worked for me, *I'd* give you time to seek love."

"It seems I'm not yet done working for the empire," he said quietly, an unexpected bleakness taking over his face.

Alisa bit her lip, wanting to go find Alejandro and slap him. Leonidas wasn't his to command, damn it. Alejandro was right—he'd been selfish to suck Leonidas into his mission.

When they reached the sickbay door, Leonidas extracted himself from her grip, looking relieved to slip away. He had never mentioned being married now or in the past, so maybe it was a touchy subject for him. Or maybe he'd just had enough of her closeness. She had to admit that the aroma only intensified when two of them were together, and he did have those enhanced nostrils.

"I'll get Alejandro out of the sanibox and send him your way," Alisa said, deciding to give him his peace rather than going in and continuing to inflict her help on him. Alejandro would be far more qualified to treat him—and probably wouldn't ask nosy questions about cyborg personal lives. He *definitely* wouldn't think about being in bed with a cyborg.

———

Alisa almost felt human again when she stepped out of the sanibox, but her head still ached, so she would return to sickbay for a painpro before crawling into her bunk. She needed to give Leonidas some chocolate too. The man certainly deserved it.

The built-in netdisc on her desk flashed, signaling the messages Mica had mentioned, but she got dressed and headed to sickbay first, leaving her soiled clothes for the automatic washer, though she was afraid they would simply have to be burned. She delved into her drawer for her stash of sweets and poked through the small assortment of choices. It was odd to be selecting one of her precious dark chocolate bars to share. They were expensive and often hard to come by in the freight lanes and on space stations. She grabbed the pecan and raisin one, figuring Leonidas might appreciate a few extra calories.

"I apologize for causing you to miss your appointment with your contact," Alejandro was saying as Alisa approached sickbay. The hatch door stood open, bright light slashing out into the night-dimmed corridor. She slowed her steps, listening.

"I'm beginning to think that the gods don't want me to—"

The way he broke off made Alisa think he'd heard her coming. Trying not to feel guilty for eavesdropping—again—she continued to the hatchway.

Inside the small sickbay room, Leonidas sat on the single medical table, his shirt off as Alejandro worked on him, using skin binders to hold gashes together while the QuickSkin sealed the wounds.

He hadn't gotten to a gash on Leonidas's forearm yet, and Alisa started, glimpsing a hint of metal and circuitry revealed by the flesh and muscle that had been laid open. Even though she had logically known that Leonidas had cybernetic implants, it was jolting to actually see machine bits inside of someone that she had started to think of as human. As normal. A person. Maybe even a friend, not a machine.

"Marchenko," Leonidas said, a guarded greeting.

Blushing because she had been caught staring, Alisa jerked her gaze up to his face. "I brought your chocolate," she blurted, waving the bar. Maybe he would forget that she'd been gaping at his cybernetic innards.

"Thank you."

Alejandro kept working and did not seem to notice the exchange. He had taken the time to finish his shower and change clothes before coming to sickbay, this robe identical to the last, except with a paucity of sewage clinging to it. Alisa found it strange to see a man in a gray monk's robe wielding medical tools. She wondered if he knew how to fix cybernetic pieces if they were damaged, but she did not want to pry.

"Will he live, Doc?" she asked, coming forward to hand Leonidas the bar.

"Yes, but he should refrain from tangling with younger cyborgs."

"He wasn't *that* much younger," Leonidas grumbled, accepting the bar and opening it with delicate precision that seemed at odds with the bulky muscles of his arms.

"Fifteen years, I'd guess," Alejandro said.

Leonidas made a face. "Damn, I've gotten to the age where fifteen years doesn't seem that long of a time."

"Must be rough getting old," Alisa teased, though fifteen years also wasn't quite the eternity for her that it had seemed when she had been younger. The forty she judged him to be would have been ancient to her when she had been in school. Now it didn't seem that far off. "Though at least you're not as ancient as the doctor. Doc, your hands steady, there? That's not an age-related tremor, is it? Can I get you something?"

He shot her a dirty look. "Do you have a purpose here, besides delivering chocolate and admiring Leonidas's physique?"

The blush that had warmed her cheeks earlier returned. "I wasn't admiring anything. I was—" She broke off, not wanting to admit to gaping at his machine parts.

Leonidas's eyebrows rose, but he did not say anything, merely snapping off the end of the chocolate bar and putting it in his mouth.

"I was coming to see if you two are staying on or want to try another city on the planet, or what you plan to do," Alisa said. "I still need to hunt down cargo and resupply, but after today, I think I better try another metropolis. The idea of staying here makes me twitchy, now that I know the imperial army is hunting for your orb."

"I'm surprised you haven't asked me to leave yet," Alejandro said quietly, his gaze back on his work.

"There hasn't been enough time to cogitate and realize the wisdom of doing that."

"Are you asking now?"

"No. I mean, not exactly. I need money, and if you're willing to keep paying, you can stay aboard." Even as the words came out of her mouth, Alisa wondered at her offer. What was she thinking? She had her own mission ahead of her, one that would be hard enough to accomplish without people constantly attacking her ship because of Alejandro's presence. But if she sent him packing, Leonidas would go with him, and she found herself reluctant to say goodbye to him forever.

Leonidas broke off a piece of the bar and offered it to her.

"Thanks," she said, accepting it. Maybe it would help with her headache. Leonidas was not the only one who had expended a lot of energy tonight.

"Have you decided yet which city you'll go to next?" Alejandro asked.

"No. I'm open, so long as I can get a cargo. I'll put out some feelers, see what's out there tonight before I go to bed. I need a few hours of sleep before I trust myself to fly us anywhere. Besides, I don't want to leave without Beck. I need to figure out what happened to him."

Alisa grimaced. She liked Beck, but he was someone else who was making her life more complicated than it needed to be. If she found out he had gotten into trouble with campus security, she would help him get out of it, but if he was simply out shopping and carousing, maybe it wouldn't be such a bad idea to leave him here and look for another security officer, one who wasn't wanted dead by the mafia.

Leonidas offered Alejandro a piece of chocolate, but he refused it, moving around his patient to seal the gash on his arm.

"Will your implants heal on their own?" Alejandro asked. "Or do I need to do something?" He waved at the exposed circuitry.

That answered Alisa's earlier question as to whether he had any experience with cyborg surgery.

Leonidas gave her a wary look before answering, as if he anticipated that she would mock him or make a snide comment. She bit her lip, distressed that she and her sharp tongue had made him expect that.

"If the implants are seriously damaged, they need to be replaced," Leonidas said, "but they do have self-regenerating capabilities that will be adequate for this." He pointed his chin at the gash.

"Good." Alejandro pulled the ragged edges of the wound together, making the cybernetics disappear. "Captain, I still need the use of a comprehensive library. Would you consider putting down in New Dublin?"

Alisa nodded. "I'll see what's available in the way of cargo there."

With her daughter missing, it seemed inane to worry about something as prosaic as cargo, but she had rejected Sylvia's offer of a loan. Perhaps that had not been wise, given her predicament. She hated to be beholden to anyone, but she would need money to keep her ship in the air so she could hunt for Jelena. She had no idea if her daughter was even here on Perun, or if they had taken her to another planet altogether. She would head to that library, too, and do what she had wanted to do earlier, look up where the local Starseers could be found. Maybe she could get a lead from them.

"Good. I will continue to pay for my cabin," Alejandro said. "And I will pay for Leonidas's too."

Leonidas arched his eyebrows. "I can pay my own way."

"I insist."

"Oh? What do you expect from me in return for such largesse?"

"Maybe he expects you to perform sexual favors for him," Alisa said, the joke coming out before she could think better of it. *This* was why Leonidas expected mockery from her. She sighed.

"That seems unlikely," Leonidas said dryly. At least he did not seem offended.

"I'll go check on Beck." Alisa left them, feeling like she was fleeing. For some reason, she was not that comfortable in her skin around Leonidas. Maybe she should rethink her offer once again and ask them both to leave at the next stop.

The sickbay hatch clunked shut softly behind her, and she paused, frowning back at it. They hadn't bothered shutting it before. What were they about to say that they didn't want people to overhear? Or was she just being paranoid? Maybe Leonidas simply did not want anyone else to walk in and stare at his naked chest. Or maybe Alejandro needed him to take his trousers off to treat wounds on his lower half.

In her cabin, Alisa slid into the swivel chair bolted to the floor in front of the desk, the computerized mesh adjusting to cup her body comfortably. She reached for the comm, the flashing light catching her eye again. She should have checked her messages right away since one might be from Beck, but she found her fingers straying as the holodisplay popped up. The captain's cabin was tied into the controls in NavCom, so she could check the course and the sensors from her bed if she woke up in the night. She also had access to the master internal communications controls. She tapped a couple of buttons, and turned on the comm in sickbay, then leaned back to listen. She felt like a creep for eavesdropping again—intentionally—but that didn't make her turn off the speaker.

"Think we can trust her?" Leonidas was asking.

Alisa felt her heart speed up as adrenaline surged through her veins. Even though she had only activated the comm in one direction, she kept her breathing soft, afraid she might get caught listening if she made a noise.

"No," Alejandro said. "She's made it clear her loyalties are to the Alliance."

A silent moment stretched, and Alisa wished Leonidas would say something to defend her. Alejandro's words were true, but she had been helping them, hadn't she? She had nearly been killed multiple times now because she had first taken Leonidas to that secret laboratory and then gone with him to the library to assist Alejandro. It seemed unfair of them to condemn her.

"I would actually prefer it if she was simply motivated by money," Alejandro said, "because I could pay her for her silence, but when she talks of fares, it's usually an afterthought." He sighed. "I'm uncomfortable with how much she knows."

"She doesn't know any more than I do," Leonidas said, his tone dry again. "Which isn't much."

"I'm concerned that she'll report what she does know to her government."

Alisa swallowed. Yes, she had been considering doing just that. The main reason she hadn't done it was that they were on Perun, and she had no idea who she would report to from here. This didn't seem like the type of information she should beam across the system to a customer service representative accessible through the virtual government site.

"I suppose it would be terribly Machiavellian of me to ask if you would be willing to make her disappear."

If Alisa's heart had been racing before, it nearly leaped out of her chest now. From Alejandro's tone, it had almost sounded like a joke, but she could imagine the man watching Leonidas, seeing if he got an amenable reaction, in which case he might consider it more seriously...

"It would be evil and villainous," Leonidas said coldly.

"I suppose so." Alejandro sighed again. "I just feel that I can't fail in this, and it's making me paranoid. I don't sleep. I lay awake all night and worry."

"Prescribe yourself something then," Leonidas said, his voice still cold.

Alisa managed a faint smile, pleased that he rejected the idea of doing something heinous to her, but it didn't last. It was chilling to hear that Alejandro, a man wearing a monk's robe, damn it, would even consider making her "disappear." Were those robes even real? Had he sworn any oaths?

Alejandro chuckled. "You're a better man than I am, Colonel. All right, we'll stay aboard, at least until I can do the library research I need to do."

"I'll remind you that I have my own quest, Doctor. I don't need you to pay my way here, nor do I appreciate you assuming that I'm yours to command."

Alisa silently cheered for him. She was glad he still sounded irked at Alejandro. Maybe he would decide to abandon the doctor and his mysterious quest and stay aboard, accepting her offer of employment.

"I don't assume that," Alejandro said quietly. "But surely you must agree that my mission is of more importance than your personal quest. You have plenty of time for that later."

"Not if I get killed protecting your ass from people who should be my colleagues, not my enemies," Leonidas said, his tone going from cold to hot. "And I still don't know what your mission is, what you and your little artifact hope to accomplish."

"I'd think that should be obvious. The goal is to put the empire back together."

Leonidas snorted. "It's not a disassembled assault rifle that can simply be reassembled."

"It can be carved out again, with the proper tools and the proper leader."

"And who might that be?"

"You know exactly who I'm talking about."

"The boy? He's *ten*. He can barely tie his shoes. And we don't know if he's alive."

"You know that's not true," Alejandro said quietly. "He already has the power to tie *your* shoes. From across the room. And I know as well as you do that the emperor got him out of the palace in time."

The emperor's son? That had to be who they were talking about. The media had reported him dead. It wouldn't shock her to find out that he had been squirreled away somehow, but how could Alejandro be so sure? Had he been there at the end? Seen the boy taken? And what was the tying shoes bit supposed to imply? That he had Starseer abilities? Alisa was hearing too damned much about those people these days.

"He's still ten," Leonidas said. He did not sound surprised by anything Alejandro was saying. "Armies aren't going to follow him."

"Not now, no, but in eight, ten more years? Our people will have had time to rebuild and gather more resources by then, and the system will have seen what a farce the so-called Tri-Suns Alliance is. It'll be our time to move then, and I plan to do my part to facilitate that."

Alisa leaned back farther in her chair, her nerves calmer now that they weren't talking about her, but the conversation was still chilling. It also occurred to her that Alejandro might start to think about getting rid of her again if he had any idea that she was listening in.

"If you're done here," Leonidas said. "I'm going to bed."

"Yes, with your accelerated healing, you should be fine in a couple of days. Go ahead."

Alisa reached for the button that would turn off the sickbay comm— the last thing she needed was for Leonidas and his enhanced ears to walk by her cabin and hear her listening to Alejandro puttering around in there. But she paused as the men spoke again.

"I wouldn't get too attached to her if I were you," Alejandro added. "I can understand not wanting to kill someone in cold blood, but if she proves herself willing to betray us for the sake of her Alliance…"

"I'm not attached," Leonidas said coolly.

The hatch clanged as he shut it.

CHAPTER NINE

Alisa sat at her desk and stared at the holodisplay of her netdisc. The brightness of the visual had dimmed since several minutes had passed since she had touched it. She'd heard the hatch to Leonidas's cabin shut out in the corridor, followed by a second clang shortly after. Alejandro finishing up in sickbay and going to his room, perhaps. She hoped so. She had forgotten to get headache medicine and did not want to run into him if she went out for some. After what she had heard, she had no idea how she would look him in the eye without glaring daggers at him.

The idea that he thought she was expendable chilled her. Even if Leonidas wouldn't be Alejandro's henchman, a doctor could easily kill someone. He would know just how to make it look like an accident. A simple injection from a needle, and she might never wake up.

She shuddered, wondering if she should arrange his death first. But she had never done something like that, and she did not know if she could. The mere idea of murder made her stomach churn. She'd shot ships down in battle, and that had resulted in people's deaths, but she was no cold-hearted killer. She liked to think she had a few shreds of honor, eavesdropping tendencies notwithstanding. She would have to hope that the mild-mannered Alejandro did not have the balls to kill someone himself.

The only thing she had appreciated about listening to that conversation had been realizing that Leonidas was no cold-hearted assassin, either. She doubted she could trust him to choose her over Alejandro and the empire, if it ever came to that, but at least he wouldn't stab her in the back. No, if he ever killed her, he would shoot her in the chest. She wished that were more comforting. She did not want him to kill her at all. She wanted him to be someone she could trust. An ally. A friend.

She groaned and sat straighter in her chair, rubbing her eyes. With her mind spinning so much, she did not know how she would ever sleep, but she needed to try to find Beck first, regardless.

When she swiped her hand through the holodisplay, the messages light flashed again. Someone had commed the *Nomad* twice, both shortly before she had returned. A late hour to be making calls.

She poked the number, bringing up a face she didn't recognize, but that did not mean much, given that she had been gone for so many years. With short brown hair, old-fashioned spectacles, and a lean, almost gaunt face, the man was neither handsome nor memorable. He *did* wear an Alliance military jacket with major's pins on the collar, and that got her attention.

"Captain Marchenko," the officer said. "I'm certain you're busy, so I'll keep this short. My name is Major Mladenovic, 14th Intelligence Division. I'm aware that you've recently returned home and found that your husband is dead and your daughter is missing. My condolences on your husband. His passing was regrettable."

Alisa shifted in her seat, uncomfortable with how much the man knew. Intelligence Division. Spies, essentially. She doubted the Perunese knew this man was down here on their planet. She couldn't imagine that the empire was inviting Alliance officers down here with open arms.

"I want you to know that even though the war is over," Mladenovic continued, "and your contract was up even before it ended, you have friends in the Alliance army. Though we are a little concerned that you've taken on some imperial passengers with dubious credentials."

Alisa was glad she was listening to a recorded message and did not have to come up with a response immediately. The man's knowledge of her affairs was unsettling, Alliance army jacket or not.

"We would like to give you the opportunity to serve the Alliance once more, even as you've now phased into the civilian life. One of your passengers has an ancient and valuable artifact that you may or may not be aware of."

"No kidding," Alisa muttered, as the major arched his eyebrows and stared directly at the camera pickup.

"This artifact could ultimately be used against the Alliance. It doesn't look threatening on the surface, but I'm told it could lead to something powerful and dangerous. I'm sure you can understand why we would prefer to have it in Alliance hands rather than grubby imperial paws."

"Everyone wants it in their hands," Alisa said, rubbing her arms, remembering the way her hairs had stood up when the orb had been out of its box.

"Since you are in a position to get it, I'd like to offer a trade with you. I can give you information on your daughter's whereabouts if you'll simply bring the artifact to me at the dawn of the first sun—6:43 in the morning, the computer tells me. Meet me at the Spaceman's Wharf. It's just outside of the base where I believe you're docked." He continued to stare into the camera—straight at her. "I urge you to come, Captain. We can't let the imperials have anything that might let them gain back any control of the system. You remember what their rule was like. Please, do what's right."

"Do what's right?" she asked as the message ended, and blackness replaced his face. "Like coercing a woman into doing something illegal, such as say, *stealing*, by dangling information about her missing daughter in front of her for bait?"

She closed her mouth, remembering that Leonidas's cabin wasn't far away and that he had that special hearing. But it was hard not to talk, to shout, to *rail*. First, the major had told her that she had friends, but then he'd implied he would only give her information if she stole something for him. What kind of friend was that? Damned superior officers. He doubtlessly only saw her as a pawn, someone to be manipulated for his gain. Maybe for the Alliance's gain, too, and while she could support that, this was *not* right. Was he even acting on behalf of his superiors? Or had he somehow caught wind of the orb himself and was now trying to get it to further his own career?

Alisa pushed herself to her feet. The captain's cabin was larger than the other ones on the ship, but not so large that she could pace comfortably. She walked four steps, pushed off the wall, then walked the same steps in the opposite direction. She would be a fool to trust this major, and yet…he *was* an Alliance officer. Or at least he claimed to be. She eyed her computer, almost sitting back down to look him up, but then realized she wouldn't have access to the Alliance military database from here. She probably couldn't look him up.

Besides, what would she do if she found out he was a legitimate officer? Do as he asked?

It would be foolish, even if she could get away with it. She wouldn't be that worried about dealing with Alejandro, but with Leonidas? After he had defended her, or at least been unwilling to assassinate her, she hated the idea of him thinking she was a traitor.

"But I'm not a traitor," she muttered. "They've openly admitted that they're working for the empire." And they had admitted in secret, unaware of her eavesdropping, that they wanted to see the emperor's son returned to power, to see the *empire* returned to power.

Alisa shuddered, almost feeling betrayed that they could want that. But they had clearly been people of power in that system, people who had been rewarded for their loyalty. Maybe they had no idea how rough things had been for the average subject—or for anyone who had a mind and wanted to speak it.

She found herself slipping out of her cabin and padding down the corridor. She glanced warily at Leonidas's hatch as she passed it, wishing he and his superior ears were down in the cargo hold with the chickens. At least Mica's cabin was on the opposite end of the corridor. When Alisa reached it, she knocked softly. In the silence of the night, she could hear soft music through the hatch to Yumi's cabin next door. With luck, she would be too busy meditating to press her ear to the wall and listen to a conversation. Not that Yumi was likely to care about orb plots. Alisa hadn't gotten the impression that she was particularly loyal to one faction or another. She seemed like someone who stayed out of the way and pursued her own interests.

Alisa had to knock three times before the hatch opened.

"I'm not lighting any more candles today," Mica grumbled, rubbing her eyes and squinting into the dim light of the corridor.

"That's good, because open flame shouldn't be allowed on a spaceship." Alisa waved toward the dark cabin. "Can I come in?"

"Of course. I can see from the clock—" Mica glanced at a digital display embedded into the wall, "—that it's well into social hour."

Ignoring the sarcasm, Alisa stepped inside. The clock promised it was only four hours until dawn and that major's meeting time. She didn't have long to make up her mind.

"I need advice, Mica," she said softly, closing the hatch behind her. Darkness fell upon them, broken only by the faint glow from the clock.

"Does it require there be lights on?" Mica yawned and shambled back to the bunk set against the far wall.

"Not necessarily, but I want to show you a message I got."

Mica fumbled on the desk, and a holodisplay popped up, providing more light for the room. "Go ahead."

"I also need to tell you about what happened to me today before the sewer incident." Alisa patted her way to the chair at the desk, sat down, and explained the trip to her sister-in-law's apartment. She hadn't fully confided to Mica before about her family problems, but she was the only one on the *Nomad* that Alisa had known for more than a month. And she was Alliance. They had served together on the same ship for a year. They had some history together.

"I'm sorry, Alisa." Mica was sitting on her bunk, leaning against the wall with a blanket wrapped around her shoulders. "I wish I could help, but I doubt I know any more about Starseers than you do. It's too bad you couldn't use the library, even though I doubt you would find anything useful in public records."

"I see you're as optimistic as ever."

"What optimism I have in my reservoir gets divided by half for every hour after midnight it is."

"Right. Sorry to keep you up, but that's not the end of my story." Alisa took a breath and logged into the computer. She pulled up Major Mladenovic's message and played it again.

Mica listened in silence, waiting until it finished before she spoke. "He's familiar. We had an intelligence unit on one of the ships I served on near the end of the war, and I think he might have been the commander some of the men spoke of, the one sending orders."

"Well, that answers one question. I was wondering if he was a legitimate Alliance officer or if he'd just beaten someone up for a jacket."

Mica snorted. "He doesn't look that athletic." She ruffled her hand through her short, tousled hair. "He looks like an asshole honestly. Most majors are."

"Guess it's good I didn't stay in long enough to get promoted to such a lofty rank."

"Definitely."

"Mica." Alisa leaned forward. "Should I do it? What do you think? I don't trust him, but if there's even a chance that he could lead me to my daughter, how can I ignore it?"

"The Intelligence Division probably knows more about the Starseers than anyone else in the army," Mica said slowly, "but maybe it would be better to comm someone else. Don't you have the comm numbers for any superior officers you liked that you served with? Maybe someone could point you to a friendly intel officer who could help."

"I suppose, but it would be days, if not weeks, to get a response here. The Perunese may even be blocking or editing outgoing communications. My sister-in-law had to physically mail a letter through a private service to get word to me about my husband."

"A problem that is easily solved by leaving the planet and taking me somewhere with more employment prospects."

"So glad your job hunt is taking precedence over your sympathy for my plight, Mica."

"Sorry. It's not that. You know, I'm just…" Mica scooted to the edge of her bunk and put a hand on Alisa's shoulder. "I'm not good at sympathy and being womanly and caring and such. You're not, either, you know. I figure that's why we ended up drinking together back on the *Silver Striker* so often."

"I thought that was just because nobody else would drink with us."

"That too. We have the kind of wit that not everybody appreciates."

"And that starts wars."

"Probably true." Mica smiled and squeezed her shoulder before sitting back against the wall again. "I don't think you should trust him, but I think you're already planning to sneak into the doctor's cabin and steal the orb."

"Why are you so sure?"

"Because Mladenovic is the only lead you've got."

Alisa thought of the conversation she had overheard, of the proof that Alejandro did not care one way or another about her and wouldn't mind if she were dead. She had to admit that she felt less bad about the idea of stealing from him after that. Oh, she did not think anything she was contemplating was truly honorable, but her choices were limited.

What worried her more than the questionable morality of what she was considering was incurring Leonidas's wrath. He would be a terrifying enemy, and if she did take the orb and hand it off to someone, he would be back here at the ship, waiting for her to return. Or he might track her down before she had a chance to reach Major Mladenovic. She would have to figure out a way to get him and Alejandro off the ship, at least for a few hours, so she could fly away. If she could get off planet, she guessed—hoped—that they wouldn't come after her. They ought to be too busy trying to find the orb. They might go after Major *Mladenovic*, but if he could not take care of himself, that was his problem. She didn't owe anything to a man who was bribing her.

"You better watch out for Leonidas if you go through with it," Mica said. "He could break you in half with his pinky fingers."

"I'm very aware of that." The memory of his exposed implant popped into Alisa's mind. "That's why I need help."

"Help? I thought you were here for sympathy."

"Sympathy, advice, help…We can't try to get the doctor off the ship and search his cabin, because he takes that orb everywhere he goes. I need to sneak in and get it from him while he's sleeping, and then I need to hustle off to this meeting. At some point, he'll wake up and realize it's missing." Hopefully not until she had already made the trade. "I would guess that he'll get Leonidas and that they'll leave the ship. Can you rig something so that once they leave, they can't get back in?"

"With the doctor, it's that way now. You and I are needed to unlock the hatch. Or Leonidas. Remember how he was on the ship for weeks before we got to that junk cave?"

"Yes."

"Well, I'm fairly certain now that he was the one doing those repairs. He also gave himself access to a lot of the ship's systems, so he can go anywhere he wants."

"Can we revoke that access?"

"*You* can. You're hardwired in as the ship's original owner."

Was she? Her mother must have done that years ago.

Mica pulled up a different program on the holodisplay. "Here, authorize this, and I'll see what I can do about revoking his access. Then you can steal the orb and go."

"*We* can go," Alisa said as she typed in the passcode for the computer, then leaned forward so it could grab a retina scan.

"Eh?"

"If you're here when they wake up, they might question you."

"I can lock myself in here or in engineering. Probably engineering so I can monitor what they're up to on the rest of the—"

"Mica, I've seen him tear open locked metal doors and grates. I wouldn't be surprised if he could get to you through a locked hatch." Alisa eyed the one in the cabin. It was sturdy and thick, like something found on a submarine that had to withstand thousands of pounds of pressure underwater, but Leonidas's arms were even thicker.

"In other words, you've determined that I'm not getting any sleep tonight," Mica said.

"You could have slept earlier instead of praying to candles on the cargo hold floor."

"We weren't praying. She was teaching me how to meditate and relax my mind and my body. Apparently, I don't do that."

Alisa wondered if Mica's willingness to subject herself to meditation had anything to do with her finding Yumi cute, something she had mentioned before in passing.

"Did you not find the meditation as rejuvenating as a full night of sleep?" Alisa stood up and rubbed her hands together. She would have to do the next step of her plan by herself.

"Oddly not. People who stank of the sewers came in and interrupted us."

Alisa headed for the hatch. "How long will it take you to revoke his access?"

"Not long."

"Can you meet me at the cargo hatch in an hour? I want to give Alejandro more time to settle into a nice deep sleep."

"It's your plan," Mica said, not sounding enthused about it or her night of lost sleep.

CHAPTER TEN

Alisa thumbed on the flashlight on her multitool, choosing the red lens out of some vague hope that the color would be less likely to wake someone up than white. Not making noise probably mattered more. She hoped she could manage that. She knew these cabins well, but if Alejandro was sleeping with the orb under his pillow, all of her knowledge would be useless.

She slipped out of her cabin into the corridor—she had turned off the usual nighttime lights, so utter darkness filled the passage. She eased out into it, guiding herself by touch. She wore soft boots and a jacket warm enough for venturing out into the night. If she succeeded in escaping with the orb, she would head straight out.

She walked past Leonidas's hatch as quietly as she could, regretting that she'd assigned Alejandro a cabin right next to his when the doctor had first come aboard. A thump came from within it as she passed, and she froze, expecting the hatch to burst open. She would be caught before she even started. Dozens of excuses whirled through her mind, but then she reminded herself that she hadn't done anything yet. For all Leonidas knew, she could be going to use the head.

Another thump sounded inside of his cabin, but the hatch did not open. The noises sounded like they were coming from the back of the room, where the bunk lay, and she remembered that she'd heard such noises coming from Leonidas's cabin before at night. He wasn't a quiet sleeper. Maybe someday, if they met again and he didn't kill her for stealing the doctor's orb, she would ask him what cyborgs dreamed about. If. An optimistic thought. She doubted they would meet again. That made her sad. She liked him a lot more than she liked Alejandro. But not enough to foolishly try to keep in touch with him after she betrayed them. The system was a large place, and she could not see herself returning to Perun. With her husband dead and her daughter gone, there was nothing left for her here.

She forced herself to continue past the room, shaking away the feelings of loss. What she did tonight was for Jelena. Alisa had to believe that it would get her closer to finding her daughter.

When she reached Alejandro's hatch, she pressed her ear against the cool metal. No sounds came from within. Despite his words to the contrary, he must not have *that* much trouble sleeping.

Alisa turned off and pocketed her flashlight, then pressed her hand to the lock pad. It lit briefly, blue light brightening the corridor. The lock disengaged with a faint clunk. She lowered her hand and pressed her ear to the hatch again. The noise had not been loud, but if Alejandro was a light sleeper—or one paranoid about losing his orb—he might wake easily.

Again, she did not hear anything. Knowing she was about to cross the threshold, she gripped the old-style latch and slid it to the side. After this, she would not be able to claim that she was simply going to the head.

It was dark inside, the sounds of soft, even breaths coming from the back. The clock on the wall glowed a faint green. It did not provide enough light to see much, but she could make out the outline of the bunk and Alejandro's form on it. She tried to see if anything lay on the floor, both because she didn't want to step on his belongings and because it would be handy if his orb satchel was simply leaning against the wall by the door. It was too dark to pick out anything against the dark carpet.

Reluctantly, she withdrew the flashlight. Using it should save her time, keep her from patting around and possibly knocking something over. But she kept a nervous eye toward Alejandro's form as she flicked it on. She skimmed the red beam along the carpet, but did not see anything. The desk and chair were also empty. There were built-in drawers and cupboards that she could open, but the metal latches and doors weren't that quiet— there were identical ones in her cabin, so she knew. Besides, she suspected Alejandro was too paranoid to sleep that far from his precious orb.

She inched across the room and risked running the beam over his blanketed form. He slept on his side, facing the exit—facing *her*. His even breathing continued, but she worried that his eyes would pop open at any moment. She kept from running the beam close to his face and angled it down toward the carpet as soon as she had seen what she needed to see. He was not using the satchel for a pillow as he slept.

Alisa was about to head to the cabinets when she remembered the presence that the orb had. She had been able to feel it, like energy humming in the air during an electrical storm, when it had been out of its box on the pirate ship. Apparently, the box provided some insulation, because she had not noticed it other times, but she also had not tried to notice it. The thing—an artifact, the major had called it—disturbed her and made her want to stay away. But she could not do that now. She backed to the center of the room and flipped off the flashlight. Though she hated taking her attention from Alejandro, she closed her eyes and tried to open up her other senses. The even rhythm of his breathing comforted her slightly.

Alisa had no idea how to use her sixth sense or whatever it was that was involved in these things. Maybe she should have joined Mica and Yumi for meditation. An altered state of consciousness might be helpful for this.

After a few seconds, she thought she sensed something. Her imagination? Gooseflesh rose on her arms. The feeling seemed to originate from the direction of Alejandro's bunk. Maybe he *did* have it under his pillow. Or under his blanket.

Flicking her flashlight on again, she eased back to his side. Carefully, she lifted the edge of his blanket. A bead of sweat ran down her spine. Searching the room was one thing, but risking touching him? That was sure to rouse him.

She crouched down to look under the blanket without lifting it higher, sweeping the flashlight through the space. She couldn't keep from imagining Alejandro waking up and staring at her, his face less than two feet from hers. But all of her worries disappeared when she spotted the satchel nestled under the blanket and against his chest, the strap hooked around his wrist with his arm draped over it. Three suns, a lover would be jealous of the thing.

She couldn't detect the sewer odor, so he must have laundered it since they had returned earlier. Or maybe he had showered with it. Paranoid bastard.

There was no way she would try to get that strap off his wrist, but she put away the flashlight and risked poking her hand under the blanket. From the way he held it, she might be able to lift the flap and extricate the box without bumping him. Maybe.

Even as she tried, she could not believe she was doing this. There was absolutely no excuse she could make to explain herself if he woke up. No, she would have to club him over the head and hope for the best. She did have her Etcher in her holster. But she didn't want to kill him, and everyone would hear that gun going off. This would have been much less crazy if she had a stunner. She made a note to herself to buy a wider variety of weaponry someday—if she ever had time to go look for legitimate work.

She slid her hand under the flap and felt the corner of the box, the hard wood slightly warm under her fingers.

Alejandro grunted, his even breathing stopping. Alisa froze. His arm moved, and she yanked her hand out, dropping to the floor beside the bunk. He stirred further, the blankets rustling slightly. She lay on her back, looking up at the dark ceiling, her heart pounding against her rib cage. If he woke fully and decided to use the lav, he would step on her on his way out.

More rustling came, then a quiet pause. His even breathing started up again, fainter than before. Even though he sounded like he had fallen back to sleep without fully waking, she waited for several minutes before risking sticking her head up. She slumped with relief when she realized that he had turned over. Not only that, but he faced the wall now, and the satchel remained on the bunk behind him, his arms no longer around it, the blanket no longer covering it fully. Maybe one of the sun gods was looking down upon her and wanted to help. The strap might still be hooked to his arm, but she could easily reach the flap, and she did so, opening it. She eased the box out, her hands shaking as she backed away with her prize.

Alisa wanted to sprint for the corridor and the cargo hold so she could get off the ship as quickly as possible, but she made herself step slowly, quietly. She would still be in trouble if he woke up.

She eased into the dark corridor, looking both ways.

A thump came from her left, and she nearly dropped the box. She whirled, turning on the flashlight, expecting to find Leonidas standing there.

The corridor was empty. The noise had come from inside his cabin, not outside of it. Good.

Alisa hustled in the other direction, more eager than ever to get off the ship. She barely kept from sprinting down the steps and into the cargo hold. A few lights were on, and Mica waited near the hatch, yawning as she fiddled with something on her netdisc.

"Open the door," Alisa said. "We're going."

Mica eyed the box tucked under her arm. "I see that."

She wasn't moving quickly enough for Alisa's tastes, so Alisa leaned past her and thumped the button for the hatch. Cold salty air rushed in as the ramp lowered. Not waiting for it to settle, Alisa grabbed an empty shopping bag and hurried outside.

"How long do we have?" Mica asked, jogging to catch up.

Alisa waved at the sensor to close the hatch, then turned toward the empty walkway outside. At least, she *expected* it to be empty at this time of night, but she almost crashed into someone striding past a lamppost. For the second time in as many minutes, she nearly dropped the box.

A hand reached toward her, and she leaped back, her nerves on edge, before it registered that she knew who this was. How many people ambled along the concourse in full combat armor?

"Beck," Alisa blurted. "Where have you been?"

She felt guilty that she had forgotten about him ever since the major's message had come in. She had meant to look up his comm number and try to reach him.

Beck glanced over his shoulder. He wasn't wearing his helmet and had it tucked under his arm. He did not carry bags of chicken feed or anything that would suggest he had been out shopping. "Extricating myself from trouble."

"With campus security?"

"First with them, yes, but all I got was a warning there for walking onto campus with weapons. But on the way back, a truck screeched out from an alley and two men with rifles tried to take me down. I can't prove it, but I think they were White Dragon. They must have people on this planet—and the word must be out that I'm wanted dead." He grimaced. "I was wearing my helmet too. I shouldn't have been easy to identify. All I can assume is that they've got me tagged somehow. I'll have to take my armor to a master smith, see if he can figure it out."

"A good quest for you for tomorrow. Why don't you come with us now?" Alisa gripped his arm and turned him away from the ship, pointing down the dark concourse. She glanced back at the hatch, making sure it was still closed. Alejandro could wake up any moment and come storming out of the ship.

"Now?" Beck blinked and looked from her to Mica. Then his gaze snagged on the box under her arm. "Uhh, what's that?"

"A long story," Alisa said, relieved he had started walking. She stuffed the box into her bag so it would be less obvious. "But your timing is impeccable. We could use someone burly and intimidating for this meeting."

"And you chose me instead of the mech?" Beck lifted his head, sounding pleased.

"Of course."

Mica twitched an eyebrow in her direction but kept her mouth shut. Maybe she was too tired for sarcasm or pessimism tonight. Alisa certainly was.

She looked back a final time before a bend took the *Star Nomad* out of sight. She dreaded returning, not knowing if Leonidas and Alejandro would have left and been locked out, or if they would still be there, waiting to punish her for her betrayal.

No, she told herself once again. It *wasn't* a betrayal. They were enemies, both of them. She was Alliance. She needed to find her daughter. All of this was perfectly logical.

The words did not keep her from feeling that she had left her honor in shreds on the floor of Alejandro's cabin.

CHAPTER ELEVEN

"Someone's coming," Beck whispered, nudging Alisa with his elbow.

She blinked, coming fully awake, hardly able to believe that she had dozed off while standing against a stack of shipping containers. She, Beck, and Mica were in a rail yard across the parking lot from the Spaceman's Wharf, the restaurant Major Mladenovic had picked for their meeting place. The sky had lightened a few shades since the last time Alisa had opened her eyes.

Numerous cars were parked on the asphalt around the restaurant, while fliers perched in a separate rooftop lot. People walked in and out of the building, the scents of eggs and baking bread wafting out, but Beck wasn't pointing in that direction. He was looking toward their left, at dark shadows inside the rail yard between two rows of shipping containers stacked three high and towering thirty feet above the asphalt.

Alisa had decided to wait here, where cargo was removed from ships and put onto trains to transport across the continent, rather than in a booth inside the restaurant, because she hoped to see Mladenovic walking in. More specifically, she hoped to see Mladenovic and however many men he brought with him walking in. He shouldn't need more than a couple of people to ensure she cooperated and to give her the information she needed. If he brought an army, she would assume it was a trap.

Following Beck's pointing arm, Alisa spotted a man in unremarkable civilian clothes walking out of the shadows. It was the major, his glasses reflecting the light of a lamp near the edge of the rail yard. Two men in mismatched combat armor strode after him.

"Thought you said this fellow would be wearing an Alliance uniform," Beck said.

Alisa had summarized the message for him on the way over here, leaving out the details about her daughter. Beck had assumed she was turning the orb in for money, or just because the Alliance had ordered her to, and it had seemed simpler to let him believe that than explaining the truth.

"I'm not surprised he isn't," Alisa said.

"He would have the police or imperial soldiers jumping on him if he wandered around here in one of our uniforms," Mica said, pushing away from the post she had been sitting on and yawning. She might have been dozing too. "There's a police flier parked over there in the restaurant lot," she added.

"Hope that means that they'll come out to help if those two thugs in combat armor try to get rough," Alisa said, debating whether she should step out of the shadows to greet the major or wait for him to cross the street and go into the restaurant. She wasn't likely to have trouble with him in an eatery full of people.

"Are you making implications about the kinds of people who wear combat armor, Captain?" Beck asked.

"Just that they probably get crabby if they spend all day and all night in all that gear."

"Actually, the padding inside mine is quite comfortable. I've been known to lock the leg servos and take a nap while standing up."

"That's a revelation that'll make me feel particularly safe with you guarding my back in the future."

"I don't nap while *guarding* people, Captain."

They weren't talking loudly, but one of the men in armor caught up to the major and tapped him on the shoulder. He pointed at Alisa's group. So much for the safety of a booth in the restaurant.

The three men veered in her direction. Mladenovic's mouth moved as he murmured something. It might have been to his men or he might have had an earstar. It was too dark to tell. Alisa did not like the idea of him reporting to some superior that he had located her. Nor did she like the idea that he might have other men around that he could be checking in with. When she and Mica and Beck had arrived, Alisa had led them on a stroll around the rail yard and the restaurant, looking for any hidden trouble—such as squads of men poised to leap out and grab her. They hadn't seen anything, but it had still been fully dark then, leaving plenty of hiding spots, especially among the shipping containers.

"Want me to look tough and menacing, Captain?" Beck asked, shifting closer to her.

"Is that hard to do when you're outnumbered two to one?"

Technically, they were three to three, but Alisa did not have anything with her that could hurt someone wearing combat armor. She did not know what Mica had. She wore her big purse and was known for carrying home-made explosives and smoke bombs in it.

"Yes, but I can manage," Beck said. "I'm a veteran."

When he got close, Major Mladenovic lifted a hand, and the two armored men stopped. He continued forward a few steps, his eyes locking onto the bag Alisa had slung over her shoulder.

"Captain Marchenko," the major said, his gaze shifting to her face.

"Major," she said.

"You're early. And not in the Wharf."

"I assumed clandestine deals went on in shadow-filled places like this rather than at cheerful booths with yellow-flowered tablecloths."

"You've been watching too many spy vids." His gaze again shifted toward her bag, but he also eyed Mica's big purse.

She was leaning against the post, her arms across her chest, looking calm. It was hard to tell if Beck was flexing his shoulders and thrusting his chest out when he was in that armor, but either way, he was looming effectively. Too bad the major's men were just as good at looming. They carried rifles as well as their built-in weapons, and in the dim lighting, she thought she saw a grenade launcher poking up over one man's shoulder. Interesting choice for a meeting at a restaurant.

"One has to entertain oneself somehow during long flights." Alisa shrugged. "While I'm enjoying the small talk, you said—"

Her comm beeped, startling her. Out of habit, she almost reached for it, but she did not want to talk now. Besides, it might be Alejandro, having woken up and realized that she, Mica, and his orb were missing.

"Not going to answer that?" Mladenovic asked mildly when it beeped again, quite insistently.

"No, it's possible that's the owner of something I recently acquired."

His gaze sharpened. "You stole it? You didn't kill the monk?"

The monk? Was that what he thought Alejandro was? Interesting that an intelligence officer wouldn't know the full story, that Alejandro had been a doctor working for the emperor's family. Of course, maybe he did know and assumed that she did not.

"You didn't mention that as a requirement," Alisa said, boggled that he seemed to find the idea of theft more unappealing than killing people. And then taking their stuff. "Look, I have what you asked for. You said you have information to trade."

Beck's helmet swiveled toward her, but only briefly before he returned to glowering at his counterparts.

"The Starseers took her," Mladenovic said.

"I *know* that. But where?" Alisa's fingers curled into a fist. If all he had was the same information she had…Hells, maybe he'd seen the same video she had seen and that was it. All of this stress would have been for nothing.

"We can help you find her, but I need to see the artifact first." He held out his hand.

Alisa did not move. She needed time to consider. Was this truly the right thing to do? So many people wanted this thing. Did the Alliance have more right to it than the remnants of the empire? Maybe neither of them should have it. If it was some Starseer artifact, maybe *they* should have it. The thought that she could possibly trade it for her daughter if necessary jumped into her mind. Not that it was hers to trade. Three suns, what was happening to her morality? Before this night, she had never considered stealing. She had always believed she was an honorable person, someone who did the right thing. But what was the right thing in this situation?

"Captain," Mladenovic said, his voice growing cold. "If you think you're going to keep it for your own personal gain—"

"I don't care anything for personal gain. I just want my daughter, damn it."

Mladenovic took a step forward, his hand still out. "And I told you: we can help you find her."

The men in armor took a few steps forward too.

"Captain?" Beck whispered, lifting one of his arms, readying the embedded weapons.

"*Can* you help me, Major?" Alisa asked. "I don't think you know anything more about her kidnappers than I do."

"Not now perhaps, but I have the resources of a battalion of intelligence officers at my disposal. I *can* help. Once you give me the artifact."

"I fought for the Alliance for four years, nearly died more than once. One would think the army would offer to help me with this situation whether I give them anything or not."

Mladenovic's jaw tightened. "Enough of this." He lifted a hand toward his men. "Take it."

Beck stepped in front of Alisa, the energy weapons on both of his forearms popping up from their ports. "Don't even think of touching her."

One of the men fired at Beck as Major Mladenovic tried to lunge around him, reaching for her. Alisa leaped back, her shoulder blades brushing the shipping container behind her, and pulled out her Etcher. She glimpsed Mica ducking behind her post and throwing something to the ground behind the major and in front of his armored men.

As Mladenovic lunged for Alisa, smoke spewed forth from Mica's weapon. Alisa pointed her Etcher at the major, but he threw something as he lunged to the side. She fired, but was distracted by the object he'd thrown, and her shot went wide. Black threads snapped out, and something akin to a giant spider's web smacked into the front of her body, the strands sticking to her skin and her clothing. An ugly version of a fluidwrap.

She jerked her arm toward Mladenovic as he approached from the side, fighting against the restrictive embrace of the web to aim her Etcher at him. An instant before she fired, he kicked out, his boot striking the bottom of her hand. She kept her grip on her gun, but pain exploded where he'd struck her, and the sticky strands stuck to the barrel. She could not aim her weapon except by turning her entire body around. She got off another shot, but it again flew wide.

The major sprang at her, crashing into her and taking her to the ground. Alisa was aware of Mica shooting from behind her post and of Beck now grappling with one of the armored men. The second one was running toward Mica, her bullets bouncing uselessly off the chest plate.

Alisa yelled, enraged that she had allowed herself to be taken down, that she couldn't help. Mica had no way to defend against an armored man. Not only was Alisa helpless to do anything, but worse, the major had her pinned. He pulled out a dagger with a serrated blade, and fear surged through her. Would he truly stab her in the chest?

No, he sawed at the strands wrapped around her—around the *satchel*. He meant to cut it out and run off with it.

Growling, Alisa bucked, trying to knock him off her.

"Stay still, you dumb bitch," he growled, grabbing her neck with one hand while he kept cutting with the other. "You should have just given it to me, you imperial traitor."

"Traitor?" she roared, too furious with her stupidity in getting herself into this to be afraid of the fingers clasped around her throat. "I risked my life to take this. For the Alliance. I've always been loyal to the Alliance. I just want my daughter back."

Mladenovic kept cutting, his face utterly impassive at her plight.

A gust of wind came down from above, some ship flying overhead. Alisa did not pay it any attention—she was too busy trying to figure out how to get out of her predicament—until it swooped lower, right over their row of shipping containers. A hatch in the back opened, and people starting firing.

"Alcyone's wrath," the major cursed, looking away from her and toward the sky.

She finally managed to land a useful blow, driving her knee upward and into his groin. He yowled and rolled away, grabbing his crotch.

Bullets and blazer bolts slammed into the ground all around them, stealing Alisa's momentary feeling of satisfaction. She couldn't get up—the cursed strands were sticking her arms to her torso—so she rolled toward the sturdy wall of the shipping container, hoping it would provide some shelter.

Wind caused by the blades of a rotary ship whipped her hair free of its braid—and the netting—so that it lashed her in the eyes. No less than four men in black with masks pulled over their faces leaned out of the hatch, shooting at the people on the ground, her people and Mladenovic's. The snipers seemed to fire without aiming, not caring who they hit.

Someone cried out. Mladenovic? It was a horrible thought, but Alisa hoped so. Better him than Beck or Mica. Or her.

A white form lunged in from the side, blocking Alisa's view of the sky. Beck.

He grabbed her and slung her over his shoulder, netting and all. She lost sight of the ship and of everything as her face was mashed against his armored back. He took off at a sprint, racing deeper into the rail yard. He fired backward as he ran, alternating between shooting at Mladenovic's men and shooting at the ship.

"Mica?" Alisa yelled, not able to see her as she bounced along on Beck's shoulder.

"She's ahead of us," he blurted, still firing. He raced around a corner and then another one. "There she is," he added, pumping his legs harder.

All Alisa could see was his back and the asphalt blurring past underneath them. A boom sounded, rattling the ground and the stacks of shipping containers.

"What was that?" Alisa asked.

"Grenade launcher."

One of Mladenovic's men had been carrying that.

"Were the people on that ship there to get *him*?" Alisa asked, trying to think even as her brain was rattled by her bumpy ride. Could the imperials have spotted the major skulking about and come after him? If they had, wouldn't they have come in a military ship and with uniformed men? Those people in black had seemed more like—

"I don't think so," Beck said. "That ship was white with a dragon snout painted on the front." He kept running as he spoke, weaving through the maze of shipping containers. "They aimed at me first, I think. Then probably fired on the major's soldiers because they fired at them. I'm not complaining, but we need to get inside somewhere. Hide until they go away."

"Sounds like a plan," Alisa said.

What else could she say? She couldn't even demand to be set down, not until she figured a way out of the web. What a mess. She still had the orb, for all the good it had done. She didn't know any more about her daughter's whereabouts than she had the night before.

CHAPTER TWELVE

"You've definitely gotten yourself in a mess, Captain," Beck said as he carefully cut away the horrible black strands that seemed to stick to every inch of Alisa's body.

"I wish I could say that it was the worst mess I'd experienced in the last twenty-four hours, but I think the sewer wins the contest."

"Yes," Mica said, wrinkling her nose.

They stood together in a family lavatory in the space base, the door locked to keep out others—the concourse had grown increasingly busy as the morning progressed. Mica leaned against a diaper-changing table while examining the remaining explosives in her purse. They were certainly a strange "family."

"This is perhaps more humiliating than the previous mess," Alisa added. "I hate being helpless. And needing to be saved." Technically, Leonidas had saved her in the sewers too. This was not her day.

"Aw, I like saving people, Captain. It's my job."

"And I do appreciate that you were quick to do it, but that doesn't make me feel better about myself."

"Well, Captain—" Beck tugged some of the sticky netting off her back, "—that's *not* my job. Maybe you could hire a therapist for the crew."

"For a crew of three?"

Alisa arched her eyebrows at Mica, realizing that her entire crew of three was spending time in a family lavatory together. If she hadn't been in a dour mood, she might have laughed. But she didn't laugh. Seeing her entire tiny team there only made her realize that nobody she truly trusted was on her ship right now, and that men who were probably in the mood to shoot her right now might be there instead. She hoped Leonidas and Alejandro had run down the ramp to look for her and had been locked out, as she and Mica had planned. She also hoped that, after they had realized they had been locked out, they had taken off looking for her, ideally in the wrong direction.

Mica waved toward the sink. "You may need to stick your head in water to get that goop out of your hair."

"No opinion on the therapist, eh?" Alisa asked.

As Beck continued to cut the threads away, Alisa grabbed some of the sanitizing gel in the dispenser and rubbed it into her hair, hoping it would break the bonding agent.

"I'm sure Yumi can give you something if you want to improve your state of mind," Mica said.

Alisa smiled bleakly. She had never experimented with drugs, unless one counted the occasional second-hand dosage acquired from walking through the rec room in the dorm at school, but the idea of using something to numb her aching brain—and ego—right now did have some appeal.

Her eyes ached, too, tired and gritty from lack of sleep. While it might have been wiser to wait a few hours—or a few days—before returning to the ship, she wanted to curl up in her bunk and pass out. She also had the notion that if Alejandro and Leonidas *were* still aboard, they might react less harshly if she returned the orb of her own free will.

Just took it out to get some fresh air, boys. You're welcome...

"Think that's as good as I can get with my knife, Captain," Beck said, stepping back and eyeing her from head to toe. "Might need a woman's touch to deal with the rest." He looked at Mica.

Mica raised a frank eyebrow. "I have paint thinner and a welding torch in engineering."

Alisa held up her hand. "I can manage the rest on my own. At least I can walk now."

"Might need to run if your cyborg buddy is waiting at the ship for you," Mica said.

Alisa picked up her bag and slung it over her shoulder, still hoping that Leonidas and Alejandro would be gone when she returned. But maybe it would be better if they *weren't* gone. Then they would take back the orb, and that would be the end of her criminal career. If they were not there, she might be tempted to enact that plan she had envisioned, of finding the Starseers and trying to trade the orb for her daughter.

They left the indoor facilities, Alisa's stomach rumbling as they passed a robot vendor selling freshly baked cinnamon stars, frosting dribbling from their points. Reluctantly, she reminded herself that she had cereal in the ship. Too bad money was in short supply. The pastries smelled fabulous.

She did veer off the path briefly when she spotted an ambulatory vending machine selling chocolate bars. They weren't the high-quality bars that she preferred, but her stash was low, and if she had to take off soon, she might not get a chance to resupply. There was no way she would risk going into deep space without chocolate.

The vending machine stopped as soon as it detected her interest, swiveling on its wheels to turn its wares toward her. She waved her chip card at its sensor before remembering that her bank account seemed to have disappeared.

"Funds inaccessible," the vendor announced brightly. "Physical cash or barter?"

Surprised it accepted physical coin, Alisa dug into her pocket, glad she had made Yumi and Alejandro pay her that way. A twinge of guilt ran through her as she wrapped her hand around a couple of the coins, realizing that Alejandro surely hadn't expected her to steal his belongings when he'd paid her for passage.

"Barter?" Mica asked.

"The team at Vendomatic Satisfaction is collecting raw materials and valuable items for the rebuilding of Perun. If you have such items, please place them on my tray for consideration. I am programmed to analyze them and offer a fair trade."

Mica plucked off some of the sticky strands still wrapped around Alisa's sleeves and back.

"I'm sure that's not what it has in mind for raw materials," Alisa said as Mica wadded them up and wiped them on the tray.

"I'm out of metals and plastics."

The vending machine sucked in its tray and hummed to itself. A scraping came from within it, and Alisa imagined the machine trying to figure out a way to dispose of the sticky strands.

"0.57 morats in credit," it announced, and lights flashed inside its case, signifying the items she could purchase.

"Huh," Alisa said.

"If you let me work on your legs, you might be able to get a bottle of FizzBurst too."

Alisa tapped the display in front of the chocolate she had been eyeing. "No, thanks. That stuff tastes like lemon-flavored takka, and I'd never get to sleep."

"Do you really want to sleep when an irate cyborg is after you?"

Alisa sighed, accepting the chocolate and heading for the door. She wished she could deny that anyone might be after her, but the bag weighed heavily against her hip as she stepped outside.

The sea air smelled of rain, and storm clouds lurked over the harbor. That did not keep people from busily streaming along the concourses, on their way to and from ships. Alisa watched the passersby for familiar faces. Beck, walking behind her and Mica, was doing the same thing, though he was surely watching for White Dragon representatives instead of Leonidas and Alejandro.

"Any idea how you can buy them off, Beck?" Alisa asked.

"Who? The mafia?"

"Yes. Surely, they have some price that they would consider acceptable."

"My life," he said glumly. "That's the price they have in mind."

"It must be costing them a lot of resources to keep sending people after you. Maybe you could bargain with them."

"I doubt they'll accept a wad of sticky webbing. As I told you before, if I could turn in a certain cyborg for an extremely handsome reward, I might have enough to pay them off."

Alisa grimaced, wishing she hadn't brought the subject up again. It just seemed that they ought to be able to come up with a way to get Beck out of his trouble. A way that did not involve betraying anyone else.

"He's too dangerous," Alisa said. "Got any other ideas?"

"If I could make it big with my sauce line, maybe I could eventually make enough money, but that'll take years, especially since I'm not able to actively work on it now. I don't have anything else of value."

Beck glanced toward Alisa's bag, but did not suggest that she give him the orb to trade. She was not surprised the idea crossed his mind. Who wouldn't be tempted by a little theft in order to get out of trouble?

"You're welcome to work on your project in your spare time on the ship," Alisa said as they stepped onto the moving walkway that would take them to the *Star Nomad's* berth.

"Making sauces?"

"The mess kitchen is a good size."

"The appliances don't work, the utensils are rusty, and there were cockroaches nesting in the stock pot when I first came aboard."

"My kitchen has a stock pot? Huh."

Beck gave her a sour look.

"At least the price is right. You would have to pay to rent a commercial kitchen."

"I suppose. When are we leaving? Maybe I could take my wages and order some ingredients for the next stage of our trip."

"Leaving might be difficult," Mica said, pointing toward Dock 87, where the *Nomad* rested at the end of a concrete pier.

The ramp was down, with the hatch open and Yumi standing at the top of it. Leonidas stood at the bottom wearing his crimson combat armor, all save the helmet, which rested under his arm. That meant Alisa had no trouble seeing the fearsome expression on his face as his gaze locked onto her. It was much different from the calm face he'd had in sickbay, looking almost innocuous as Alejandro tended his wounds. Now he looked like... an enemy.

Alisa did her best not to squirm as the moving sidewalk took her closer. His hard gaze never left her face. His mouth moved as he spoke, probably to his earstar rather than to Yumi, who was tinkering on her netdisc. Three suns, she wasn't holding the door open for him, was she? To ensure he wasn't locked out? Maybe he had figured out the problem and had forced her to do so, though she appeared calm as she poked at a holodisplay, not under any duress.

"It's not too late to turn around and run the other way, Captain," Beck observed, apparently also the recipient of Leonidas's flinty gaze.

Alisa sighed. "Yes, it is."

She had seen Leonidas run. He could catch them easily.

As Alisa stepped off the sidewalk and headed down the pier toward their ramp, she glimpsed Alejandro running toward them from farther up the concourse, pushing past people as he raced the wrong way on the moving sidewalk. His expression was more panicked than flinty, and she shrank within herself, feeling guiltier than ever for taking his artifact. Even if it wasn't his and had only been lent to him on behalf of the empire. She imagined how she would have felt if something of such value had been taken from her. Hells, she felt that way now, about Jelena.

She reached Leonidas first, who, thankfully, was not pointing any weapons at her. Not that he needed a weapon to strangle someone. She removed her shopping bag and offered it to him—Alejandro was still running in their direction, his robe flapping around his ankles.

"Couldn't get the price you wanted?" Leonidas asked coldly.

"That's...more accurate than you know. Here, take it." Alisa tossed the bag to him and took a step toward the ramp, not wanting a lecture from him or from Alejandro.

Leonidas caught the bag, but he also caught her arm, his steel grip keeping her from escaping into the ship.

"If you make a habit of stealing from your passengers—"

"I don't." She tugged at her arm, though she well knew that she wouldn't get it back unless he let go.

Beck stepped forward, though hesitantly. He did not want to tangle with Leonidas, and she could not blame him.

"Don't let her go," Alejandro blurted, racing down the pier toward the ramp. "We'll turn her in to the army headquarters here in town. They can question her, find out what she's told the Alliance."

Alisa spun toward him, as much as she could with Leonidas holding her arm. "Look, I brought it back. I haven't told anyone anything. You're passengers on *my* ship, *my* guests. You don't get to turn me in to anyone."

Beck intercepted Alejandro before he could run up the ramp, catching *him* by the arm.

"You brought it back," Leonidas snarled. "That makes it acceptable that you snuck into the doctor's cabin and stole it out from under him while he slept?"

"I didn't have a choice, all right?" She yanked at her arm again, hating the disappointed look that he turned on her. "Get off me, mech."

It was the wrong time to use that derisive term, and she knew it as soon as his blue eyes clouded over, as stormy as the sky above the harbor. She didn't care. Panic swelled in her breast as she imagined them carting her off to some imperial interrogation headquarters.

"Yes, I'm sure someone *made* you steal it," Alejandro said. "While aboard your own ship, a ship you could simply fly away in at any point. We can play the cameras, but I highly doubt armed men stomped onto the craft and held guns to your head and told you to take it." He tried to yank his arm away from Beck, but with his combat armor, Beck was just as immovable as Leonidas.

"Mladenovic said he knew where my daughter is, damn it," Alisa growled. "I don't have any other leads. I had to do it, all right? But he lied. Just like everyone on this damned planet lies. He's probably been brainwashed into being an asshole by too much time down here in the empire." She scowled fiercely at Leonidas and Alejandro, the scowl of the righteous. The scowl of the wronged. Or the wrong. She was being defensive because they had a case, and she knew it, but she didn't care. She just wanted to get out of this hole and find her daughter. "Beck, let him go. You two don't like how things work on my ship, then get off. Maybe you shouldn't have lingered here so long. It's not a suns-damned hotel."

To her surprise, this time when she tried to yank her arm away, Leonidas let her go. She almost fell on her ass. She flailed her arms and kept from toppling, then spun and stalked up the ramp. Yumi was watching it all, her mouth open, her eyes wide.

"The empire has your daughter?" Leonidas asked, his tone masked now, hard to read. "Why?"

Alisa almost chose not to answer, having the urge to keep walking, to hide in the cargo hold and shut the hatch before Alejandro could make another attempt to have Leonidas cart her off to the imperials. Yet, in her frustration, she answered before she could debate the wisdom of doing so.

And maybe a part of her hoped they would understand why she had done it if they knew, that they wouldn't continue to think of her as a lowlife thief.

"Not the empire. The Starseers. I saw the video myself. They took her right out from under my sister-in-law's nose. And I have no idea where to even start looking. It was months ago. Mladenovic said…Oh, it doesn't matter. It's all lies." Her frustration was threatening to bubble over into tears. This time, she did stalk inside, turning her back on all of them and fleeing to her cabin.

Nobody stopped her. She locked the hatch and dropped onto her bunk, yanking the blankets over her head.

CHAPTER THIRTEEN

It was hunger rather than a desire to see anyone that eventually drove Alisa to contemplate leaving her cabin. She had slept some, having nightmares of Jelena in a dark, cobweb-filled monastery being indoctrinated by the Starseers and turned into a monster who did not recognize her own mother. She'd woken from those horrible dreams, eaten the chocolate bar, then lay on her bed awake, her knees curled to her chin as time ticked past, barely noticed.

Twice, someone had knocked at her hatch, but she had ignored it. With so many dangerous enemies looking for the people aboard her ship, she ought to be making plans to leave, but she had not felt like being that mature. She also wasn't sure that Alejandro was not out there, plotting a way to drag her away and turn her over to his imperial thug allies.

Her stomach growled, longing for real food, the chocolate forgotten. The smell of something cooking drifted through the vents, making her notice her hunger even more.

Alisa rolled out of bed and headed for the lav. In the future, she would keep food and water stashed in her cabin for the days when she wanted to lock herself in and sulk like a toddler. She washed up, putting on her last change of clothing and hoping that the laundry machine could get the rest of that sticky stuff off the things she wadded up and stuck in the chute.

When she ventured farther afield, she did so quietly, hoping she would find that Leonidas and Alejandro had packed up their belongings and left. She did not want to deal with either of them, did not want to see that disappointed expression in Leonidas's eyes again. Better if she never saw either of them again. All they had brought was trouble. If they both left, then all she would have to deal with was Beck and his mafia issues. Even though the White Dragon people had tried to shoot them all just that morning, it seemed a simple problem in comparison to the artifact and the empire and all that Alejandro wanted to do.

The tantalizing smell of freshly grilled meat and vegetables led her to the mess hall. Voices came from the room, and she was tempted to turn around, to wait a couple of hours more and hope for leftovers. But the food smelled too good to resist.

Beck had his portable barbecue unit out, some kind of seasoned burgers cooking over the flames. A few were finished cooking and rested on a plate in the center of the table where Yumi and Mica sat. Leonidas was also there, leaning against the wall, no longer in his combat armor but no less intimidating in plain clothes. Alisa groaned to herself. If he was still here, Alejandro was probably still here too. What did she have to do to get rid of these people?

Avoiding his gaze, she ducked past him to grab a bun and a burger. She avoided Mica's and Yumi's gazes, too, beelining for the rec room. The wide hatch usually stayed open, but she unhooked the chain and closed it behind her.

She sat down at the table, ignoring the flashing lights on the surface that invited her to play one of the games programmed into it, and made it halfway through her meal before someone knocked. She closed her eyes, tempted to ignore it, to stay quiet and pretend she wasn't in there. But she had walked past three people, and it was not as if there was a back door she might have escaped through.

The knock came again, not hard and demanding but a soft rap, such as one might make with a couple of knuckles.

Hoping it was just Mica—she did not want to talk to Alejandro—Alisa called, "It's not locked."

She could not bring herself to offer more of an invitation. She did not want company. She knew she had done a dishonorable thing, and she did not need anyone pointing it out. If she had gotten her daughter's location, or at least some concrete information on who had her, it might have been worth it. But she hadn't.

The hatch opened. She focused on her burger, taking another chomp. Battered morals or not, she hadn't eaten much in the last twenty-four hours, and her stomach would not stand for being ignored. Even so, she almost lost her appetite when she saw who loomed in the hatchway. It wasn't Mica.

"Figured you'd be gone by now," Alisa said, staring straight ahead at the table.

Leonidas looked at her, then looked over his shoulder—Yumi's and Beck's voices floated in, along with the scent of a fresh round of charbroiled meat. Lamb, Alisa had decided as she had been eating, heavily spiced with orakesh. It was a favorite dish from the southern continent here, though Beck had added an interesting twist, a hint of orange and pepper.

Leonidas stepped inside and closed the hatch.

Alisa licked her lips for reasons that had nothing to do with the spices. She remembered Alejandro's statement that she should be interrogated. He had suggested dragging her off to some imperial facility for it, but maybe he had decided to settle on having his local cyborg do it. The day before, Leonidas might have objected to the idea of assassinating her, but that had been before she had stolen the doctor's orb.

She kept her gaze forward, pretending indifference to this enforced privacy, but she watched him out of the corner of her eye. She picked up the burger for another bite, not wanting him to think she was worried.

"Yumi gave us some interesting information after you went to your cabin," he said. His voice was level, not threatening. He walked to the opposite side of the table and sat across from her. If he was still angry, he was hiding it.

"Oh?"

"She says she knows the location of one of the main Starseer temples."

Alisa froze, her burger held in the air before her, juices running down her wrists. Was it possible? That *Yumi* of all people might be a resource in this? "I wouldn't have guessed that she knew the location of more than the closest colony of *jashash* growers."

It was a snide thing to say, and Alisa was glad the hatch was closed. Yumi had proven she had knowledge about more than her quirky hobbies.

"I wouldn't have guessed, either," Leonidas said, "but she claims one of the largest temples is on Arkadius."

"On Arkadius? The Alliance seat of power and one of the oldest and most populated planets in the system? I think someone would have noticed during the Order Wars if there was a Starseer base there."

"The Starseers are good at not being found."

"Tell me about it." Alisa set her burger down with more force than required, and crumbs tumbled off the plate and onto the table. She had not even started looking for her daughter yet, and she was already frustrated with the Starseers.

"I've spoken to Alejandro, and he believes the Starseers may have the answers he seeks since the artifact is of Starseer origin. Getting those people to give him the answers without taking the orb from him will be a challenge, but he thinks it's worth the risk. He could spend the next five years researching in libraries, assuming he can get close to any more libraries without being captured by soldiers, and not find what he's looking for."

"Why are you telling me this?" Alisa finally met his eyes, more than a little worried about the sharing of information that they had heretofore been secretive about. Maybe they had plans to kill her, after all, and figured it didn't matter what she knew now.

"It's not obvious? We need a ride."

"A ride?" she mouthed. How could they possibly want to continue on with her now? Surely, there were other ships heading that way, and if not, it seemed that Alejandro had money enough to bribe someone to change course for him. "Alejandro wants to continue to be my passenger?"

"No, but he's realized, or he did after I pointed it out to him, that the reason we were likely allowed down to the planet in the first place was not because of some special stature he has among the remaining imperials. Someone knew he had the orb and wanted a chance to get it."

Someone. Senator Bondarenko?

"I didn't figure it was the doctor's winning personality or ability to quote scripture that got him invited down," she said. "But why fly with me? There are other ships."

"We're here already. And *Yumi's* here. She's the one with the map to the temple in her head. Oddly, she wishes to stay aboard while she looks for employment."

Alisa snorted. "Did you try to bribe her to get her to leave with you?"

"Alejandro may have."

She snorted again. Alisa could not imagine why Yumi cared one way or another who she rode with, other than that her chickens were settled in here, but she found herself smugly pleased that Yumi had turned down Alejandro's bribe.

"There's also an implication that she can get us an invitation in to see the Starseers," Leonidas said. "Since their usual modus operandi is to diddle with the minds of the people who try to find them, causing them to become lost, that could be useful."

"You believe she has this knowledge and these connections? When you don't know anything about her?"

"We have no reason not to trust her." His tone chilled a few degrees. "It's not as if she's tried to steal from us."

"Not us, *him*," Alisa growled. "I haven't taken anything from you."

"I have nothing of value. Unless you count what's under my skin, and those implants wouldn't be worth much these days. Old tech, you understand."

"You act like I'd slice you open to make two tindarks." For some reason, his disdain affected her more than it should have, and she found her throat tightening with emotion, a mix of frustration and something else she couldn't identify. "Look, I'm not a thief. I'm just—"

She swallowed and looked away, unable to get more words out. It would have been an excuse, anyway. *Wasn't* she a thief now? It did not matter that she'd brought the orb back. She wouldn't have if the original plan had worked out.

"Never mind," she said when she found her voice again. "Fine, whatever. You want a ride, it's another two hundred tindarks each. I need to pay Beck and get supplies for the voyage."

"Don't forget to save for a down payment on your combat armor."

She smiled bitterly, remembering how he had said that with her mouth, she would need a set. He probably believed that now more than ever. Tears threatened to form in her eyes, and she looked away, waving him toward the hatch, hoping he would accept that the conversation was over and leave. She let out a breath of relief when he stood and headed toward the mess room.

Still looking toward the far wall, she lifted her hand and wiped her eyes. She didn't want anyone to see her cry, not when she had no one to blame but herself for her current mess. If she hadn't joined the Alliance four years ago—

"You never mentioned you have a daughter," Leonidas said quietly from the hatch.

He hadn't opened it yet.

Alisa swallowed, lowering her hand, not wanting him to guess at her tears. "It's nobody else's business."

"How old is she?"

She meant to harshly say, "Why do you care? Go away." What came out was a sniffle and, "Eight." She hated bothering other people with her problems, but a part of her wanted him to know so that he might understand, so he would not condemn her for the choice she had made. "It's been a year and a half since I've seen her in person. I was a pilot and made the choice to help the Alliance when they sent out the recruiting papers. I left Jelena and my husband because I thought I was joining a worthy cause, doing something that would make her life better. And his too. He didn't have the freedom to do the research he wanted, and I know it ate at him, frustrated him. But it was a hard choice—what kind of mother leaves her daughter for four years when she's that young? At the time, I didn't know it would be that long, but...I've regretted the choice many times since then." She wiped her hand down her cheeks, smearing away the tears that had escaped, keeping her head turned away from him. She wagered that cyborgs never cried.

"We all make choices we regret," Leonidas said quietly.

A part of her wanted to stay silent, in the hope that he would go away. A part of her was curious and didn't want him to go away.

"What do you regret, Leonidas?" she asked.

He hesitated. Not sure he wanted to share with a thief? Her mouth twisted as she looked down at her plate—she was tired of looking at the wall.

"Among other things," he said, "I have no children."

"You still have time for that, if you don't let Alejandro get you killed."

"Perhaps." He said it the way someone says something to be agreeable, not because they really mean it.

Odd. It wasn't as if he was ugly. Alisa was sure there were plenty of women who would drool over his big muscles, and he had a handsome face when he wasn't glowering.

"She might like you," Alisa said.

"Who?"

"My daughter. Her favorite cartoon character is Andromeda Android." Realizing he might take offense to being compared to an android, Alisa hurried to add, "If you haven't seen the show, Andromeda was created by the empire to do its bidding. She broke free from a mad scientist's laboratory and now lives in the underworld on Perun, solving crimes and helping the downtrodden. She has a psychic cat named Boo. That's possibly the reason Jelena liked the show so much, especially when she was four. Hm, you should probably get a cat, Leonidas."

She glanced at him to check his reaction. His brow was wrinkled as he gave her one of his I-find-your-humor-perplexing looks. Well, at least he did not appear offended.

"Jelena and I used to watch the cartoon together when I was home from my delivery runs. In the middle of the day, while Jonah was at work. It was our time."

"I see." He waited, perhaps to see if she would say more, and then tugged on the handle to open the hatch.

"Leonidas?" she asked.

He paused. "Yes?"

"I'm sorry I called you a mech."

"You're not the first."

"No, but…" Alisa groped for a way to say that she had come to think of him as a friend—whether that was wise of her or not, all things considered—but she found that hard to admit. Perhaps because she doubted he would admit it back, not now. Maybe not ever. "I always thought of myself as honorable. But I guess it's easy to be honorable when your life is normal and your needs are met. It's when you get desperate that your morality really gets tested, isn't it?"

"It is," he agreed.

"Do you have any family, Leonidas?" She wasn't sure why she kept using his name when there was nobody else in the room. Maybe as an apology for calling him something else earlier, implying he was less than human.

"My parents are gone. I have two younger brothers."

"I was an only child. I always wanted brothers or sisters. Someone to play with on the ship during the long voyages. I never knew my father, and when my mom didn't make it back from her last freight run—well, that was hard. I was glad I had Jonah by then. It seems wrong that now, years later, I have less than I had before. Aren't you supposed to accumulate more things—more friends, more family—as life goes on?"

"Not in my experience." Was that a hint of regret in his voice? If he truly wanted children, why hadn't he tried to find someone? Had he been too busy with his career as a military officer?

"Are the brothers at least good company?" Alisa met his gaze, this time for more than a second. Her eyes had dried, and it seemed safe to do so.

He scoffed.

"Surely, they don't pick on you." She waved at his brawny arms.

"Neither of them have any interest in talking to their half-machine brother." He smiled, as if in indifferent dismissal, but it did not look that sincere. "One of them joined the Alliance."

"That *is* a crime."

He glowered at her, though it seemed more of a mock glower this time. It made her smile. She doubted he would forgive her for taking the orb, or trust her going forward, but at least he wasn't threatening to pull her toenails off to make her talk.

A knock came at the hatch. Leonidas opened it, and Mica poked her head in, eyeing them warily. She leaned back out again.

"They both have their clothes on," she announced.

Alisa felt her eyebrows fly up. *That* was what people had been speculating about out there? Not that she was in here being tortured for information?

"Really," Leonidas said dryly and walked out.

Mica came in and took his vacated spot. "I ordered supplies today while you were hiding—"

"I was sleeping."

"Where no one could reach you. Our groceries and the parts that were available have been dropped off. I'll have to make do with some things until we have time to wait for delivery of a special order. That's all fine, but what I came to tell you is that we may have trouble."

"How extraordinarily novel for us."

"Yes." Mica slid her netdisc onto the table and thumbed the holodisplay to life. "That's the camera by the hatch."

Two men were standing at the base of the *Star Nomad*, poking at the controls next to the hatch. Someone had raised the ramp, so they had no way to get in, but Alisa did not like the looks of them. They wore bland, forgettable khaki and white clothing, but they had the lean faces and short hair of soldiers.

"Are they trying to comm us or get in?" Alisa asked.

"Both. They started out comming. We haven't answered."

"That's antisocial of us." Alisa grabbed her plate and stood. It looked like it was time to take off.

"Nobody wanted to share the lamb burgers." Mica followed her into the mess hall.

"Last one out of the mess hall does the dishes," Beck announced. He was cleaning his grill, but a stack of crumb-filled dishes sat on the table. Yumi and Leonidas had disappeared.

"I have to fly us somewhere," Alisa said.

"Oh? Where?"

"Apparently, we're going to visit a Starseer temple on Arkadius."

"Well, that's one place where the White Dragon thugs won't likely find me."

"I don't think anyone finds you in a Starseer temple," Mica muttered.

"You have reservations about going?" Alisa asked, assuming she had heard Yumi sharing her information earlier since she did not sound surprised by the announcement now.

"Many. Want a list?"

"Not really. I need to talk to any Starseers I can find."

"What's the point when they'll just wipe your mind of the conversation later?"

"You sound like you have personal experience."

Mica hesitated, then shook her head.

"I'm surprised we're going," Beck said. "Why would the doc believe Yumi could lead us to a Starseer temple? It's not as if she's been waving her hands and doing magic."

"You didn't see him take her napkin?" Mica asked.

"Huh?"

"The doctor was sly about it, but he slid it off her lap while she was eating. I wouldn't be surprised if he went straight to sickbay to analyze her DNA."

"We don't have a gene sequencer in sickbay," Alisa said. "You're lucky if you can find bandages."

"Maybe he has one in his cabin. He brought a big duffel aboard."

"I assumed it was full of gray robes."

"Either way, he came back a few minutes later and told Leonidas they were going to Arkadius," Mica said.

Alisa grimaced, more at the idea of Leonidas going along with Alejandro than at the notion that Alejandro might have found Starseer genes in Yumi's spit. She wanted him on *her* side, damn it, not on the side of the imperial lackey who kept implying that he wanted to get rid of her. Except when he decided he wanted her to fly him somewhere. Then Alejandro did not seem to mind her presence.

She supposed she would be safe as long as he could keep using her. After that, she would have to watch her back.

CHAPTER FOURTEEN

The stars were muted, outshone by the city lights sprawling along the harbor. Alisa did not care. They would be much brighter soon. She'd taken off a few minutes earlier, leaving those two men banging at the hatch and ignoring a couple of comm messages flashing on the console. Maybe she would answer them once the *Nomad* had broken atmo and the chance of the authorities catching up to them dwindled. Maybe she wouldn't.

She was relieved at the idea of escaping some of her problems by shooting off into space, but she did worry that Jelena was with Starseers here on Perun and that she would be taking an extra journey for no reason if she headed to Arkadius. Instead of rocketing straight up into the atmosphere, she cruised over the ocean, waiting for the person she wanted to question to join her before committing to this new route. Unless her passengers had their noses pressed to the portholes, they should not notice that she was flying mostly laterally for now.

Alisa tapped the internal comm. "How are things looking in engineering, Mica? We got enough gas to make it to Arkadius?"

"Gas? This is an RG-classic mobile fission reactor. It uses—"

A soft knock came at the open hatch to navigation, and Alisa cut the lesson short with a question of, "Well, we got enough of it?" She waved for her visitor to enter.

"We have enough, but don't plan any side trips."

"Who, me?" Alisa murmured, thinking of the research-lab-pirate-ship fiasco.

Yumi walked into NavCom and sat cross-legged in the co-pilot's seat, arranging her dress over her knees and tucking her boots underneath her. "You wanted to see me, Captain?"

"Just wanted to have a chat with my unofficial science advisor."

Yumi gave her a wary look.

"Who it now seems may potentially be an advisor on Starseers as well as chemistry and the metaphysical," Alisa added.

"I know a few things," Yumi said, that wariness creeping into her tone too. It was strange to hear from the bubbly and open woman. So far, she had been willing to talk about any topic.

"You heard me mention that four men in Starseer robes and with some interesting mental powers kidnapped my daughter from my sister-in-law."

"You didn't get into specifics when you were hollering at Leonidas, but yes."

"I wasn't hollering. I was arguing defensively."

"Of course."

"Can you think of any reason why the Starseers would take an eight-year-old girl?"

"Only if they wanted to train her as one of their own." Yumi looked curiously at Alisa, scrutinizing her as if she could see through her skin and into her DNA to check for gene mutations.

"*I* don't have any Starseer blood," Alisa said. "I'm positive about that."

"Your husband?"

Alisa hesitated, still not certain she could quite believe Sylvia's revelations on that matter. How could she have known Jonah for more than ten years and never have stumbled across that secret?

"The main order of Starseers has a government and laws they abide by," Yumi said when she didn't answer. "They're not necessarily the same as imperial laws—or now, Alliance laws—but they aren't without morality and structure."

"Are you saying that my daughter shouldn't have been kidnapped?"

"I'm saying that those may have been rogue operatives. Or they may have had permission to come get her."

Alisa frowned. Permission? Surely, Jonah would not have given that. They had both signed legal documents before she shipped out to join the army. At the time, they had been more worried about assigning custody if *she* didn't come back alive, but he'd also given her full custody of everything they had if something happened to him, and they had named Sylvia as Jelena's guardian, should something happen to both of them. She was damned sure there hadn't been anything in those documents about Starseers being given permission to tote their daughter away.

"I understand you told Alejandro that a Starseer temple on Arkadius would be the place to look for information, both for him and for me," Alisa said.

"It's where the seat of their government is, and there's also a teaching academy there for youths."

Alisa chewed on that. Did that mean it was the kind of place where a kidnapped girl would be taken to be trained?

The lights of an island passed below them, its population sprawling all the way up the side of an active volcano. If what Yumi said was true, would Alisa be safe in plotting a course to Arkadius now?

"There's no such teaching academy here?" she asked.

"Not that I'm aware of. There are Starseers that live here—you can find them on any planet of sufficient population—but they're likely spies watching over the government. It was the empire, after all, that was instrumental in rendering their world uninhabitable and killing thousands and thousands of them in the Order Wars."

"Yeah, I've heard that some of them hold a grudge, even centuries later." Alisa gave Yumi a sidelong look, wondering where her passenger/ science advisor fit into the Starseer community. She had already said more than was common knowledge.

"That is true," Yumi said softly. "Even those who don't hold grudges are often aloof with... the non-talented." She gazed toward the view screen, watching the dark ocean sail past beneath them.

"Would you care to explain how you know so much about them?"

Yumi continued to watch the ocean, not speaking, her hands resting on her knees. If her eyes hadn't been open, Alisa might have thought she had lapsed into one of her meditation sessions.

"Is it necessary?" Yumi finally asked. "Will you trust my guidance without knowing?"

Alisa snorted. Trust was in short supply around here right now, but she assumed that *she* was the one most people were questioning. Yumi hadn't stolen anything from anyone.

"You seem to have given Alejandro enough that he's convinced that you know what you're talking about," Alisa said.

"Is his opinion something that would sway yours?" Yumi smiled slightly, the blue, green, and white glow of the console buttons and displays highlighting her face. "I wouldn't have guessed that."

"At the moment, we both seem desperate to gain information that the Starseers may have, so I guess so."

Alisa studied the controls for a minute, then pulled back on the flight stick. The ocean disappeared from view as they shot toward the starry night sky.

"You can go if you want," Alisa said, flicking her fingers toward the hatchway. "Thanks for coming up to talk to me."

Yumi looked toward the corridor, then back toward the view screen, and finally over to Alisa.

"My mother was—is—a Starseer," she said quietly.

"But you're not?" Alisa asked, not surprised by the revelation at this point.

"I never manifested the abilities, despite trying very, very hard as a girl. And later too." Yumi's expression grew wry, and sad as well. "My mother wasn't around much when I was growing up—Father didn't have powers, either. It's not that uncommon for Starseers to have relationships with normal humans, since there are so few of their people left, but the powers often cause rifts and resentment, especially if the woman is more powerful than the man."

"So your mother left when you were young?"

"She came around a lot until I was about ten. The records tell us that's the latest age any children have come into their power. If they don't display any abilities by then, it's unlikely that they ever will. Some people have a bit of prescience and the like, but no telekinesis or mind manipulation abilities."

Mind manipulation. Alisa shuddered, remembering the way those men had caused Sylvia to freeze in the hallway, to let Jelena be taken in front of her eyes.

"I thought my mother was a very glamorous and amazing person," Yumi said, "so I tried very hard to develop those powers, hoping she would come back permanently, or that she would take me away to train me. My father was a good man, mind you, a scientist who taught me to love biology, chemistry, and the other branches, but I thought it would be incredible to join her and visit her world."

"Have you ever been? To the temple you're directing us to?"

"No. What I know is from the stories she told."

Stories that would be at least twenty years out of date now, Alisa judged with a sinking feeling coming to her stomach.

As if guessing her thoughts, Yumi added, "My understanding is that the temples have been where they are for hundreds of years, so it's not likely much has changed."

"Ah," Alisa said neutrally.

Yumi unfolded her legs and stood up. "Once you've allowed the computer pilot to take over, you should join me for some meditation. It could help you with your anxiety."

"So would shooting the people who took Jelena."

"Meditation is more easily achievable."

"I don't know about that." Alisa remembered trying a guided meditation exercise after a class once. She had not been able to keep her mind from racing all over the place when she'd been supposedly focusing on her breath and stilling her thoughts. She glanced back as Yumi started toward the hatch. "Say, is that why you got into the mind stuff? To try and find some powers?"

Yumi turned back, that sad smile on her face again. "Yes. The meditation, the psychedelics. I thought that perhaps if I could alter my way of thinking, the power that lay untapped within my genes might be released."

"Has it ever?"

"A few times I've thought…" Yumi shrugged. "Not in any significant way, no."

"Maybe you should try fondling Alejandro's orb. It oozes power when it's not in its box."

"I gather that he doesn't want anyone touching that artifact. And I know—I can feel its power even when it's *in* its box." Yumi tilted her head. "Can't you?"

Alisa remembered the way she'd felt it in his cabin, but only after closing her eyes and thinking about it, almost having to be in a meditative state herself. "A little bit. But it's really noticeable when the lid on the box is open."

"I should like to see it sometime."

"Do you have any idea what it is?"

Yumi hesitated. "I have *ideas*. Nothing solid."

Alisa opened her mouth, intending to ask Yumi to share if her ideas became more solid, but the proximity alarm went off, and she cursed, spinning back to the controls.

An imperial ship loomed up ahead of them in a high orbit. It looked like one of the ones she had played cat and mouse around on the way into Perun. She hoped its crew wasn't holding a grudge.

She changed her course to take them past it at an angle. A casual angle. She didn't want to screech off in another direction and draw attention, but she knew they would have grab beams, more powerful ones than that Fang had possessed. If the captain had heard about the orb and was also on the hunt, he could easily catch them.

Intent on the view screen and the sensors, Alisa barely noticed when Yumi slipped out. She sat tensely, sending glances at the comm, expecting to be hailed any moment. The sensors showed another imperial ship in orbit farther away. She wasn't sure how many they kept up here, protecting the planet, but in a fight—or more accurately, a *flight*—the *Star Nomad* wouldn't be a match for even one of them.

The closest ship continued along its path, not detouring as Alisa piloted her freighter past them. Only when it switched from being in her side cameras to her rear cameras did she let out the breath she hadn't realized she had been holding. Either one hand wasn't talking to the other in their fleet, or it was the night shift up there, and whoever was on the bridge had not gotten the message that clunky old freighters were trouble and should be detained.

As the blackness of space stretched ahead and the imperial ship grew smaller in her rear camera, Alisa allowed herself to slump back in her chair. They had made it off planet with less trouble than she had expected. Maybe her luck would hold, and they would make it to Arkadius without trouble too. They had to fly across the system first, since Arkadius orbited Opus instead of Novus Solis, but thanks to Mica, they had supplies. Maybe she would be able to relax and catch up on some sleep. Beck could stop wearing his armor around and take her up on the offer of turning the mess into a commercial kitchen for his sauce making. So far, everything he had created had been good, so she wouldn't mind tasting the results of his experiments.

The proximity alarm beeped again, and Alisa sat upright.

"I knew it," she grumbled. "I *knew* it couldn't be that easy."

She expected to find that one of the imperial ships had turned to pursue them, but the sensors detected another vessel up ahead, coming out of the shadow of Draco, Perun's green moon. It was a big ship, larger than the imperial cruisers and even the dreadnought, and she thought of the mining craft that the pirates had taken over.

Alisa altered her course. On the unlikely chance that it was simply flying to Perun, she would give it a wide berth.

Her shoulders sagged when it altered *its* course. To cut her off.

She changed course again. Some of her sense of defeat vanished when it grew close enough for the sensors to identify. It wasn't a mining ship; it was a big salvage tug. It would have the speed of a Perunese legless toad.

The comm flashed. Alisa highly doubted she wanted to talk to anyone hailing her, but she was bolstered by the knowledge that she should be able to outrun that vessel.

She answered it with a terse, "Captain Marchenko, commanding the *Star Nomad*."

"Good evening, Captain," a female voice replied. "This is Commander Bennington of the Alliance salvage tug *Laertes*."

Alliance? Alisa wanted to feel relief, but after her dealings with Major Mladenovic, she wasn't sure she could trust her own people, not with this orb nonsense.

"Nice to see you, Commander," Alisa said, keeping her tone cordial in case these people might have good, or at least neutral, intentions. "Is there a reason you're heading in my direction? We're not in need of a tow, though I can see why you might think that, given the *Nomad's* slightly advanced age."

A chuckle came over the comm. "She does look like she could have brought the first colonists over from Earth."

Alisa's tone lost some of its cordialness when she said, "She's not *that* old."

"We're not coming to tow you. Simply to be in position if you accept my offer to trade."

"What kind of trade?" Alisa doubted she would like the answer, but found it slightly promising that the captain was offering to barter rather than simply demanding to take the orb. Bennington probably knew she couldn't catch the *Nomad*, old ship or not.

"I've been informed by an operative on Perun that you have something the Alliance has been looking for."

Yeah, she had something *everyone* had been looking for.

"Since you're a former Alliance officer yourself," Bennington went on, "I'm hoping you'll be amenable to a fair trade. I have been authorized to barter. I can't give you the entire price, of course, since I'll be taking on the security risk of taking it back to Arkadius myself, but what would you say to a hundred thousand tindarks? In exchange for us relieving you of your burden?"

Alisa felt her mouth gape open. A hundred thousand tindarks for the orb?

With that much money, she could *buy* information on her daughter's whereabouts. Well, maybe not. Would the Starseers care about money? With their mental powers, they could simply arrange to win at the casinos on Primus 7 if they needed coin. Besides, while money might make her life a little easier, it wasn't exactly her heart's desire. She wanted her daughter, and she wanted to keep the empire from rising again. If she gave up the orb to the Alliance, it would be to help with the latter. Still, she almost hated to lose the thing, having the notion that she might somehow barter it to the Starseers if necessary. And then there was the complication that she didn't truly *have* it. It was back in Alejandro's quarters, and she couldn't turn it and Alejandro over without making an enemy of Leonidas. As it was, she was surprised Leonidas was still talking to her. She would hate to lose that forever.

"Can you be more specific on which burden you want?" Alisa asked, realizing she hadn't responded and that Bennington might find that suspicious. "I'm not trying to be funny here, but I have several burdens right now."

The tug was still angling toward the *Nomad*, moving to overtake it—or come up beside it for an airlock transfer perhaps. Alisa could have shot straight out into space and left the Alliance craft behind, but she did not alter her course again, not yet. She was within the tug's firing range—salvage ship or not, it had likely been used during the war and would be outfitted with weapons—and she did not want to take a butt full of buckshot if she could help it. Besides, she was curious about the commander's offer.

"Your life sounds complicated," Bennington said, her tone still friendly. "Why don't you let us simplify it?"

"How?"

Alisa was debating on mentioning that Alejandro had the orb and wouldn't let her simply walk it to the airlock when Bennington responded with the unexpected.

"Let us come alongside you, attach to your airlock, and bring some men over. We have an aerosol sedative that will knock out your passenger. I assume you have him chained or otherwise restrained somewhere?"

Alisa snorted. She wouldn't mind chaining up Alejandro, but that hardly seemed necessary. It wasn't as if he was a fighter. She could probably just lock him in his cabin. The real threat was Leonidas.

Thinking his name sent a jolt through her, and she felt like a dunce as she realized what "burden" the commander wanted to relieve her of.

"You're looking for Leonidas?" she blurted before she could stop herself. That tone of surprise would tell Bennington too much, that she had something else of value on board.

"I assume you know that's a pseudonym, Captain," Bennington said, some of the friendliness disappearing from her voice, "and that you're harboring Imperial Cyborg Corps Commander, Colonel Hieronymus Adler aboard your ship."

"No. I mean, yes. I mean, he paid his fare." Alisa rubbed her face. Could she possibly sound more daft? This was throwing her off balance; she had been so certain they wanted the orb. "And he neglected to give me his real name."

Alisa didn't hear a noise behind her; it was more a sense of being watched that made her turn in her chair.

Leonidas stood in the hatchway, his arms folded over his chest as he leaned against the jamb. His face was impassive as he listened.

"I'm not surprised," Bennington said, "though I am a little surprised that you took a cyborg on as a passenger, knowing fully well that they serve the empire."

"Well, he didn't advertise what he was," Alisa said, glancing at Leonidas's jacket with the Cyborg Corps patch on the front. It was the same jacket he had been wearing the day they met, the day he leaped thirty feet off the top of the *Nomad* and landed in the dust as if he'd hopped down from a curb.

Leonidas raised a single eyebrow.

"Captain, I hope you're not implying that he's walking around your ship of his own free will. Cyborgs are extremely dangerous, and he's one of the most dangerous. The war crimes he's committed…"

Alisa hardly felt in the position to judge anyone for war crimes. Especially Leonidas. Since she had known him, he'd acted much more honorably than she had. Admittedly, she hadn't known him long, and she had no idea what caused those nightmares he seemed to have on a regular basis.

"You're right that he's dangerous, Commander," Alisa said, now wishing she had been smoother and faster to think when the officer had first revealed what she wanted—things might have been easier if she'd just said that Leonidas had gotten off on Perun. "And I'm afraid I can't accept your offer. Especially since I know the bounty on his head is *two* hundred thousand tindarks."

Leonidas's other eyebrow rose. He didn't seem surprised to hear about the bounty, but was perhaps mildly surprised to hear that Alisa had known about it. Granted, she hadn't known about it long, and it had slipped her mind during all the chaos on Perun.

Bennington huffed out a breath. "I *knew* you knew who he was."

"I'm sorry I can't accept your offer." Alisa wasn't sorry at all. She would hand Alejandro and his orb over if it would help the Alliance and keep the empire from regaining power, but she couldn't betray Leonidas. Her conscience wouldn't let her. More than that, she was certain *he* wouldn't let her, not when he was standing right there listening to all this. Had he been there since the beginning? She wouldn't be surprised if he had.

"Is that your final decision, then, Captain?" Bennington asked. "You won't accept…one hundred and fifty thousand tindarks for him?"

"Not to be impertinent, Commander, but do you even have that kind of money to offer? I know the Alliance isn't that flush with cash yet, being too busy recovering from the war, and quite honestly, I don't understand why this cyborg is worth that much." This time, she was the one to raise an eyebrow, directing the gesture at Leonidas.

He didn't give her anything in return. He merely gazed at the tug on the view screen, his face a mask.

"I assure you that I am authorized to provide the funds," was all Bennington said.

Alisa doubted it very much. She adjusted the *Nomad's* flight path and increased to maximum speed. It was time to leave that tug back there kissing the moon. "Sorry, Commander, but I want the full two hundred thousand."

"You greedy little smuggler," Bennington growled. "You would extort the Alliance? Even after you served in the war?"

"I'm not extorting anyone. You just can't have him. He's mine." Feeling a little silly for not having a better excuse than that, Alisa shut off the comm before the officer could answer. Having Bennington think her greedy and that she wanted the full bounty for herself was better than having her know the truth, that she *liked* Leonidas and didn't want to hand him over to her government or anyone else's. And honestly, it made her feel like more of a traitor than just wanting the money would have. Cyborgs were imperials, and imperials were enemies. She wasn't supposed to *like* them.

"So, it turns out that the Alliance is looking for you," Alisa told Leonidas, as if it would be news to him. She didn't look back at him to check his reaction. She was watching the tug in the camera as the *Nomad* sped away.

The big Alliance craft was lumbering right after her. But, as she had guessed, the *Nomad* was faster. Alisa raised her shields in case the tug tried to fire. She didn't think they were close enough for the vessel to use a grab beam, but it would have a lot of range and power for towing, so she couldn't be sure.

"I know," Leonidas said.

He stepped into navigation and surprised her by laying a hand on her shoulder. She was too busy flying to analyze how the gesture made her feel, but it seemed to be one of thanks, and she appreciated it. He could have easily threatened her during that conversation, but he must have known that he didn't need to. But had he believed it was because she wouldn't be foolish enough to try to make a deal for him while he stood there listening, or had he realized that she'd come to care about him and wouldn't have betrayed him even if he *hadn't* been there listening? She wished she could find a way to let him know it was the latter, but she didn't know how. Even if she tried, would he believe her, after she had stolen from Alejandro?

Leonidas removed his hand and sat in the co-pilot's seat. She was just thinking that it would be nice to have some company for a while when the proximity alarm went off again.

"*Now* what?" she groaned. "I do *not* have enough chocolate on board to deal with all of these hassles."

The tug was still following them, but it had fallen behind, so that wasn't the source of the alarm.

"If you had a crate of chocolate, would that be enough?"

She snorted, wondering if he would be willing to bribe her with chocolate if she avoided the Alliance ships that were after him all the way to Arkadius.

Not one but three large blips appeared on the radar. They flew out from behind the moon, as the salvage ship had done earlier. These weren't slow, bulky vessels, and Alisa groaned again as she recognized them. Alliance warships.

"No," she whispered. "Not even a crate would be enough."

CHAPTER FIFTEEN

Leonidas saw the warships and immediately headed for the hatchway.

"Any chance you're going to get me chocolate?" Alisa asked, scanning the space around them, wishing a comet or a rogue band of meteors would stray into range so she would have something to hide behind, someplace to run from those ships. But the green moon was the only body nearby, and the Alliance warships, coming from that direction, would easily intercept her. The featureless sphere held few hiding spots, anyway, and she doubted the domed moon stations would invite her to dock.

"I'm getting my combat armor," Leonidas said, his voice grim.

"Leonidas." Alisa turned toward him. "Even if I had weapons, I couldn't...I *can't* get in a fight with Alliance warships."

It was cheeky of them to all show up this close to Perun and that orbit full of imperial warships, but there they were, nevertheless.

"I'm not asking you to. They want me alive. They'll have to come get me." A fiercely defiant expression crossed his face before he ducked out of view, jogging to his cabin.

The comm flashed, and Alisa sighed. Was there any point in answering? It was probably Commander Bennington again, prepared to be smug now that her backup had arrived.

It flashed relentlessly as the warships closed, no question as to their destination. Like the tug, they were on an intercept course with the *Star Nomad*.

Feeling cranky, Alisa swatted the button. "What?"

"What?" an amused male voice on the other line asked. "Is that really how you answer the comm now that you're a civilian, Marchenko?"

Alisa gaped at the console. The man's voice was familiar, as was the way he had said her name, but it took her a few seconds to place it. "Captain Tomich?"

"It's *Commander* Tomich now. There were lots of promotions after the war ended and the temporaries mustered out. Look at what *I* got."

Alisa linked the comm signal with the ship it had come from, the Viper-class warship in the lead. She was a beauty, newer and bigger than the two trailing it, though any one of those ships could have pulverized the *Nomad* in seconds.

"Not that you're smug about it," Alisa said.

"Not at all," Tomich said, a familiar grin in his voice. It had been two years since they had served together—he had been her squadron leader when she'd been assigned to the *Merciless*. He was practically the one who had taught her that snark was expected from military pilots, not that she hadn't already had a knack for it.

"I can't believe they gave you a ship that big. You could barely land your cobra without scraping the paint off on the hangar bay doors."

"This ship has bumpers."

Alisa snorted.

"So, are you truly a greedy little smuggler these days," Tomich asked, quoting Bennington, "or are you in an awkward situation?"

"Awkward doesn't even begin to describe my week," Alisa replied before she had fully parsed the nuances of the question. She realized he might be asking if she was a prisoner on her own ship, with Leonidas being the one in charge.

"I see," he said, annoyance replacing the smile in his voice.

He was not, she sensed, annoyed at her. It pleased her that Tomich thought well enough of her to assume she was not a traitor, but it didn't necessarily change anything for her. Well, it might if she was willing to sit back and let them board and take Leonidas. If she did, they might let her go on her way after that. But it would be intolerable to hand him over to the army, even if it was her army, to be interrogated for who knew what reasons. What did he know that they wanted to know? It had to be information that they sought or they wouldn't care if he was turned in alive or dead. That warrant specifically said he had to be brought in alive for the reward.

"Is he there with you now?" Tomich asked quietly.

Alisa leaned out of her seat so she could see through the hatchway. The short corridor was empty.

"He's...around," she said. She would not say that Leonidas was putting on his combat armor, though it probably didn't matter. Surely Tomich would expect that.

"Is the boy with you?"

"Boy?" She was sure the puzzlement came through in her tone. All she could think of was Alejandro, but the retired surgeon was surely not a boy.

"I'll take that for a no." Tomich sighed. "Unfortunate."

"I'll pretend I know what you're talking about, so we can move on to the more personally pertinent part of this conversation. Is there any chance I'm going to get out of this alive?"

"The Alliance has no quarrel with you or your...I'll be generous and call that a freighter. Is it hard to fly that after a Striker?"

"Is this really the time for you to be mocking my ship?"

"No, perhaps not." Tomich lowered his voice to a whisper. "Lay low, Alisa. Stay out of the way, and don't let yourself get turned into a meat shield. We have to get him."

She dropped her face into her hand, feeling utterly helpless. She highly doubted Leonidas would use her as a shield, so that wasn't her concern. Sitting here and doing nothing and letting them take him was. But what choice did she have? Even now, with the *Nomad* cruising away from the moon at top speed, the other ships were closing on her, moving to flank her. There was nowhere to run.

And as much as she had come to like Leonidas, a selfish part of her admitted that her life would become much, *much* simpler if the Alliance simply took Leonidas and Alejandro and the orb off her hands. It wasn't as if they had paid her to protect them. All they had paid for was fare. Granted, she would feel a little bad if she kept their money after they'd been hauled off by the army less than two hours after taking off, but again, what choice did she have?

"None," she muttered.

"Pardon?" Tomich asked.

"I'll do my best to cooperate," she told him.

"Just keep yourself from getting hurt. I have a lot of young twitchy infantry boys with big guns that I'm sending over there."

"Thanks for the warning."

"I'm sorry I can't do more." He sounded like he meant it. "The tug is coming to lock onto you and keep you in place, so you don't fly off. I remember your skills well."

"You needn't worry about them. There's no place to hide, and this freighter doesn't have any weapons."

"Doesn't it? You should have retrofitted it. I don't think the Alliance is going to be as anal when it comes to civilians with weapons, especially when we don't yet have the people and resources to patrol the entire system."

"I wasn't planning to have such controversial passengers. I'm a freighter, Tomich. A *freighter*. There are *chickens* in the cargo hold."

"We'll try not to disturb them."

Sure, they would sleep right through the blazer bolts zipping over their feathered heads.

Disgusted with the entire situation, Alisa closed the comm. She turned in her seat and found Leonidas standing in the hatchway, his crimson armor gleaming, everything except his helmet on.

"Meat shield?" He sniffed. "Cyborgs do *not* hide behind civilians."

"What about behind other cyborgs?"

"That's slightly more acceptable. I don't suppose you have any on board?" He smiled at her. Out of all of the emotions she would have expected from him in his present situation, amusement was not one of them.

"No, and I think my tendency toward inappropriate humor is rubbing off on you."

"You may be right. That's disconcerting." He smiled again.

Three suns, he wasn't looking *forward* to going into battle against those young twitchy infantry boys, was he? Alisa didn't think she had ever seen him in such a good mood.

But why not? Those Alliance soldiers were enemies to him. He probably enjoyed the idea of taking out as many of them as he could. After all, they had destroyed his empire.

They were not enemies for her, though. The thought of this confrontation horrified her. She could not expect him to let them take him without a fight, but with the way he fought, he would likely take out twenty of their people before they managed to subdue him, especially since they wanted him alive. If she had a doctor who was on her side, she could have asked him to come up with a concoction to knock Leonidas out, as the tug commander had implied they had. But her gut twisted at the idea of doing that to Leonidas, even if she could. She didn't want to hand him over. She wanted to go on her way, find Jelena, hire Leonidas to work for her, and proceed to live a normal life.

White flashed on the view screen, and the *Nomad* shuddered. The tug's grab beam wrapped around them. The warships had caught up, too, and fenced them in, one in front, one behind, and one to the side. With the tug on the other side, she felt like a lion in a cage in a zoo.

"I'll wait at the airlock and charge onto their ship if I can," Leonidas said. "I suggest you call the rest of your people up here and lock the hatch. The soldiers shouldn't have a reason to harass the rest of you. *Most* of you." He looked down, checking the battery pack on the blazer rifle slung over his chest. "I know you must have thought about handing Dr. Dominguez over, too, but since they haven't inquired about him and the artifact, I'd appreciate it if you didn't volunteer anything about him. Of course, I can't stop you if you do." He inclined his head and turned toward the hatchway.

"No, damn it."

Leonidas looked back, his eyebrows raised.

"Stay right there. Let me think a second. This is ludicrous. There has to be an alternative."

"We're clearly trapped." He waved toward the view screen full of ships. "But once they have me, they should leave your ship alone."

"I'm not worried about my ship. Those are my people you're about to blast into. I don't want them killed. And you're my passenger. You paid your fare. I don't want you killed, either."

"There's no alternative," he said softly, holding her gaze with his.

Maybe it was her imagination, but she thought she read regret in that gaze. Despite his eagerness to leap into battle, maybe he regretted that he had to go out this way. Maybe he even wished he could stay on the *Nomad* and accept her offer of employment.

"Sure, that's it," she muttered with a snort.

"What?" Leonidas asked, even though he had probably heard her.

"We're making an alternative." Alisa hit the internal comm button. "Stay," she told Leonidas, pointing at the deck as if commanding a dog.

His eyebrows twitched.

"Mica, you keeping abreast of the situation?" Alisa asked.

"I have a porthole down here."

"I'll take that for a yes. How familiar are you with that tug over there?"

"It's an IM-7 Digger-class salvage tug with the imperial numbers filed off and Alliance paint covering the hull. It has improved power systems over the IM-6, with twin Z-drive 3619C engines that have a towing capacity of over 100,000 tons."

"So, you're vaguely familiar with it."

Maybe she, like the gangly young boy Alisa had met on Perun, had a model of it.

"Vaguely," Mica agreed.

"If you got aboard it, would you know how to break the grab beam?"

"I can break anything on any ship."

"How is it that employers weren't storming our hatch, trying to get you on their team? All right, good. Get whatever tools you need and meet us at the airlock."

"The airlock that's already getting a tube and clamps extended toward it?" Mica asked.

Alisa winced. "Yes, hurry. Leonidas?"

"Yes?" he asked warily.

"I need you to talk pretty to Alejandro. Tell him to get on the horn and call those imperial ships we passed on the way out of orbit. Tell him to let them know that his orb is about to fall into Alliance hands, so they might want to come out here and make sure that doesn't happen."

"I don't think—"

"I don't care. Do it anyway. Go. Shoo, shoo." She waved her hands at him, then turned back to her console. She doubted Tomich would tell his people to bother her ship, but she would lock down the controls so nobody but she could access them.

"You really want those imperial ships to come over here?" came Mica's voice from the corridor. She stepped past Leonidas as he was going the other way. "You're not trying to start another war, are you?"

"No, but we need some chaos if we're going to have any chance of escaping. There are three other ships out there with grab beams. Didn't I tell you to meet me at the airlock?" Alisa added, her hands flying over the controls.

"I got ready more quickly than you." Mica patted her satchel, but looked over her shoulder. "You sure this is worth it? Does the Alliance care about us, or do they just want the doctor?"

"Leonidas."

"Pardon?"

"They want Leonidas. Remember that warrant?"

"I remember him being a colonel in the army that spent four years trying to blast us out of the sky and, oh, a lifetime oppressing us so that we lived in fear of spitting."

"You're not going to get pessimistic on me, are you?"

"Of course not. What's there to be pessimistic about?" Mica waved at the various camera displays, all of them full of warships. "I'm just saying that maybe we should give him—both of them—to our people."

A clank sounded against the hull. The ship shivered, and Alisa imagined giant talons wrapping about the hull, grasping it tightly to the tug's side.

She finished and pushed away from the controls. "They paid their fare. We're not giving anybody to anyone."

Mica grabbed her before she could head through the hatchway. "Alisa, don't be ridiculous. If we openly side with them, the Alliance won't forgive us. I don't want my family suffering for the choices I make here. I already spent four years worrying about that during the war."

"We're not openly siding with them," Alisa said. "We'll be…"

"My prisoners," Leonidas said, returning to NavCom.

They turned together to look at him. He had donned his helmet, and one of his hands rested on the blazer rifle strapped to his torso. As it always did, seeing him in full combat armor—the armor of the enemy—made Alisa uneasy.

"If you insist on coming along, that is," he added, his frown making it clear that he didn't think that was a good idea.

"We do," Alisa said, as Mica shook her head. Alisa nudged her with an elbow. "Some intellicuffs for our wrists would be good, though. Then if we're spotted, it would be obvious we're prisoners."

She did not like the idea of making Leonidas seem like a villain—more of a villain—in the Alliance's eyes, but Mica was right. It would be foolish of them to make themselves enemies of the Alliance on his behalf. She had no trouble snubbing the remnants of the empire, but this was different. As she had said, these were her people.

Mica sighed. "I have some old-fashioned metal handcuffs in my cabin. I'll get them."

"That'll have to do," Alisa said, stepping past Leonidas to follow her to the crew quarters. He came right behind her.

"I've put together something special too." Mica dug a small device out of her pocket—a remote control?

Before Alisa could ask what it controlled, Beck ran out of his cabin, his combat armor on. "We're getting boarded, right?" he asked as Yumi poked her head out of her own cabin across the way. "I assume you want me to wait somewhere, fully armed and ready to spring into action when they come in?"

"Actually, I was hoping you could give yourself a black eye, then tie yourselves up." She nodded toward Yumi and also waved toward Alejandro's hatch, which had just opened.

"These aren't the usual requests made to a security officer."

"I'm an unusual employer."

"Not arguing, Captain. Not arguing." Beck *did* look like he wanted to argue about staying out of the fighting, but Yumi stepped forward and took his arm.

She started to guide him back toward the cabins, but Mica called out from her own room, "Have anyone who's not involved in this scheme stay in NavCom with the hatch locked. I've got a surprise rigged."

"A surprise we'll like?" Alisa asked.

"A surprise those boarding us *won't* like."

"You heard her." Alisa waved Beck toward NavCom.

"There's no place in this freighter we could *hide*?" Alejandro asked from farther down the corridor, his satchel clutched to his side. "That cubby in the cargo hold, perhaps? I'm sure navigation will be the first place they look."

"They'll be busy looking at *me*," Leonidas said.

"Because you'll be shooting at them?" Alisa asked. "Or because of your blinding handsomeness?"

He frowned at her, no hint of a smile on his face.

"If it's the first thing, I'd prefer we do this without killing any Alliance soldiers," she said, holding his gaze.

"What are we doing exactly?" he asked.

"Boarding them while they're busy boarding us," Alisa said, "disabling their grab beam, making a messy distraction on their ship somewhere, perhaps with explosives, and then coming back to the *Nomad* and flying away. *Without* killing anyone."

Leonidas stared at her, and she thought he would say something along the lines of, "That's ludicrous," or "If they shoot me, I'm shooting them back." Instead, he said, "If they're in armor, I may be able to break it down without killing them."

"What if they're not in armor?"

"I can target their knees."

Alisa grimaced, remembering that both of her kneecaps had been shattered in that last crash on Dustor. She had passed out before enduring the pain for long, but she vividly recalled those few minutes before she had.

"Better than their heads, I guess," she murmured.

Mica stepped out of her cabin. "His and her models." She waved the two pairs of metal handcuffs at Alisa. "Which do you want?"

"Well, you're the one with short hair and a surly disposition."

"Ha ha. If we had more time, I'd clobber you for implying you're more feminine than I am." Mica tossed a set of cuffs into Alisa's hands.

"I'm not sure that statement corroborates your claim of femininity."

A clank sounded, and an alarm went off, the warning that someone was forcing the airlock door. Alisa hurried toward the cargo hold.

"Are there keys to these?" she asked, noting the physical keyhole.

"I don't have them anymore," Mica said, "but if you get them lubricated enough, you can slip out."

"Ew." Alisa clasped one side of the cuffs around her wrist, leaving the other free for now.

"Maybe your new cyborg buddy can help you."

Despite the direness of the situation, Alisa flushed with embarrassment. She hoped *that* wasn't why Mica thought she was taking this risk. Alisa just wanted to protect her people and the Alliance soldiers.

"I can break them easily," Leonidas said, either ignoring or completely missing the innuendo.

"You must be fun in bed," Mica said dryly.

His brow wrinkled behind his faceplate. Alisa almost laughed, but there was no time. They had reached the airlock door, and the bangs and thumps coming from the other side promised it would be open soon.

"They're going to burst in here with their guns on autofire, aren't they?" Alisa asked, noting with some amusement that Yumi had found the time to stack crates all around her chicken pen and reinforce the netting stretched atop it with more layers. She couldn't blame her and hoped nothing happened to the birds.

"Likely." Leonidas pointed to a corner protected by a beam and more crates. "I'll charge into them. You hide."

"I have a better idea." Alisa grabbed his arm. "We'll all hide." She tugged him toward a concealed door in the bulkhead, the same spot where they had hidden when the ship had been boarded by pirates. "Just long enough for them to come in and spread out."

Mica did not hesitate to rush to the spot and open the door. Alisa followed her, crouching to squeeze in behind her, but she paused when Leonidas did not follow. A hiss-clank came from the airlock. The soldiers would force their way in any second.

"Leonidas, come *on*." Alisa jerked her thumb into the dim storage space.

He must have objected to the tone of her voice, or the order itself, because he said, "You're not my commander, Marchenko."

"I'm the captain of this ship, and you're on this ship. Look, I'm trying to save all of our butts. Get over here. Please."

"It'll be easier to make those kneecap shots when they're spread out and you can sneak up on them," Mica added.

"You can't sneak up on a man in combat armor." Leonidas waved to the back of his helmet, probably indicating the camera embedded there.

"Oh, I think you'll be able to," Mica said cryptically.

"Come on, Leonidas," Alisa said. "I'll rub your ears if you join us." Maybe bribery would work better with him than commands, since he seemed to believe his former military status as a colonel meant he outranked her, even on her own ship.

After a long look back toward the airlock, he finally strode across the hold. The doorway to the hidden compartment was just large enough for his broad armored shoulders to fit through. As soon as he squeezed in, Alisa pulled the door closed behind him. Darkness fell in the cubby, a spot meant for hiding valuables in case of a pirate boarding, not for hiding people. The door did not have a peephole or any way to see what was happening in the cargo hold, though the clangs from the airlock reached Alisa's ears.

"Despite your interest in comparing me to a cat, a bat, or some other animal, I prefer shoulders," Leonidas said.

"Pardon?" Alisa asked.

"Shoulder rubs."

"Oh. I'll keep that in mind."

"I bet you will," Mica muttered.

Alisa might have flushed again—she would definitely have to set Mica straight in regard to her feelings toward Leonidas—but a final ominous clang came from the airlock. After that, silence fell. Alisa imagined soldiers in combat armor streaming into the hold, rifles pointing in every direction as they searched for enemies.

Something touched her hand, Leonidas's gauntleted fingers. He gently but firmly snapped the second side of her handcuffs around her wrist. A faint click sounded as he did the same to Mica.

Soft thuds came from the other side of their door. Someone walking past—or walking toward them. Alisa held her breath. She knew the door concealed this cubby from plain sight, but she had also heard that some models of combat armor had special visual sensors that gave the wearers access to night vision and thermal vision. What if the door panel was not insulated enough and their body heat registered to such a scanner?

"Unleashing the surprise," Mica whispered, her voice so soft that Alisa was not sure she had heard correctly.

Not wanting to make any noise, she did not ask for clarification.

A startled exclamation, the voice muffled by a helmet, came from the other side of their door. Someone barked an order from the far side of the cargo hold. Alisa, crouched with her back to the wall and Leonidas between her and the door, felt her feet lighten. A hint of vertigo washed over her as they went from feeling light to lifting off the floor.

"Your surprise was to cut gravity?" Alisa breathed, bracing herself with a hand on the ceiling of the compartment and a foot against something else.

Was that Leonidas? If so, he hadn't moved. He still crouched in front of the door. His combat boots would have magnetized soles for fighting on the exterior of a ship or in situations without gravity. So would those of the men outside. Alisa grimaced, doubting Mica's surprise would do anything, other than to warn the soldiers that someone was up to no good on the ship.

"And the lights," Mica whispered. "I left power on in NavCom, but that's it."

Thinking of helmets with night vision, Alisa did not know how much help that would be.

"I like it," Leonidas breathed, but did not explain further. He shifted closer to the door, almost dislodging Alisa's foot. Maybe it would add a degree of uncertainty or confusion to the other side, and he would have an easier time sneaking up on them. And if he tackled someone, it might knock the person's magnetized boots free from the deck.

"Did Alejandro comm the imperial ships?" Alisa murmured.

"I don't think so," Leonidas whispered. "He said he wouldn't. I pointed out that any help would be useful, even that of Senator Bondarenko's people. He may change his mind."

Leonidas did not sound confident on that last note, and Alisa's stomach sank with a feeling of defeat. If the imperial ships did not come over to at least make threatening noises in the direction of the Alliance ships, nothing they did on the tug would matter. Even if they managed to free the *Nomad*, the warships would simply recapture it.

The squawks of alarmed chickens came through the door, and Alisa imagined them floating up into the netting above their pen, terrified and confused. Poor things. As much as she had enjoyed the morning omelets, she didn't think livestock should be riding along when the *Nomad* had been encountering trouble so often. She hoped none of the young idiots with guns would find it amusing to shoot the chickens.

A couple of minutes passed, and Alisa did not hear anything besides the squawks. Had the men moved to search the rest of the ship? Their cubby was near the steps, so she ought to have heard people clanging up the metal treads, but they might be stepping carefully—softly—if they were worried about flying up into the zero gravity air.

"There are only two left in the cargo hold," Leonidas whispered. "I'm going out. Stay here until I come for you."

"Kneecaps," Alisa told him, though if the soldiers were all in combat armor, she knew he would have to do more than that. "And be careful," she added.

It was too dark to see anything, but she imagined Mica giving her a curious look.

Alisa did not hear him open the door, nor could she see anything outside, but he moved away from her foot, leaving her scrabbling for another hold, and she knew he was gone. She had barely registered it when the squeals of blazer fire erupted near the airlock. Streaks of crimson lit up the cargo hold briefly, but from her spot, she could not see anyone or tell who was firing.

The fight ended almost as soon as it had begun. Alisa was tempted to poke her head out, not that there would be anything to see in the dark, but a touch to her shoulder made her twitch in surprise.

"Stay," Leonidas said. "The others will be here any second."

Not waiting for her response, he refastened the door, leaving Alisa and Mica alone in the dark.

CHAPTER SIXTEEN

The sounds of fighting had drifted away, perhaps moving up toward navigation. Alisa, her feet and hands braced awkwardly so she could stay in place, leaned her forehead against the cool metal of a bulkhead. It seemed foolish to hope or believe that Leonidas could take care of all of the soldiers who had boarded without killing any of them. Or without being killed himself. Tomich knew exactly what he was dealing with. He must have sent a couple of squadrons of his best men, and if they reported that they needed backup, he certainly had the means to send more over.

If Alejandro had been willing to contact the imperial ships, then they might have had a chance, but if he was objecting to reason, then they had no hope. Poised there in the dark, it was hard not to loathe him. Had Tomich's people been boarding to get the orb, she had no doubt that he would have done anything within his means to start a brawl so they could slink away. But because the Alliance was here for Leonidas, Alejandro was just going to hide under a console in navigation and do nothing while they took his only ally. As long as they weren't here for him, he didn't care. After all the help Leonidas had given him. It was unconscionable.

"Bastard," Alisa growled.

"Which one?" Mica asked.

"Alejandro. He's a coward. Unless someone threatens to kick the wheels off his wagon, he doesn't care about anything except his mission."

"As opposed to people who needlessly get themselves involved in the affairs of others?"

"I know you're not sniping at me, Mica, because that would be insubordination."

"Only on a military ship. We're civilians now."

"Damn. I never thought I'd miss the army."

Mica sighed. "Will you hate me if I admit I would prefer it if our cyborg passenger got himself killed and the doctor got himself captured, so we could go on our way without any more drama?"

"It's not an illogical thought," Alisa admitted. "Trust me, I've had it myself."

"And then you imagined the cyborg in bed with you and decided to throw logic to the stars?"

"I did *not* imagine that. Look, I don't know what kind of notions you've got rattling in your skull over there, but I'm not developing feelings for him. He's imperial, he's a cyborg, and he probably killed thousands of our people during the war."

"You don't have to have feelings for someone to want to ride him like a comet."

"He's not even my type."

"Please, I saw him with his shirt off in sickbay. He's a walking fantasy."

"Only if you're into ridiculously brawny men."

"With the kind of delicious delineation of muscle and perfect symmetry that sculptors pay for in their models."

"Maybe *you're* the one obsessed with him," Alisa said.

"He's even less my type."

"Right, I forgot. Yumi is the cute one."

"Yumi doesn't have any armies chasing after her. It's definitely a perk."

Alisa had thought Mica's preferences went both ways when it came to relationships, but it wasn't the time for that discussion. All she said was, "You'll have to get in line with her. I think Beck is interested."

"It doesn't matter where his interests are; it's where hers are."

"Could we not talk about this now?" Alisa asked as the sounds of more gunfire drifted down from the deck above them. Her stomach was in knots, and she wished that Leonidas had not locked her cuffs. With her wrists bound together, she would have a hard time getting the door open to climb out. "I'm trying to come up with a plan."

"Another one? We've barely enacted the last."

"I'm afraid it's not going to go well. Not unless…" An idea popped into Alisa's mind, and she dug awkwardly into her pocket for her comm.

"What are you doing?" Mica asked, perhaps hearing the rustle of clothing.

"Kicking the good doctor's wagon wheels." Assuming he had his comm on him, Alisa called up his code. She'd gotten them from her passengers when they first boarded.

"Yes?" Alejandro whispered. It sounded like his airway was restricted. Either someone had a hand around his throat, or his neck was scrunched up because he had stuffed himself under a console to hide.

Alisa hoped he was sitting on his orb box, and that it was poking him in the ass. "You three doing all right?"

"So far," he replied. "Two of them tried to get in here, but they were dragged away before they could break the lock on the hatch. We're hiding, so they shouldn't have seen us through the window. I assume that's Leonidas out there—we can hear the sounds of combat."

"He's fighting the intruders single-handedly."

"I'd help if you all would let me," Beck said, a few feet away from the comm.

"Hold that thought," Alisa said. "First, I need to know if you made that call, Doctor."

Alejandro's hesitation told her all she needed to know. She ground her teeth.

"No," he admitted. "As far as I can tell, this isn't about the artifact. I would like to keep it that way."

"By letting them have Leonidas? The only person here who cares one iota about you?"

Distant energy blasts sounded over his comm, and Alisa winced at the idea of Leonidas by himself against all of those men. The ship had alcoves and struts and hatches one could take cover behind, but it was not designed like a warship with built-in bottlenecks and bulkheads that could be lowered to thwart intruders.

"He cares about honoring the emperor's dying wishes," Alejandro said. "It has nothing to do with caring about me. He would be the first to agree that I should keep silent to keep my mission safe. He would be willing to sacrifice himself for that."

"Well, I'm *not* willing to sacrifice him, damn it." The ferocity in her voice surprised her. By Rebus-de's fiery left tit, Mica wasn't right, was she? Alisa wasn't developing feelings for Leonidas, was she? She shook her head. It was something to worry about later. "You comm those ships right now and get them over here, Doctor, or I'll comm Commander Tomich on the lead Alliance warship and tell him all about your artifact and what I know of your quest."

Alejandro hesitated again. Then he scoffed, or tried. It wasn't very convincing. "I doubt their commander has time to listen to a civilian freighter operator when he's in the middle of trying to subdue a dangerous cyborg."

"Guess again, Doc. We served together in the war. We've already had a chat today, and he's concerned that I'm Leonidas's prisoner. Maybe I'll tell him that you're the brains and I'm really *your* prisoner."

"Captain…" Alejandro groaned, sounding truly pained.

Alisa supposed it was petty to smile viciously at his distress, but it was dark, and nobody could see her. That made it all right to be petty.

"You going to make that call?" she asked.

He sighed. "Yes."

"Beck, are you still listening?"

"I'm here, Captain."

"If our passenger has any trouble getting his comm to work, you help him, understood?"

"Yes, ma'am."

Bangs sounded, dozens of footfalls pounding the deck—reinforcements coming in through the airlock.

"Marchenko out," Alisa whispered and closed the comm.

She leaned her forehead against the bulkhead again, grimacing more deeply as the footfalls grew louder, heavy combat boots ringing out on the metal deck. The soldiers ran straight for the stairs, clanging up them and into the core of the ship. More soldiers rushing up to help their comrades against Leonidas. How many could he defeat? The darkness and the lack of gravity would not give him *that* much of an advantage.

"Maybe we should sneak aboard their ship while all of their men are charging onto ours," Alisa muttered, not truly entertaining the idea. If they were caught over there, and Leonidas wasn't leading them, they couldn't pretend they were prisoners.

"Or maybe we should stay in our box and do nothing," Mica said firmly. "This isn't our fight."

"They have my ship."

"And I'm sure they'll let go of your ship as soon as they have their cyborg."

Alisa wanted to argue, but Mica was right. Besides, what were the odds that two women in handcuffs could sneak all the way to engineering on that tug without being seen?

A soft tapping came from the other side of the door. Alisa lost her grip on the wall and spun awkwardly in the zero gravity cubby.

A pop sounded as the panel was tugged free. She groped for something to use to push herself backward in case it was one of the soldiers. Not that hiding farther back in the cubby would save her from them.

"It's me," Leonidas whispered, his voice barely audible through his faceplate.

Only after he identified himself did he move the panel fully. Had he expected to find them in here with their guns pointed at the door? Alisa doubted she could even unholster her Etcher with her wrists linked together.

She pulled herself out of the cubby, grabbing Leonidas's arm to keep from floating away. The darkness was still absolute in the cargo hold—Mica had rigged it so that even the emergency lights had not come on—but it stank of smoke, and Alisa thought she could feel something in the air swirling against her skin.

Energy blasts echoed from up above.

"If you're here, who are they fighting?" Alisa whispered. Beck hadn't leaped out into the fray, had he?

"Their imaginations," Leonidas said. "I had some smoke bombs and rust bangs, so they're struggling to see. The smoke works on sensors as well as eyes. Still ready to go to the tug?"

Alisa wrinkled her nose. "More than ever. Mica?"

A hand latched onto Alisa's shoulder. "If it'll get me out of zero grav, I'm ready. Three suns, I get sick in this crap."

"Turn your head if you're going to throw up."

"We don't have much time." Leonidas started walking across the hold, his boots keeping him affixed to the deck.

Alisa felt silly floating along behind him like a tethered balloon. Mica, attached to her instead of Leonidas, probably felt the same way.

"Check down there," came an order from above, near the head of the walkway.

Alisa tightened her grip on Leonidas's shoulder. If someone stepped out on the walkway, all of the cargo hold would be in view if that smoke wasn't as thick as he had implied. Unable to see or walk, she felt utterly helpless.

Leonidas quickened his pace, though he was careful not to make any noise, and he set each foot down carefully before lifting the other. It wouldn't do for them *all* to be floating around down here.

The control panel inside the airlock hatchway came into view, an irritated red button flashing that something had been damaged when the soldiers forced their way in. At least their tube was securely attached. A camera display on the panel showed suction lines like octopus arms holding the two ships together, the tube stretched in the middle of them.

Boots clanged on the walkway, followed by a thump and a noisy grunt. "Will someone figure out how to get the suns-cursed gravity and lights back on? And clear this damned smoke."

Must have been an officer. Someone who didn't want to do things himself.

Leonidas pulled Alisa and Mica into the airlock tube. Usually, Alisa's stomach did not object to zero grav, but there was a weird mix inside, gravity wrestling with null gravity and creating currents. Mica made a gagging sound, one she immediately tried to smother.

"Who's down there?" the officer barked.

Alisa found herself pulled farther into the tube, as Leonidas brushed past her and Mica. He fired at the same time as the man on the walkway did. Alisa banged into the hatch that led into the tug. The lighting in here wasn't much better than in the cargo hold, but she groped her way to a control panel.

"Let me," Mica whispered, shouldering her aside.

Alisa let her take over and pushed herself up so she could peer through the small circular window in the hatch. She should have expected that someone would be guarding it, but surprise and fear lurched through her when she found someone staring back at her.

"Help us," she mouthed, remembering that she was supposed to be a prisoner. She lifted her cuffed wrists to the window while widening her eyes and glancing back. She didn't have to feign her fear much, because red beams splashed against the rim of the hatchway on the *Nomad's* side of the tube.

"Can you get that open?" Leonidas asked, ducking back into the shelter of the airlock tube as more beams ricocheted off the floor and the jamb. For now, the men on the walkway did not have a good angle to fire straight in, but if that changed, Alisa and Mica, lacking any kind of armor, would be much more vulnerable than Leonidas. "They know where I am now," he added. "They'll all be down here in a second."

"How many?" Mica asked, fiddling with the controls.

"All of them," he said grimly. "Since I wasn't shooting to kill."

On the other side of the window, the armored soldier was talking to someone.

Alisa shook her wrists again and mouthed, "Please. Help us."

No need to specify that the help she needed was in escaping her own people. The soldier glanced over his shoulder. Four armored men appeared in the distance, trotting around a corner and into his corridor, all carrying blazer rifles that looked big enough to blow a hole in Leonidas's chest plate. The closest soldier gave her a firm nod, but held up a finger.

"I'm trying to get them to open the hatch for us," Alisa said, making sure to hide her mouth from the window. No need to let the Alliance men know she was helping her cyborg captor.

"How's that working?" Mica grumbled.

The soldier turned away, looking at the oncoming men again.

"We may need to look more helpless and needy," Alisa said.

No less than eight beams of red energy struck the hull and deck all around Leonidas, forcing him away from the hatchway. Alisa grimaced. The hull of the *Nomad* could take a lot of abuse, but if the flexible material of the tube was struck, she and Mica might be sucking space dust.

Leonidas backed farther, forcing Mica and Alisa against the tug's closed hatch. Mica was still fiddling with the control panel. Leonidas turned toward the similar control panel next to the *Nomad's* entrance. He punched a button, and the hatch swung shut with a clang and a sucking noise, the seal activating to make the ship airtight.

"Uhh," Alisa said, not sure they wanted to be trapped in the airlock tube with enemies on either side.

A hiss-suck came from behind her, and the tug's hatch opened, sliding sideways. Since she was still leaning on it, Alisa would have tumbled through, but Leonidas leaped past her, pushing her down. Mica joined her on the floor of the tube as he sprang through the hatchway, slamming into the soldiers waiting there with the speed and deadly power of a lightning bolt.

Alisa felt that she should help, but as soon as those rifles started going off, she grew acutely aware of how vulnerable she was with nothing but clothing to protect her. Some protection. She rolled to the side and curled up in the corner of the tube, trying to make herself small enough that the exterior of the ship's hull would protect her. Mica occupied a similar spot on the other side of the hatchway, glancing up at the control panel over her head, perhaps thinking about shutting the door.

A bang came from the *Nomad's* hatch, barely audible over the fight in the corridor of the tug, Leonidas battling the soldiers hand-to-hand, intentionally staying close enough to prevent them from aiming weapons at him. The faceplate of an armored soldier appeared in the window of the *Nomad's* hatch. Alisa couldn't see the man's face through two layers of glastica, but she held her cuffed wrists in front of her and tried to look helpless. It wasn't hard.

She hoped the soldiers would not charge in and start firing with two civilians hunkered in the tube. They could probably get the hatch open, since they had already forced their way onto the ship once. At the least, the locking mechanism would be broken.

The soldier on the *Nomad* watched the battle taking place in the tug's corridor and must have seen something he didn't like. He waved someone over, and from the way his head bent, Alisa knew he was working on the controls, trying to get the hatch open. So much for not charging in with civilians in the way.

"Got a plan, Captain Optimism?" Mica asked, almost shouting to be heard over the clangs of gauntleted fists and boots striking armored torsos. One man flew against the corridor wall, his helmet striking it with such force that his head must have been ringing like the clapper in a bell. He slumped to the deck, not moving. Another man leaped on Leonidas's back, an arm snaking around his neck.

"We're going to have to get in there." Alisa waved at the corridor where the men fought. "Then withdraw the tube, so the rest of them can't join in."

"That strands *us* on the tug. And leaves all of those angry soldiers on *your* ship."

"No choice."

Alisa made sure nobody was aiming at the open hatchway, then slipped around the corner. A fallen soldier, still alive as evinced by the moans coming from his cracked faceplate, lay sprawled on the deck. His rifle had fallen from his fingers, and Alisa was tempted to pick it up. But if she did, and if she did not then aim it at Leonidas…

She bit her lip. She wanted to help him, but she could not shoot Tomich's people—*her* people.

Instead, she lunged across the corridor to the controls inside the hatchway. She doubted she could release her ship from here, as the grab beam still held it tight to the belly of the tug, but—yes, there was the button for the tube. She jabbed it, hoping it wouldn't demand a passcode.

The hatch on the *Nomad* flew open at the same time as the hatch on the tug slid shut. The soldiers—there had to be at least twenty of them crowded at the airlock now—started forward before they realized what was happening. Red light flashed inside the tube, and they skittered backward, nearly falling over themselves to get back to the *Nomad's* cargo hold. They managed to get inside and slam the hatch shut a half second before the tube detached, the darkness of space visible as it withdrew back into the hull of the tug.

Realizing it had grown quiet behind her, Alisa turned around. Mica was staring at her from a spot pressed against the wall with a soldier moaning at her feet. Leonidas stood in the center of the corridor, dents and black burn marks in his crimson armor. The rest of the soldiers were down around him, some moaning, some not. She hoped he was still trying not to kill anyone, as her conscience was already in knots over this mess. She told herself that if she had let Leonidas go without helping him, and without extracting his promise to try not to kill, it would have been worse.

"We'll have to get to engineering to release the grab beam," Mica said. "What you want to do after that, I have no idea, because we won't be able to get back to the ship."

"We'll just have to take over the tug," Alisa said.

"Oh, I'm sure that will be easy."

"This way," Leonidas said. "You can talk on the way."

He turned down the corridor, not asking for directions. Maybe he had the specs for all of the Alliance and imperial ships in the system memorized.

"Better keep your prisoners in front of you," Alisa whispered, striding after him. "If there are cameras, someone might wonder why we're not wandering off."

Leonidas paused, waving for them to pass him. Alisa glanced at a fallen rifle again, this time wondering how good of an idea it was to leave all these men behind, still armed. If all they were was wounded, they could get up and join the fight again. But taking their rifles probably would not matter, since they had extra weapons built into their suits, and it wasn't as if she could simply tie a rope around someone in combat armor. The men would easily break free. Besides, she didn't have any rope.

Worried they would end up facing those people again, she hustled to join Mica in the lead. Her face was bleak, but she strode quickly down the corridors, presumably heading toward engineering. Alisa had never been on a tug and had no idea where anything was.

Her comm beeped. She might have ignored it, but that was Beck's number.

"What?" she whispered, glancing down corridors as they passed through intersections. The passages stood empty now, but she doubted it would take long for the tug's commander, that Bennington woman, to realize what had happened and to send down reinforcements.

"Some angry-looking soldiers are trying to force their way into navigation," Beck whispered. "Is Leonidas dead? Where are you?"

"We're with him on the tug. We had to pull the airlock tube."

"Leaving all these pissed soldiers with us?"

"Sorry. They might be less pissed if you just let them in and they don't have to break down the hatch. And I would appreciate it if there weren't any more broken doors on my ship than necessary."

"Not like you'd be the one fixing them," Mica grumbled.

"Tell them you're prisoners and that you were hiding up there to avoid the fighting."

"I'm in my combat armor, Captain."

"So?"

"You think they'll believe I'm a prisoner?"

"You can point out that Leonidas can best you whether you're in combat armor or not and he wasn't worried about it."

"That's not a thing I'm eager to point out to people, Captain."

"Just make up a plausible story." Alisa followed Mica into a lift, where she pressed a diagram of the ship, the big section at the bottom marked engineering. The doors shut. "I don't have much time to talk, but stay safe and be careful. Tell them you fought for the Alliance in the war."

Banging sounds came over the comm.

"And am I telling them that our doctor fought in the war too?" Beck asked quietly. "He's sitting on his box and looking concerned."

"Did he comm the imperials?"

The doors opened, and Alisa glimpsed a large open room with high ceilings before Leonidas stepped in front of her, waving for her to stay put as he slipped out.

"He did," Beck said. "But he's not sure if they're coming, or if they believed him."

"That's reassuring. Tell him to hide the box under my seat and lie to them. I'm sure he can manage that."

"Yes, ma'am."

Weapons fired somewhere in front of Leonidas, and Alisa cut off the comm. Once again, she felt helpless as she pressed herself to the wall next to the lift doors. Mica had her thumb on the touch-display, keeping those doors from closing.

A bolt of energy sizzled between them, slamming into the back wall. Alisa crouched and threw her arms over her head and neck.

Silence soon fell outside, only the hum of machinery and computers breaking it.

"Clear," Leonidas called.

Alisa eyed the smoking and melted wall at the back of the lift, then stepped out. Mica turned left and strode straight toward a workstation.

Alisa joined Leonidas in the middle of engineering. He had disarmed two men in uniforms, ripping up one's shirt to make strips of material to tie them together, back to back in the middle of the deck. From the way their heads lolled, neither appeared conscious. Leonidas kept them in his peripheral vision, but he watched the lift and another door that must lead into the rest of the ship.

"If this works, what's next?" he murmured, not looking directly at her. Maybe he had cameras on his mind too.

Alisa feared that someone who sat and watched a video of this would immediately be suspicious of how easily she and Mica were going along with Leonidas, especially since he had not pointed a weapon at them once. A stranger might simply think they were cowed, but Tomich knew her. If he saw this, he would wonder why she wasn't trying to get away—and also why she wasn't making rude gestures and throwing sarcasm and insults at Leonidas.

What's next, Leonidas had asked. Alisa feared it would be an arrest warrant for her, assuming they somehow managed to get away. She wasn't sure how that would happen right now, unless she left her ship and her people behind and stole the tug. That would *definitely* result in an arrest warrant. Or more likely a shoot-on-sight warrant.

"Marchenko?" Leonidas prompted.

"I think you can call me Alisa now."

"Seems overly familiar for a captor-prisoner relationship."

"What about for a captain-passenger relationship?"

"Are you going to keep Dominguez and me as passengers if we get out of this? I thought you might make us walk the plank."

"He paid your fare to Arkadius. You're staying."

"You're an interesting woman, Captain Marchenko."

He said that in the way a scientist spoke of an unexpected result from a specimen rather than in the way a man spoke of a woman he wanted to get to know better, perhaps over dinner and subsequent recreational activities. She told herself that was fine and looked around the engineering space, searching for inspiration. Their predicament was slightly more important than thoughts of dinners.

They couldn't steal the tug. Even if it did not have a crew of dozens, if not hundreds, it would not have been logical. No, they had to force the tug to release the *Nomad*, disable the grab beam, and somehow get back to her ship. Oh, and they would still have to deal with the squadrons of soldiers that were currently banging at the door to NavCom.

"What are the odds of finding spacesuits that fit us down here, Mica?" Alisa asked.

Mica, busy cursing and scowling at a console, did not answer the question. Instead, she said, "This is locked down. I need a retina scan from someone with access. Or a computer hacker."

Leonidas promptly strode toward his tied men. Alisa headed for the first storage cabinets she spotted. She was certain there would be spacesuits somewhere on the ship, as exterior repairs sometimes needed to be done, but she worried they would be close to an exterior hatch rather than here in engineering. Still, engineers would be the likely ones to go out on repairs. Maybe she would get lucky. She could use some luck this week.

"They should have attacked by now," Leonidas said from the console—he had toted the two men over, lifting both rather than untying them—and had one's face turned toward a scanner. A slender beam shot out as he pried the man's eyelid open.

"I'm pleased that they haven't," Alisa said.

"They must know we're here."

"Might be planning some other trouble for us," Mica said.

"How about some optimism here?" Alisa asked as she poked through cabinets. "Maybe they're confused as to what's going on. Maybe they think we're still on the *Nomad*, and they haven't figured out that we're here molesting their engine room."

A click sounded, followed by a faint hiss.

Leonidas's helmet spun toward the direction of the noise, his gaze locking onto a vent near the ceiling.

Mica scowled at Alisa. "I hate optimism. It has no place in space."

CHAPTER SEVENTEEN

"Gas," Leonidas barked. "It won't affect me, but—"

"We're dead takka?" Mica demanded, glaring toward the vent.

Alisa could not see anything coming out of it, but she trusted that Leonidas's helmet sensors told him it was there. "Can you identify it?" she asked, rummaging through another cabinet as efficiently as possible with her hands cuffed. She was on the verge of asking Leonidas to break the chain, but she didn't want to waste the time.

"No."

"So it might be knockout gas, or it might be more deadly?"

Alisa tried to breathe lightly. The engineering room was big, so it should take a while to disseminate, but if it was something extremely potent, even a small amount could affect them. Affect them, or kill them.

She hoped that the commander wouldn't choose such a drastic measure when two of her own people were in here. Of course, the commander might believe that her people had already been killed.

Leonidas strode to the lift doors and waved at the sensor to open them. Nothing happened. He roared and forced them open, metal screeching and warping.

"While we're impressed with your strength, I doubt the lift is going to work now," Mica said. "If anyone cares, I've disabled the grab beam."

"You're right," Leonidas said with disgust, poking at buttons.

A computer voice informed him that the damage to the doors made the lift inoperable.

Mica coughed and wiped her eyes as she glowered at the vent. She was closer to it than Alisa and moved to the opposite side of the room.

Finding the cabinet empty, Alisa ran to a pair of doors between two workstations. One with giant warning labels on it led to the reactor. The second was unmarked. She tugged that one open, and the gleam of light reflecting on faceplates met her eyes.

"Mica, over here." Alisa practically leaped into the closet space to paw at the uniforms, hoping to find ones that would fit women, though she would risk shambling around in something twice her size as long as she could make it airtight.

"I'm checking the door," Leonidas said, running out of the lift and toward the other exit. Alisa wagered it, too, would be locked. Likely guarded as well. The soldiers out there might expect him to be able to force his way out.

Mica crowded the closet doorway behind her. "Shove one out here," she rasped, coughing again. "I think that's prienzene in the air."

Alisa did not recognize the name of the drug. "Is it deadly?" She grabbed the two smallest suits and pushed them out of the closet.

"If the dose is high enough and unless the antidote is administered in a timely manner, yes."

"Great. Leonidas—we need your strong hands." Alisa thrust her cuffed wrists into the air. She would not be able to climb into the suit with her hands fastened together.

Leonidas stood with the side of his helmet pressed against the door—listening to troops in the corridor outside? He left his position and raced across the room to grab her chain. He snapped it easily, not hurting her at all, then turned to do the same for Mica.

"They have men lined up in the corridor outside the door," Leonidas said. "They're certain we'll charge out to escape the gas."

Alisa did not answer. She was trying not to breathe since she could feel indicators of the gas, a dry tickle in the back of her throat, a burning in her nostrils. She dove into the suit she had selected, fumbling with the fasteners, not sure whether her hands were shaking as a side effect of the gas or out of fear. Who knew if the commander would bother administering the antidote to the prisoners who had just broken her grab beam?

Leonidas stayed beside them, helping with the suits and helmets. Mica was dressed first—she was probably more experienced at donning space-suits for exterior repairs—and she strode off to poke into one of the cabinets Alisa had searched earlier. She must have seen something useful inside, though Alisa couldn't remember what. She'd had a singular purpose in mind.

As soon as her helmet was in place, she activated the internal life support system, hoping she hadn't already breathed in too much of the tainted air. How long until one passed out after exposure? The rough tickle in the back of her throat worried her, reminding her of an allergic reaction to something. If her airway closed off, all the oxygen in the suit's tank would not matter.

Alisa leaned on Leonidas to tug on the boots and tried not to worry about the rest.

"Stay behind me when we go out," he said, plucking at the flimsy material of her sleeve. "This won't stop weapons fire."

"Is going out a good idea?" Alisa asked. "When there's a squadron of soldiers waiting out there? You can't play cat and mouse with them when they're expecting you." She eyed the burn marks on his suit. How much more damage could it take? "Unless Mica can find the lights and gravity controls for this ship too."

"I found something better," Mica said, backing away from a cabinet full of tools.

She grinned wolfishly at them through the faceplate of her helmet. In both hands, she gripped a big tool with a tank and fuel hose and nozzle.

"Is that a flame thrower?" Alisa asked.

"A blowtorch for welding breaches in the hull." Mica strode toward the workstation she had been at before. An orange flame flared from the muzzle of the tool. Without any apparent discretion, she torched the controls.

"I see that retina scan was crucial," Leonidas said, eyeing the tied men on the floor beside the workstation. One watched Mica's blowtorch with woozy concern.

"It was," Mica said. "That was to make the tug let go of our ship. This is to ensure it won't be able to reacquire our ship."

A clank came from the door, and Leonidas turned his rifle in that direction.

"They'll soon grow impatient with waiting and simply walk in," he warned.

After she finished destroying the station, Mica jogged to a wall opposite the door and the lift. "There should be a corridor back here." She glanced at Leonidas, as if for verification.

He nodded. "Yes, and there's another lift that way, too, but I don't know if you'll be able to burn through—those walls are full of conduits and wires."

"I can do it." Mica laid into the bulkhead. "And they can bill my captain for the damages."

"Lucky me," Alisa murmured.

The door to engineering slid to the side. Leonidas fired instantly, reacting before it fully opened. He stepped in front of Alisa, blocking her view—and blocking her from harm. She peered around his shoulder in time to see armored men jump out of the way out in the corridor. The door slid back shut again.

"That won't stop them for long," Leonidas said. "They'll realize I just have a blazer rifle and that they can charge it with their armor on."

"It might not be your *gun* that they're afraid of," Alisa said.

He gave her a wolfish smile, his eyes gleaming.

"Working as quickly as I can," Mica announced.

Leonidas took Alisa's arm and led her to the bulkhead where Mica was working, wielding the blowtorch like a professional. That did not mean the process was quick. The bulkhead was thick, and as Leonidas had said, she was cutting through insulation and conduits too.

The lights flickered, then went out.

"Was that you?" Alisa asked. "Or are they trying to confuse us?"

Something snapped inside the wall, and flames leaped from the bulkhead. Alisa stumbled back, her movements awkward in the spacesuit. It lacked the balance servos of combat armor.

"It might have been me," Mica admitted, waving away smoke.

Alisa could see it by the light of the blowtorch, but she couldn't smell it. That was good, reassuring her that the gas should not be getting inside of her suit, either.

Mica ignored the dancing flames and went back to melting a hole in the bulkhead. A thump came from the door. Were the soldiers preparing to charge in?

"That's enough," Leonidas said, when Mica had cut a semi-circle into the bulkhead. He planted a hand on her shoulder and pushed her to the side.

"Really," she said, eyeing him like she was considering applying the torch to his armor.

He ignored her, slipping his gauntleted fingers into the gap she had made. He found a grip he liked and pulled. Metal squealed and ripped as he tore open a piece of the bulkhead. Wires and broken conduits spilled out, along with a flame retardant insulation. He tore it away, shreds of metallic fluff flying into the dim light.

"I'll have to burn a hole in the other side too," Mica said, waving the blowtorch.

"No time."

Leonidas turned sideways and slammed a side kick into the bulkhead. His boot went through the wall, the noise making Alisa jump. His foot got caught, but he maintained his balance, extracted it, and kicked three more times, battering a bigger opening. Then he grabbed it and tore the metal away further, making the hole large enough so he could wedge his armor through. Light streamed in from the corridor on the other side.

"You're a beast, Leonidas," Alisa murmured.

He looked back at her for a second, giving her that expression she had seen before, the wistful one he got sometimes when he told her he was as human as she was.

She groped for a way to say she had meant the words as a compliment, but he was already climbing through the hole. He fired at something—or someone—in the corridor, so Alisa hesitated to follow him.

"Clear," he said a couple of seconds later.

Alisa pulled herself through the hole, her oxygen tank catching on the ragged rim. She managed to wriggle through and fell out on the other side without any grace. She almost landed on someone in a uniform who was rolling around on the deck, grabbing his knee. Leonidas picked up the rifle that the soldier must have dropped.

Alisa climbed to her feet, wincing in sympathy at the man's gasps of pain. Mica clawed her way out, still carrying the blowtorch.

"This way to the lift," Leonidas said, pointing for them to lead the way, as he walked sideways beside them, watching both ways, a rifle in one hand and a pistol in the other.

Alisa and Mica jogged through the corridor, likely sharing similar thoughts, that they weren't cuffed anymore, that Leonidas was clearly protecting them, and that the odds of anyone thinking they were prisoners were slim. It couldn't be helped now. They would just have to get out of here and back to their ship as quickly as possible. Alisa wished she had figured out how they would do that.

They made it to a lift without encountering anyone else, but shouts from behind them suggested the soldiers had burst into engineering and found them missing. It would not take long for them to figure out which way their intruders had gone.

"We're heading back to the airlock, right?" Mica asked, reaching for the lift controls. "To see if we can reattach to the *Nomad*?"

"Wait," Alisa said.

"I don't think this is the time for that."

"All those soldiers will still be on the *Nomad*, probably back in our cargo hold, ready to shoot at whoever presses a nose to the window of the hatch," Alisa said. Further, she had no idea if the imperial ships were on the way. For all she knew, one of the Alliance warships might already have noticed the *Star Nomad* adrift and latched onto it. She doubted Beck, Alejandro, or Yumi had tried to pilot it anywhere.

"I don't see what we can do about that from here," Mica said.

Alisa faced Leonidas. "I was never in the infantry, but I seem to remember there being master controls for the Alliance and imperial combat armor, so that someone on their ship could walk the suit back to safety if a soldier was knocked out."

"Many ships' armor sets have such controls," Leonidas said.

"Is there any way we could do something to disable all of the soldiers' suits at once? Even if it wouldn't do anything to the men inside, they would be forced to get out of their armor if it didn't work, right? And then they would be easier targets for you if you charged into the cargo hold."

He was shaking his head before she finished speaking. "The operators can override those auxiliary commands. No man would want to potentially be a puppet for a puppeteer."

Alisa resisted the urge to point out that all imperial soldiers had been puppets for their emperor, deciding he might not appreciate that. "Is there any way to break something before they have a chance to recover and take control?"

"What if you demagnetized their boots?" Mica suggested. "Assuming the gravity is still out over there, they'd float away from the deck, and even if they got control back quickly, it would take them some time to get reoriented again and back to a surface they could grip."

"Not that much time," Leonidas said. The lift buzzed. He had his thumb on the button keeping the doors shut, and he frowned down at it. "It wouldn't be a bad tactic if I was at the hatch, about to charge in, but if even a minute passed, they would be able to recover. They'd also be able to fire from free fall. That wouldn't affect their ability to shoot."

"But it would discombobulate them," Alisa said, "give you an advantage."

"Yes. Briefly."

"So someone has to stay at the suit controls while you run back down to the airlock."

"Splitting up would not be wise," Leonidas said firmly.

"No, but I can't think of anything wiser."

Mica muttered something under her breath. It sounded pessimistic.

Alisa clung to the hope that they would be able to think up something creative to do to the soldiers' combat armor that would buy her team more of an advantage. "Any idea where that master control panel would be?"

"The bridge," Mica and Leonidas said at the same time.

"Oh," Alisa said. "Any chance the way there won't be well guarded?"

"No." Leonidas sighed and hit the button for the bridge.

CHAPTER EIGHTEEN

The route to the bridge wasn't as heavily guarded as Leonidas had suggested, perhaps because half of the ship's complement of troops were on the *Nomad* and the other half were still on the engineering level, trying to figure out where their intruders had gone. Alisa doubted that would take long. The tug wasn't exactly state-of-the-art, but it would have better internal sensors than the *Nomad*. She wagered the crew would be able to pick out the lone cyborg running around the ship.

Leonidas took out two more soldiers' kneecaps on the way to the bridge, but that was the only resistance they faced as they ran through the long corridors. Double doors at the end of one of those corridors came into sight, and Alisa's comm beeped.

"Now isn't a good time, Beck," she said as a greeting.

"Just thought you should know that the doc's imperial buddies are on their way."

"How many ships?"

"Three. Big ones too. They look like an even match for the Alliance warships."

"All right, thanks. We're trying to figure out a way to get back over there to join you so I can fly us away."

"We'd appreciate that, Captain," Beck said. "The doctor, especially. He's fiddling with his pendant and praying. Or that might be cursing. Not quite sure. He likes to mix the two."

"He's not the paragon of religiosity that we first thought," Alisa said, slowing down as they approached the bridge doors and Leonidas strode into the lead. "I'll talk to you later."

Leonidas paused before the double doors, a firearm still in each hand, but he had traded the pistol for a rifle he had taken from a soldier. Between the two weapons and his armor, he looked like the scourge of death. Alisa was glad she was behind him and not in his way. It was not a good day to be an Alliance soldier. She wished he were mowing down imperials instead.

"Stay here," he said, nodding to the wall beside the doors.

They had not opened at his approach. He lowered the rifle attached to him with a strap and leaned the second against the wall next to Alisa and Mica. He didn't hand it to them, perhaps still trying to help them by pursuing the prisoner ruse, but he put it within their reach. Now that they were in spacesuits instead of cuffs, Alisa doubted anyone would mistake them for prisoners. Unfortunately.

Leonidas stood so he could flatten his hands against the door and pull. He ripped it open as if it were made from rice paper. He charged inside, his rifle back in his hands. Shouts and blasts from blazers went off inside.

Alisa pressed her back to the wall and eyed the rifle propped next to her. Even though she didn't want to fight against Alliance people, she felt cowardly for hanging back while Leonidas risked himself over and over again.

"Don't even think about it," Mica said, her voice punctuated by weapons fire from beyond the doors.

A streak of orange shot past, escaping into the corridor, and making Alisa glad she had her back to the wall. "I'm not," she said.

The sounds of weapons discharging ceased, replaced by gasps and sobs of pain. Alisa winced. If she got out of this, she was going to find the money to outfit the *Nomad* with an armory full of stun guns. If they'd had any, Leonidas would not need to be blasting the kneecaps of everyone on board the tug.

"Captain Bennington," his voice came from within the bridge, an unexpected iciness to his tone.

Alisa did not know if it was safe, but she crept through the doors. Several men and women were down around the room, many whimpering and clutching at injuries. Others were unconscious. She hoped they were *only* unconscious.

In the middle of it all, Leonidas towered in his red armor, a rifle pointed at the chest of a woman sprawled on the deck at his feet. From the doorway, Alisa could not see his face, but the chill that had been in his tone made her rush forward.

"Problem here?" she asked, carefully laying a hand on Leonidas's armored forearm. "Ah, her kneecap is lower. And I believe she's Commander Bennington now. We chatted earlier."

Leonidas did not acknowledge her humor—or her. Standing next to him, she could now see inside his faceplate, to the ice in his blue eyes, and she felt certain that he was contemplating shooting.

"Leonidas?" Alisa whispered, glancing around to make sure nobody was grabbing for a weapon or leaping to their feet while Leonidas was distracted. Bennington, her graying red hair clipped short around an angular face full of terror, lay unmoving as she stared up at Leonidas. Nobody else was moving either, not yet.

Mica eased along the upper bridge, checking the workstations. Alisa nodded at her, glad she always stuck to business. A beeping came from a communications station, probably someone wanting an update on the capture of Leonidas.

As Alisa looked back to him, she noticed movement on the massive view screen that stretched from deck to ceiling and side to side at the front of the bridge. The *Star Nomad* was visible in the bottom corner of the screen, her engines silent, the ship adrift. Though she clearly wasn't going anywhere, one of the warships must have seen that she had broken away from the tug. It was veering toward the *Nomad*, its massive body moving to come alongside the freighter, blocking out the influence from the sun, leaving her ship in shadow. Despite Beck's words, Alisa did not see any sign of the imperial ships yet.

"That's going to be a problem," she said, wanting to ease past the tableau of Bennington and Leonidas and toward the helm, but she dared not leave his side. "Leonidas, will you tie her and the others up, please? And find a way to secure the doors? I'm sure her infantry soldiers will figure out where we are any second now."

"She killed an entire platoon of my people," Leonidas said, that coldness still in his voice, barely contained rage.

"In the war," Alisa said slowly. "Right? The war is over now. Our peoples signed a treaty."

"If the war was over, they wouldn't be trying to capture me," he said, his finger tight on the trigger of his rifle. "*Commander?*" he sneered. "She surrendered her last command. Her ship—the *Basilisk*, wasn't it?—was all but destroyed, adrift in space. She surrendered to us, said she had hundreds of injured and that her sickbay was inoperable. We accepted her surrender, sent over a team of medics with my people to protect them and secure the ship. Her people were there, but she wasn't. She fled in the only working life pod, used the cover of wrecked ships in the battlefield to slip away unnoticed. She had a remote and ordered a self-destruct of her ship from a distance, with *my* people on it. And hers."

Leonidas never breathed hard, even after running and fighting, but Alisa could hear his breaths now, deep angry breaths as he stood poised, reliving that moment perhaps, debating whether to unleash his rage. Alisa groped for something to say that would calm him down. Just being here, she would be seen as a traitor to her people, but if they killed the commander, if she abetted in that killing in front of witnesses—and there were a half dozen of them conscious, writhing in pain but also watching the confrontation—she might never be able to set foot on an Alliance planet again.

"I had the prime minister and the chief financier backing the Alliance on my ship," Bennington said slowly, staring defiantly at him and not begging for her life, though maybe she should have. Alisa doubted Leonidas would kill someone pleading for mercy. A soldier defying him might be another story. "I had to get them to safety. I couldn't let them fall into your hands."

"And so you blew up your *ship?*" he demanded. "With your people on it? With *my* people on it? The fighting was over and you'd surrendered. What you did was reprehensible. Inhumane."

"It bought us the time we needed to get away, didn't it? All of my people swore oaths to give their lives if necessary to overthrow the empire."

"And they rewarded you with a promotion for that?" Leonidas asked in disgust. "For using the lives of hundreds of people to protect your financial backer?"

Alisa wanted to slide into the seat at the helm, to navigate the tug to block the ship easing closer to hers, but she feared if she stepped away from Leonidas, he would shoot. And that it wouldn't be at a kneecap.

"Leonidas," Alisa whispered, trying to press down on his arm to move the rifle away from Bennington's chest. It did not budge. She might as well have tried to move a granite boulder.

"We didn't have the resources at that point to risk losing anyone who could pay our troops," Bennington said.

"No need to pay your troops if you kill them all before payday."

"What do you know about it, mech? You never had to worry about money, you with your hundreds of thousands in implants. How many impoverished workers were taxed to starvation to pay for that?"

Three suns, this woman had the self-preservation instincts of a rock.

"You know, I can see you're busy," Alisa said, making her tone light, hoping it would distract Leonidas from his anger. "Why don't *I* tie her up?"

She glanced at the view screen. Her window of opportunity for intercepting the warship was closing. Soon, it would be close enough to clamp onto the *Nomad*, to fasten its own airlock tube and send more troops over. Alisa would never be able to get her team to engineering to disable the grab beam on that warship. Meant for battle of every kind, it would have five times the troops that the tug claimed.

Yet, she did not lunge for the helm, too afraid of what would happen here if she did. With her hands shaking from fear and uncertainty, she knelt and eased between Leonidas and Bennington. As she grabbed the woman's hands, intending to pull her up, she was well aware that she had put the muzzle of his weapon right between her shoulder blades. The spacesuit would do nothing to deflect a blast from the blazer rifle.

Leonidas made a disgusted noise and pointed his weapon toward the ceiling. "You're a maniac, Marchenko."

"And you would have already fired if you believed killing her was the right thing to do," she said, her voice sounding more confident than she truly felt. She hauled Bennington to her feet. "I don't think you have it in you to shoot someone who is defenseless."

He grunted. "Don't think too highly of me. I'm just a man."

Bennington's lip curled at that proclamation, as if she wanted to protest him being a "man," but she was finally smart enough to hold her tongue.

"Man enough to find some rope and tie these people up?" Alisa asked, glancing again to the view screen.

This time, Leonidas glanced at it, too, finally seeing her problem. "Yes. Do what you mean to do." He shouldered his rifle and grabbed Bennington's arm. He ripped the front of her jacket off, making her gasp in pain, though her pain was surely less than that of the men and women he had shot. Swiftly, he tore the jacket into shreds to fashion makeshift ropes.

Trusting that the moment had passed and that he wouldn't use one of those ropes to strangle her, Alisa leaped into the main pilot's seat, clunking her oxygen tank on the back. Though she was far more familiar with one- and two-man Alliance fighter craft, she got the gist of the console layout quickly.

"Any luck over there, Mica?" she asked, calling up power from the engines. She did not want to ease into position the way the warship was. Instead, she gently fired the port thrusters, shifting the alignment of the tug's blunt nose.

"I've pulled up the controls for the suits," Mica said. "I can see where their people are on our ship."

"Did you say *our* ship? Does that mean you're staying with it instead of job hunting elsewhere?"

"After this? You *are* a maniac."

"Was that a no?" Alisa had the nose of the tug lined up perfectly. She buckled her harness. They would probably just bounce off the warship's shields, but with luck, her surprise would be enough to divert the craft away from the *Nomad* before it could clamp on.

"I think I've found the controls to do what we talked about," Mica said, ignoring Alisa's question. "To demagnetize their boots. I wonder if—hm, maybe I can short something out and make it permanent. I'm not sure. But either way, I'll have to do it one at a time."

"Hold that thought. And brace for impact."

"Impact?" Mica blurted, spinning in the chair she had claimed.

Alisa did not pause to explain further. The warship might have noticed their movement by now. She brought the thrusters to maximum for a short burst.

The tug did not surge forward like a racehorse springing from the gates, but it moved quickly enough to take everyone by surprise, including her target. The warship did not have time to veer away as the tug roared in. It slammed into the side of its sister craft with a jolt that would have thrown Alisa from her seat if she hadn't buckled herself in. Someone *did* hit the deck behind her as the sound of the crash, warping and crumpling metal, filled her ears.

They had not simply hit the warship's shields and bounced off, as Alisa had expected. The other ship must have lowered its shields so that it could latch onto the *Nomad*. She smiled viciously as her console lit up, and alarms started wailing in the tug. That warship wouldn't be latching onto anything now.

Barely checking the alarms, she reversed the thrusters, planning to back them up so she could maneuver the tug alongside the *Nomad*. She, Mica, and Leonidas still had to get back, so they needed to be close enough to extend the airlock tube.

But the tug did not move. The painful grinding of metal on metal sounded, and that was it.

"Alisa," Mica groaned. "You got us *stuck*."

Alisa tried the thrusters again, but the console only beeped alerts at her. The ship itself was unresponsive.

"Something that will be sure to delight *them*," Mica added, pointing at the screen.

The damaged Alliance warship filled most of the view, but a swath of starry space was visible in the corner. Another ship was coming into sight in that space. An imperial dreadnought.

CHAPTER NINETEEN

The screech of blazer fire shook Alisa from the stare she had locked onto the imperial ship. She leaped from the pilot's seat, ignoring the alarms wailing and the lights flashing all over the consoles on the bridge. Leonidas stood to the side of the double doors, shooting down the corridor. If the tug's soldiers hadn't known where their intruders were before, they surely did after that crash.

"Mica?" Alisa ran to her station, both to check on her progress with the suits and because it would get her out of the line of fire from the doorway.

"I disabled two of them," Mica said. "I'm not sure if it's permanent or not. I tried to make it that way."

"How many men left to do?" Hiding in the dark cubby on the *Nomad*, Alisa had gotten the impression of close to twenty men stomping around, engaging in cat and mouse with Leonidas.

"Nineteen."

"Ah." Alisa had hoped she had overestimated—that would be a lot of angry soldiers waiting in the cargo hold upon their return. Even though Leonidas had clearly shown he could play cat and mouse with the best of them and that he could handle superior numbers, that seemed a lot to ask, even for a cyborg.

"There are more of them coming," Leonidas said over his shoulder as he ducked behind the wall to avoid fire. Crimson and orange beams lanced through the doorway, one striking the view screen. It exploded with an angry snapping of electricity. Smoke streamed into the air, and the view went black.

"Can you fight a way through them so we can get to the lift?" Alisa asked. She looked around the bridge, hoping to spot some back door that she had missed, but there was only the one exit.

"Not a chance," Leonidas said, "but we might be able to get to the first intersection there. They haven't advanced that far yet. If I remember the layout of this ship correctly, there are some maintenance ladder wells that could take us back down to the airlock level."

Alisa winced at the idea of trying to navigate rungs in the clunky spacesuit. Would Leonidas even be able to fit inside a ladder well in that big armor of his?

"We better go soon if we want to have a chance," he added. "Their whole crew will be here in a minute."

Another red beam sizzled through the doorway, this time smashing into the helm.

"Mica?" Alisa asked. "How much time do you need?"

"Ten minutes and a foxy lady," Mica said, her hands flying over a set of holo controls.

"I'd get you one if I could. Ah, you are referring to the drink, right?"

"Yes."

Leonidas unleashed another barrage of fire while muttering something about having used up all his rust bangs on the *Nomad*. He raised his voice. "They're regrouping, and I think more men just arrived. Marchenko, we have to go *now*."

"Come on, Mica."

"Just three more."

Alisa pulled Mica out of the seat. "It'll have to be good enough."

They joined Leonidas beside the doorway, staying out of the soldiers' line of sight. Leonidas fired a couple of shots down the corridor, but he also held something in his left hand, a blazer pistol he had snatched from a fallen bridge officer. In the seconds when nobody was firing, Alisa could hear it humming softly.

"What are you doing?" she whispered, gripping Mica's arm because she kept glancing back toward the station she had been using.

"Overloading it," he said as the humming increased. His mouth moved, like he was counting, then he leaned out, and fired his rifle several times before throwing the pistol down the corridor.

It skidded along the deck like a hockey puck belted across the arena. Just before it reached the corner where the soldiers were firing from, it blew up, exploding with enough force to make the walls tremble.

"Come on," Leonidas said. "Stay *right* behind me."

He charged into the corridor, not waiting for a response.

Trusting Mica to follow, Alisa raced after him, running as fast as she could in the awkward spacesuit. She did her best to keep up with Leonidas, who blitzed toward the black smoke filling the corridor, firing as he went. Return shots zipped toward him. One slammed into his shoulder. That one might have struck Alisa if he hadn't been there.

Firing wildly, he stopped just past the intersection he had mentioned. Thanks to the explosion, pockmarks damaged the deck ahead of him, and soot coated the walls. The smoke still clogging the air did not keep the soldiers from firing. Alisa sprinted around the corner, ducking as a blazer bolt streaked past Leonidas. As she went, she waved frantically for Mica to follow. She needn't have bothered. Mica crashed into her in her haste to avoid more blazer bolts lancing down the corridor.

"This way," Mica said, passing her to take the lead.

Leonidas ducked around the corner, but did not follow them. Instead, he kept leaning out and firing at the soldiers, keeping them from charging up to the intersection.

Alisa hesitated, not wanting to leave him behind. His shoulder smoldered from where he had taken that direct hit, and a dozen other dents and scorch marks marred his armor. Had any of the attacks reached flesh? How injured was he under that armor?

"Go," Leonidas barked, pointing his chin toward Mica's retreating back.

Reluctantly, Alisa obeyed. Even if she stayed, what could she have done to help? Besides, he knew the layout of the ship and where they were going. He could catch up.

Mica led them around two turns, almost sprinting past the ladder well.

"Here," Alisa called, pointing to the compact hole in the side of a corridor.

Mica cursed as she skidded to a stop and backtracked. "Your armored buddy will never fit in that."

Alisa, staring at the narrow ladder well, was thinking the same thing.

"He'll have to find another way down then," she said, though she hated the idea of leaving him where he would be forced to fight so many, forced to kill if he wanted to avoid capture. That was everything she had hoped to avoid by coming along.

Someone cried out in the distance, and the sounds of the firefight continued to echo through the corridors.

Mica swung onto the rungs, her large, awkward spacesuit boots slipping off more than once as she descended. Her oxygen tank banged against the wall behind her, and the welding blowtorch she still carried caught in the ladder.

"You might want to leave that behind," Alisa said.

Mica grunted, freed it, and continued down, not relinquishing the tool. Maybe she planned to make more doors along the way. Alisa followed her, having little more luck navigating in the spacesuit. More than once, she almost fell, but they made it to the bottom deck, the one that held the airlock hatch.

They did not run into anyone as they raced through the long, white corridors. All of the soldiers must have been on the bridge level, trying to get to their commander, trying to defeat Leonidas. Alisa did not see how he could find his way back down here to join them, especially if he could not fit inside the ladder well. She blinked back tears, focusing on the way ahead. This wasn't the time to mourn. She needed to get back to her ship.

Mica ran around a corner and came to the dead end where they had boarded earlier. Drying blood stained the deck, but the soldiers Leonidas had shot had disappeared, dragging themselves to sickbay or up to join the fight.

Mica pressed her palms to the hatch on either side of the window, clunking her faceplate as she peered out.

"Can you see the *Nomad?*" Alisa asked, crowding behind her.

"Yes, but there's no way the tube will reach over there. You should have been steering us closer to the ship instead of crashing into another one."

"That other one was about to lock its grab beam onto the *Nomad*. We wouldn't have had *any* chance of getting to it if they'd hauled it away."

"What chance do we have now?" Mica demanded, stepping back so Alisa could look.

"Plenty. We're in spacesuits, and that's space." Alisa waved at the gap between them and the *Nomad*.

"Are you crazy? We don't have rocket packs. We can't steer ourselves over there. We'll just end up floating helplessly until our oxygen runs out and we die of asphyxiation."

"Quit being so dramatic. All we have to do is make sure we push off in a straight line."

"A straight—that ship must be a thousand meters away, easy. Nobody can jump that straight."

"It's not like we need to land on a half tindark coin," Alisa said. "Anywhere on the freighter, and we can grab on, magnetize our boots, and walk along the hull to the hatch."

"You *are* crazy. What happens if we miss?"

Shouts sounded down the corridor behind them, along with the firing of weapons. They had left that noise behind as they descended the ladder well, so if they were hearing it again now, that meant that soldiers were down here, on this level. Alisa and Mica didn't have much time.

"And what happens if we make it?" Mica demanded, grabbing Alisa's arm. "There's a huge squadron of very irritated soldiers with boot problems in there. They'll shoot the first thing that comes in the door."

Heavy footfalls thundered in a corridor near them, someone running in their direction.

"Inside," Alisa whispered, tugging open the hatch to the airlock. The outer hatch remained shut—it would take a minute for the ship to depressurize the inside so they could jump off. She hoped they had that minute.

Mica unleashed a stream of curses as she shoved herself into the airlock. As Alisa stepped across the threshold after her, a familiar figure raced around a corner and sprinted toward them. Smoke wafted from the back of Leonidas's crimson armor, his faceplate was cracked, and he was limping. None of that slowed him down.

Someone fired around the corner toward his back, but he spun and loosed a few bolts, driving the soldier back into hiding. He lunged into the airlock, barely keeping from knocking Alisa over as he hit the button that made the hatch slide shut behind him.

"Cycle the lock," he barked.

"Already on it," Mica said.

Alisa made sure her magnetic boots had a hold on the deck as air hissed out of the chamber.

"I can't help but notice the tube isn't extended and that your freighter is way over there," Leonidas said, breathing only slightly heavily after his crazy run.

"That's because cyborgs are extremely observant," Alisa said. "We're jumping."

A red beam streaked down the corridor, slamming into the thick door.

"Soon, I hope," Alisa added. "Mica?"

"Any way to keep them from overriding the hatch controls?" Leonidas said, facing the window.

His shoulder blocked most of Alisa's view, but she glimpsed armored soldiers sprinting down the corridor now that Leonidas couldn't shoot them.

"Move," Mica said, hefting the blowtorch.

Wordlessly, Leonidas did so, flattening his back to the wall. Mica welded the metal around the spot where the hatch slid into the wall. The first of the soldiers reached the controls on the other side.

"I'm opening the door," Leonidas said, shifting to the outer hatch while Mica continued to work.

Alisa knocked on the window. The soldier trying to open the inner hatch looked at her. She had absolutely nothing to say to him and was only trying to buy Mica time, so the metal would melt—or harden. Alisa didn't know exactly what Mica was doing, but she widened her eyes and pointed behind the man. He scowled at her and returned to the controls.

"Well, that bought us almost a second," Alisa muttered.

Mica backed away, turning off the blowtorch as the outer hatch opened, and the vastness of space stretched before them. Since the airlock chamber was already depressurized, there was no tug or any sensation of currents stirring. However, a faint hiss reached Alisa's ears.

She crept up behind Leonidas, touching a hand to his back. "Is that you? Is your suit damaged?"

"Is it *damaged*?" Mica asked, joining them at the outer hatch. "He looks like he got run over by a herd of Senekda buffalo."

Clunks and thuds came from the hatch behind them. Mica must have succeeded in jamming it. Either that, or the men realized they couldn't open it now, not with the outer hatch open. Of course, they might be able to override the interior controls and close that outer hatch.

"I'm venting air," Leonidas agreed. "We're jumping? Is that the plan?"

"Yes, how's your aim?" Alisa asked.

"Probably better than yours. Hang on to me." He grunted and stepped to the edge, gripping the jamb with both hands and looking back at them.

"Your cyborg isn't modest, Captain," Mica said.

"I don't think modesty is listed as a desirable attribute on cyborg recruiting posters." Not sure where to grab him, Alisa opted for the strap of the rifle slung across his torso. He wouldn't let *that* fall off, she was sure.

Mica, still carrying the blowtorch, wrapped her free arm around his neck and climbed onto his back. Alisa almost made a comment about her revising her bedroom fantasies, but more thuds came from behind them, and Leonidas crouched to push off. Alisa swallowed, fear riding in her chest despite her proclamation that the freighter was huge and hitting it would be easy.

Leonidas pushed off more gently than she expected, stretching his arms out above his head, like a swimmer diving into a pool. They sailed into the blackness of space, stars suddenly visible in all directions. The view took Alisa's breath away even as it terrified her.

If Leonidas miscalculated and they missed…

Fortunately, they seemed to be on track to hit the freighter. It grew larger as they sailed across the void, the other Alliance warships, along with two imperial vessels, coming into view to the sides.

"We're going to make it," Alisa said.

She gripped Mica's arm with her free one and caught an amazed expression on her engineer's face as she gazed around them. Alisa felt that same sense of wonder. She knew they still had to deal with the soldiers inside the *Nomad*, but for now, utter peace and silence surrounded them, their suits protecting them from the cold.

Until Alisa felt something pop.

Alarm surged through her. Had something happened to her suit? No, a reverberation came through her hand where she was touching Leonidas. A tiny stream of air shot out from his damaged suit.

Alisa's first thought was to worry that he wouldn't have enough oxygen to make it. Then Mica patted her frantically on the shoulder and pointed ahead of them. That tiny stream of air, released under pressure, was altering their path slightly. And they were still far enough from the *Nomad* that a slight change of angle mattered.

Alisa's earlier alarm turned into terror as their path changed—it would take them over the top of the ship and out into space. She shifted her grip so she could clamp her hand over the leak, but it was too late.

They would overshoot the *Nomad* and be stranded until someone noticed them and picked them up. Or didn't.

Leonidas's helmet swiveled toward Mica. As they continued to sail through space, he reached back and grabbed her arm. Alisa frowned in confusion. Then she realized it wasn't her arm that he had snagged but the blowtorch. She let him have it. He must have pressed something because a razor popped out of the wrist of his armor. He jabbed it into the gas tank on the blowtorch, then twisted it and his arm back at an awkward angle. The force emitted from the tank must have been greater than what was coming out of his suit, because their course soon adjusted. Once again, the *Nomad* lay within their path.

Mica grinned and thumped him on the shoulder.

Alisa smiled smugly at her, wishing she could say that *her* cyborg, as Mica had referred to him, had no need to be modest.

They approached the hull of the freighter, Leonidas angling them toward the back of the craft. Alisa lost all feeling of smugness, of anything except for shock, when the cargo hold hatch came into view. It wasn't shut, as it should be. Instead, it gaped open, the dark interior of her ship open to the elements of space.

CHAPTER TWENTY

Alisa crawled as quickly as she could along the exterior of the *Nomad* without losing her boots' magnetic grip on the hull. She had to get to the cargo hold, see why the hatch was open, and figure out if the rest of the ship had been closed off or if…it hadn't. If it hadn't, everything would have been blown out into space. Even if it had, everything in the cargo hold would be gone. She grimaced, thinking of Yumi's chickens.

Leonidas, who was leading their crawl along the hull, stopped, tapped her shoulder, and pointed down. Though impatient, Alisa paused to look. And gape. A soldier in combat armor drifted past, arms waving, a rifle still gripped in his hand. She tensed, thinking he might manage to shoot, but he appeared too distressed by his situation to notice them.

Leonidas continued toward the hatch, maneuvering around the edge and disappearing from sight. Mica and Alisa reached the spot at the same time. Alisa poked her head around the edge, not sure what to expect. She glanced at the dim corner where the chicken pen had been kept. The birds and the makeshift fencing and netting Yumi had erected were gone, as were some items that hadn't been bolted down.

Shaking her head, she climbed down the edge of the hatch until she could set her boots on the deck. Leonidas was already halfway across the hold, heading for the stairs leading up to the walkway. Landing behind Alisa, Mica planted her feet, then hit the button to close the hatch.

Alisa barely noticed. She strode after Leonidas, trying to see up to the corridor leading into the crew areas. Was the hatch up there open? Closed?

With his long legs, Leonidas made it up the stairs first. Alisa scrambled after him, almost tripping. She cursed the awkward suit, even if it had kept her alive so far in the vacuum of space.

She caught up with Leonidas at a hatch that was thankfully closed. He was knocking at it with the butt of his rifle, probably ready to spin the weapon around if anyone unfriendly came to check on them.

Mica had headed toward engineering instead of joining them. Lights flickered on, and machinery clanked, the oxygen regeneration system being activated and gravity being restored. Alisa appreciated her dedication to getting the ship in working order again, but she was currently more worried about Beck and Yumi. She bumped Leonidas inadvertently as she tried to see through the small window in the hatch.

He stepped aside so she could peer through. Alisa almost laughed at what she saw. Two chickens were running amok in the corridor as Yumi chased after them, trying to gather them up. Beck stood in his combat armor, leaning against the wall, holding up a finger toward the window. He held a rifle in his other hand. Had he played a role in getting rid of the soldiers? He must have.

"Life support has been returned to the entire ship," came Mica's voice over the comm speakers.

Beck ambled forward and opened the hatch.

"What happened?" Alisa blurted, rushing in and gripping his shoulder. She would have given Yumi a squeeze, too, but one of the chickens escaped and was heading toward the cargo hold. Yumi groaned and chased after it.

"A little chicanery," Beck said, "and some time spent going over the operations training videos for a *Nebula Rambler 880* to learn how to override the ship's safety system and open the hatch to space when people are inside the cargo hold. People that were oddly floating around and cursing a lot even before we got the doors open." He tilted his head and raised his eyebrows toward her. "Do you have any idea how hokey and out-of-date those videos are?"

"Yes..." A chicken ran past Alisa's boots. "How did you get the chickens out of the cargo hold while not letting the soldiers out?"

"Yumi said she had to feed them a while back." Beck shrugged. "The soldiers weren't really mad at *us*. They did pry us out of navigation so we couldn't fly anywhere, as if those horrible videos could have shown us how. Did you know the woman speaking in them wears striped polyester pants and has collar lapels that flare out almost to her elbows? Was that what passed for fashion in the last century?"

"All you need to do is look at the rec room carpet to know the answer to that." Alisa frowned. "How did Yumi go from feeding the chickens to getting them up here?"

"She took them up one at a time, saying they needed their medication." Beck shrugged again. "She's got a sweet and innocent smile. They believed her. I did feel a little bad sending the soldiers out into space after they were fairly reasonable with us—even if they were swearing up and down that they were going to strangle the mech and anyone sympathizing with him—but I figure their armor will keep them alive long enough for their ships to pick them up."

"Captain?" Alejandro said, leaning out of the hatchway to NavCom. "I'd appreciate it if you saved the briefing for later and piloted us out of trouble before anyone figures out what's going on."

"It's good to see you, too, Doctor," Alisa said dryly. "By the way, is there any chance you have the antidote to prienzene gas in your medical kit? Mica and I breathed some in." She did not know if it had been enough to cause long-term damage, but she could still feel the uncomfortable swelling in the back of her throat along with a dull ache behind her sternum.

"The antidote? No."

"Not enough room in your bag after packing that orb?" She did not manage to keep the bitterness out of her voice. What had she expected? That he would anticipate running into people that would hurl poisonous gases at him during his journey?

"I can make a compound to accelerate and enhance your body's ability to flush exogenous toxins," Alejandro said. "You don't look that bad, so that should suffice."

Should. Alisa was not sure if she should find that word comforting but decided to do so. She also decided not to think about how he had been contemplating that her death might be convenient for his mission. He shouldn't have a reason to want Mica out of the way, so with luck, he would make the same substance for both of them.

"Good," she said and gave him a warm smile in case it would help endear her to him. "Thank you."

Alisa patted Beck on his armored shoulder—he was looking concerned over this talk of poisonous gas—then headed to NavCom. If Alejandro would fix up a special compound for her, the least she could do was comply with his suggestion to pilot them out of the area. Besides, she agreed with the sentiment. The sooner they got out of here, the better.

"*We're* glad to have you back, Captain," Beck said firmly, waving at his chest and pointing in the direction Yumi had gone—he also waved to include the wayward chicken darting around. "I'll prepare a celebratory dinner if you can get us away from all of these party crashers."

"I'll do my best."

In NavCom, Alisa slid into the pilot's seat—she wanted to collapse and take a few minutes to gather herself, but there was no time. Her fingers flying, she steered them away from the tug and the warship she had crashed the tug into. The warship was in the process of extricating itself, and Alisa wanted to be far away when it regained room to maneuver. She had no doubt that its commander would be livid with her as soon as he or she found out who had been responsible for that mess.

The other two Alliance warships still flanked the *Nomad*, but they did not attempt to pursue, nor did they maneuver to use their grab beams, not with the three big imperial ships looming in a triangular formation in front of them. Any ship that wanted to grab the *Nomad* would have to lower its shields to do so. Alisa's plans for escape hinged on the hope that neither side would trust the other enough to risk that. She wasn't about to comm anyone to ask. She simply guided her freighter downward, away from both sets of ships. The green orb of Perun's moon filled the space ahead, and she headed for it, figuring she would disappear behind it and get out of the other ships' lines of sight—and out of their commanders' minds—before once again setting a course for Arkadius.

The proximity alarm beeped as one of the imperial cruisers charged away from the pack. It flew past the Alliance ships, arrowing straight after the *Nomad*.

"Damn it," Alisa cursed, pushing the engines to maximum, no longer worrying about stealthily sneaking away.

The cruiser surged to *its* maximum, which was far greater than the freighter's. Alisa weaved as she flew toward the moon, hoping vainly that providing a busy target would give their grab beam operator a hard time. Something brushed against the *Nomad's* shields, a first attempt to snatch them. She flew like a drunk, a calculating drunk. Maybe if she could reach the moon's orbit and—

The second attempt to latch onto them worked, and the *Nomad* halted with an alarming jolt.

"Not again," she groaned, slamming her fist against the console.

"More trouble?" Leonidas asked, walking into navigation, his helmet under his arm, his crimson suit so battered and soot-marked that it looked like he had dragged it out of a junkyard. Or a dumpster.

"You could say that. Any chance I can talk you into rolling down a window and throwing the doctor's orb outside for them?"

Leonidas lifted an eyebrow.

The comm flashed, and she slapped her palm on the button, giving it a surly glower.

"Captain of the civilian freighter *Star Nomad*," a male voice said. "As you are no doubt aware, we have restrained your ship."

"Must be your people," Alisa muttered, not bothering to mute the comm. "They have the bureaucratic gift for using a lot of words to state the obvious."

"You will be permitted to fly away, despite damages done to our university library, but we require that you leave behind a sphere-shaped artifact. We are preparing to board and pick it up. If you wish our generous offer to release you to remain in effect, you will have it waiting and will not resist us."

Not surprisingly, Alejandro showed up in the hatchway behind Leonidas to hear this. Alisa scowled at him, then ignored both men to reply to the imperial bureaucrat.

"This is Captain Marchenko," Alisa said. "If you try to board my ship, I'll blow up your sphere-shaped artifact. It's been a nice paperweight for my desk, but I'm sure I can replace it with a moon rock."

Alejandro smacked a palm to his forehead and ran his hand down his face. The faintest hint of a smile curved Leonidas's lips upward.

"If you destroy the artifact," the imperial speaker said, "we will destroy *your* ship."

"Then it's going to be a bad day for all of us." Alisa leaned back in her seat, prepared to wait out his bluff. She *hoped* it was a bluff.

"Captain," Alejandro said slowly. "May I suggest—"

"No."

Alejandro's eyebrows rose.

"Leonidas, I do wish you'd accept my offer of employment," Alisa said, "because I'd love to be able to order you to carry wayward passengers out of NavCom for me."

Alejandro scowled at Leonidas, as if he'd been the one to make the impertinent comment. Alisa did not see if he returned the scowl, because her sensors showed one of the other ships moving away from the cluster. It was one of the Alliance warships.

The grab beam disappeared as the imperial ship raised its shields, rotating to turn its weapons toward the newcomer.

Alisa did not question her luck. She immediately reengaged the thrusters, returning them to her original course. The other ships would have trouble locking onto her if there was a moon in the way.

"They let us go?" Alejandro asked.

"Clearly, my threat made them tremble in distress," Alisa said.

Focused on the path ahead, she did not look back to see if he rolled his eyes at her or made a rude gesture.

The comm flashed again. Alisa thought about ignoring it, but the call was coming from one of the Alliance ships rather than the imperial craft.

"Yes?" she answered.

"Well, that's slightly more professional than answering with, 'What?'" a familiar voice said. Tomich.

Alisa did not know whether to be relieved by his contact or not. She had left him with a mess.

"Commander," she said carefully. "Are you going to let us go?"

She realized that it was his ship that had advanced on the imperial vessel. They were now facing each other, posturing.

"Us," Tomich said, his voice flat.

He must have seen enough or heard enough in his reports to believe she had been working with Leonidas. She did not see any point in denying it now. He would think less of her if she lied. They had been colleagues once, sharing more than a few drinks over lost comrades, and she did not want to intentionally give him a reason to feel distaste toward her.

"For the moment. They paid their fare. I'm taking them to—" Alisa glanced at Alejandro, "—where they want to go."

Tomich was silent for so long that she glanced at the comm to see if the channel was still open. She also checked the sensors to make sure he hadn't decided to give chase, imperial ships notwithstanding.

"The next time we meet," Tomich finally said, "you owe me one."

"I will be glad to buy you a sake while we watch a forceball game."

"One sake? That's it?"

"Two? I'm just a lowly freighter operator now, you know. I don't have a regular Alliance paycheck to rely on."

Tomich grumbled something under his breath, then sighed. "I have a feeling I'm going to regret this day."

"Thank you, Commander," she said, taking all hints of sarcasm and irreverence out of her voice.

The comm light winked out. Alisa suspected that the next time she ran into Tomich, he would be as likely to punch her as accept a drink from her. It was also possible that his superiors would punish him for letting the *Nomad* go—and put out a warrant for her arrest.

She sighed and looked back at the two men in her hatchway, wondering about her sanity for continuing on with them.

EPILOGUE

Alisa stood up, turning the autopilot on to navigate the start of their journey to Arkadius. The stars were bright and clear, and the sensors showed no sign of pursuers, imperial, Alliance, or otherwise. She decided she could risk a shower. Maybe even bed. The lights had dimmed a while ago, signaling the ship's night cycle, and she had finally stopped having to run to the lav. Apparently, Alejandro's toxin-clearing potion had involved kicking her kidneys into overdrive.

It had been a couple of hours since they had cruised away from Perun's moon, leaving the damaged Alliance ships glaring across the stars at the imperial ships. She trusted they wouldn't start a war with each other. The Alliance could call in a lot of allies, and with the *Star Nomad*—and Leonidas and Alejandro—gone, the imperials had nothing left to fight over. She just hoped she would be allowed to approach Arkadius when they arrived in a week. Just because Tomich had let her go didn't mean that his superiors would not put out the word for her capture.

"Marchenko," Leonidas said, stepping out of the dim corridor and into NavCom.

He wore soft black gym pants and a gray T-shirt, no sign of his uniform jacket tonight. The T-shirt fit him like a second skin, and Alisa made herself look away, thinking of Mica's admonitions about letting her feelings get them into trouble. As if Alisa couldn't get into plenty of trouble without feelings ever coming into play. She admitted that her actions might not have been the wisest, even if they had possibly resulted in less loss of human life than if she had simply let Leonidas charge onto the Alliance ship with rifles blaring, no thoughts of choosing non-vital targets in his mind.

"Still not calling me Alisa, eh?" she asked.

"If I did, you might take it as a sign to call me Leo." His mouth twisted with distaste. "You've defaulted to that a couple of times."

She had defaulted to "mech," too, which she regretted. "I could call you Hieronymus," she offered, since that was the name on his arrest warrant, even if it was a mouthful.

His mouth twisted further. "I don't know if I'd answer to that. It was my grandfather's name, and I always thought it was horrible. My fellow officers just called me Adler."

"What do your brothers call you?"

"Mech."

Alisa blinked. "Seriously?"

He had said that he and his brothers did not get along fabulously, that one had even joined the Alliance, but this sounded like outright antagonism. How could they feel that way about him? Even if he was supposed to be the enemy to her, she couldn't imagine him ever acting with anything but honor. She wished she could look at her own record and know she had always acted so.

"Not to my face," Leonidas said, "but I've heard them talking to each other about me when they thought I couldn't hear."

"They sound like lovely people."

"They're quite a bit younger than I am. They don't know why I joined." His hand flicked toward his forearm, maybe to indicate more than joining, but also the implants.

"Why did you?" she asked, looking into his eyes.

He did not meet her gaze, instead staring at the stars on the view screen. Alisa knew there wasn't much exciting to see out there—she had checked and double-checked before allowing herself to think of showering.

"I need to stop at Starfall Station on the way to Arkadius," Leonidas said. Pretending he hadn't heard her question? "There are tech smiths there. I need to get my armor repaired and thought it would be good to do so before we visit Starseers unannounced."

Alisa nodded. "That's not a problem. As you said, it's on the way."

The *Nomad* could use some new parts, too, as Mica was quick to point out on a daily basis. And the airlock hatch needed repairs. They were lucky the ship was still spaceworthy after the soldiers had forced their way in.

"The doctor seems certain that we'll find trouble on Arkadius," Leonidas said dryly.

"Trouble finds him wherever he and his orb go."

"Odd. He said the same thing about you."

"Me? As if getting waylaid in the library was my fault. Or getting jumped by Alliance ships trying to leave the planet."

He winced. "No, that was because of me."

"I just try my best to improve uncomfortable situations." Alisa shifted and patted the seat of her chair, where a stretch of engineer tape held a rip together.

"Uncomfortable situations? That's an understatement, isn't it?" His gaze shifted from the stars to her face.

"Not to an optimist. Right now, I'm optimistically being positive that we'll reach the Starseer temple on Arkadius and both find what we're looking for."

"You believe your daughter is there?"

She wished that were the case, but she was tempering her optimism on that matter. "That would be ideal, but at the least, I believe they'll know where I can find her."

He was holding her gaze now, his eyes warm with sympathy. She hadn't seen that from him, and she didn't know what to say. Maybe she wasn't expected to say anything. The urge to lean against him for support crept into her, but she did not give in to it. She was the captain. Captains did not lean on others for support, certainly not their passengers.

"I spoke with Dominguez earlier," he said quietly. "He told me about how you threatened him on my behalf."

"Oh?" Alisa wouldn't have been surprised if Alejandro had lied to Leonidas, implying he hadn't wanted to abandon him. But then, she hadn't quite figured Alejandro out yet. One moment, he was pretending religion meant something to him, and the next, he was proving that he would do anything and sacrifice anyone to complete that mission of his. "And are you annoyed? He said you would happily sacrifice yourself for him and his orb quest."

Leonidas did not appear annoyed. He looked mellower than she had ever seen him. Maybe because the lighting was dim, and he was wearing the clothes he probably slept in. Except he would take the shirt off to sleep. She remembered the time he had answered the door in the middle of the night with only pants on, then found herself blushing at the memory for some reason. Perhaps because it was easy to picture him that way again with that T-shirt hiding little of his musculature.

"Perhaps not *happily*," he said, one corner of his mouth curving upward. "I appreciate that you cared enough to help." His head tilted to the side, his expression turning faintly bemused. Apparently, he hadn't had the same revelation that Mica had shared in regard to *why* Alisa wanted to help him. He stepped forward and rested a hand on her shoulder. "Thank you."

"You're welcome," she whispered.

She licked her lips, aware of how close he was. She could almost feel the heat radiating from his body. There was nothing sexual about his gesture or the look he was giving her—if anything, his grave nod seemed to be a gesture that one gave to a comrade. An appreciated comrade, perhaps, but nothing more.

That was fine, she told herself firmly. As she had stated on several occasions, he definitely wasn't her type. He didn't get her humor, and she didn't even think he could laugh. Besides, she had not been at Jonah's funeral, hadn't had time to formally sit down and say goodbye. It was far too soon to think of relationships with other men. It would feel like a betrayal to his spirit to turn her back on him so quickly.

As logical as her thoughts were, her body did not quite grasp them, and she found herself thinking about how long it had been since she'd had sex. Jonah might not have been gone from the universe for long, but it had been nearly a year and a half since she'd been home on leave. The warmth of Leonidas's hand on her shoulder made her imagine his touch in other places, and she wondered if kissing him would be similar to or different from kissing another man. What would he do if she tried? Be surprised and step back? Be surprised and enjoy it? Not be surprised? He was perceptive enough in other matters, so it seemed crazy to think that he wouldn't be aware of the effect he could have on a woman.

A throat cleared in the corridor.

Alisa jumped back, heat flushing her cheeks as if she had been caught doing something she shouldn't. No, just thinking libidinous thoughts…

Leonidas simply lowered his arm and turned, no hint of red tingeing his cheeks. Probably because he *hadn't* been thinking libidinous thoughts.

"Leonidas," came Alejandro's voice from the corridor, his tone neutral.

Had he seen Leonidas with his hand on her shoulder? Had he seen her drooling on him?

"May I speak with you?" Alejandro added.

"Yes." Leonidas gave her that nod again and said, "Goodnight, Marchenko—Alisa."

She leaned against the back of the pilot's seat, watching him walk out and once again told herself that she was not developing feelings for him, and she definitely wasn't melting into a puddle because he had deigned to use her first name.

He and Alejandro disappeared down the corridor toward their cabins. Their conversation wasn't going to be held anywhere so open as the mess hall.

Alisa checked the sensors and told herself to get that shower she had been thinking about—perhaps there was a reason Leonidas and his enhanced olfactory senses hadn't given her anything more than a friendly pat on the shoulder. Yet, she found herself glancing at the comm console, thinking of eavesdropping again. It had given her some good intelligence last time—and shown her what an ass Alejandro was. If he was planning something that could affect her and her ship when they got to Arkadius, shouldn't she know about it? Or was it just that she wanted to know what he was saying about her, if anything?

Grumbling about her questionable morality, Alisa closed the hatch, slid into the pilot's seat, and flipped through the switches to open the comm in Alejandro's cabin.

"She said we could stop at Starfall," Leonidas was saying.

"No mention of an extra fee?" Alejandro asked dryly.

"No."

"All right, good. I don't trust the Starseers to have any interest in the empire or want to help us. Having your armor repaired to 100% could be important."

"I may not be very useful against them," Leonidas said. "My mind is no different from yours."

"Some of their attacks and defenses strike the mind. Others strike the body. I'll do my best not to pick a fight with any of them, of course, but we need to be ready."

"I'm always ready."

"The gods themselves can be surprised on a beautiful day," Alejandro said, quoting scripture.

"Is that supposed to be a warning about letting my guard down?"

"Advice only. I want to part ways from Marchenko and this ship when we reach Arkadius."

Alisa frowned at the comm station. She would be happy to let Alejandro part ways—he would be lucky if she didn't fly over one of Arkadius's many oceans and dump him in. But even with the warrant on Leonidas's head and the fact that it would make her ship a target, she would regret having him leave.

"Did you get Ms. Moon to agree to come with us independently?" Leonidas asked, making Alisa wonder what kinds of conversations Alejandro, Yumi, and Beck had shared back here on the ship while the soldiers had been tramping around.

"No, but I've had enough of the captain interfering with my quest."

"She's been ferrying you around to *further* your quest."

"Fine, I've had enough of her threatening me, then. She knows too much. Leaving her with what's in her head is almost as unpalatable an idea as staying with her, but I assume your stance hasn't changed."

"It hasn't," Leonidas said coolly.

"We'll get what we need to know from Yumi, then hire someone else to taxi us around if need be." Alejandro grunted. "I suppose it's too much to hope that what I seek is on Arkadius."

"Since I still don't know what you seek, I couldn't say."

"I'll tell you when we get there. You will come with me, won't you? I can pay you for your time. It is my hope that this can be finished in a few months, and then you can return to your own quest."

Alisa willed Leonidas to tell Alejandro to stuff his payment and his quest, that he was going to accept her job offer and stay here to help her with *her* quest. If he helped her find her daughter, she would fly him wherever he needed to go to find what he sought. Damn, she wished she had told him that when they had been alone together. Instead, she'd been thinking about kissing him.

"If the emperor's dying wish was for you to fulfill your quest," Leonidas said, "I'll help you do it. There's no need for payment."

She heard the hatch clang softly, and Alisa straightened in her seat, realizing he had walked out. She flicked the comm button off, then looked toward the corridor, hoping Leonidas would return to keep her company. But nobody walked into NavCom to join her. Her heart was heavy at the idea of him going with Alejandro and disappearing from her life once they reached Arkadius, but so be it. She had to find her daughter. Being caught up in the dying wishes of an emperor she had done her best to dethrone would only delay her—or worse.

"This is for the best," she told herself. "It's for the best."

THE END

Bonus Short Story

STARFALL STATION

Hieronymus "Leonidas" Adler waited until late in the space station's day cycle to walk down the ramp of the *Star Nomad*, his hover case of damaged combat armor floating behind him. He could have carried the two-hundred-pound case easily, but he was a wanted man—a wanted cyborg—and he did not wish to call attention to himself by displaying inhuman abilities. Not here, not on a space station controlled by the self-proclaimed Tri-Sun Alliance.

His mouth twisted with bitterness. Almost everything was controlled by the Alliance now. When the empire had maintained order over the dozens of planets and moons in their vast trinary star system, Leonidas would have walked proudly onto the station, his head high as he wore his Cyborg Corps military uniform. He wouldn't have waited until the lights dimmed for night to skulk into the concourse on his errand.

Alert for trouble, Leonidas spotted Alisa Marchenko, the captain and pilot of the *Star Nomad*, when she was still hundreds of meters down the concourse. This did not take enhanced vision since she was leading a train of hoverboards, each piled more than ten feet high with crates. Her security officer, Tommy Beck, also walked at her side, his white combat armor bright and undamaged. Why wouldn't it be? He had spent most of their last battle hiding under the console in the navigation cabin.

Leonidas waited at the base of the ramp for them to approach in case they bore news that could affect him. Such as that squadrons of police officers or Alliance army soldiers were roaming the station, looking for stray cyborgs.

"Evening, mech," Beck called to him as they approached, his expression more wary than the cheerful tone would have implied. "Are you waiting to help us load these boxes into the cargo hold?"

"No," Leonidas said, his own tone flat. He would help if Marchenko asked him to, but was a passenger, not crew. Besides, he had little interest in assisting the security officer, a man who had served in the Alliance army during the war and who preferred to call him *mech* rather than use his name.

"Going to get your armor fixed, Leonidas?" Captain Marchenko asked, giving him a warm smile and waving at his case.

Alisa, he reminded himself. She had asked him a couple of times to use her first name, though he found the familiarity difficult. She, too, had been in the Alliance army, and she'd referred to him simply as "cyborg" for the first week after they had met. Still, they had been through a lot since then, and she had fought to keep the Alliance from capturing him during the Perun battle. She'd said that he had paid his fare for a ride on her freighter and that was that, but she had risked her life, doing far more than most civilian captains would do to protect a passenger. For that, he could certainly address her by her first name.

"I am," Leonidas said. "I made a late-night appointment with an excellent tech smith in Refinery Row."

"Better watch out for yourself, mech," Beck said, lingering instead of leading the train of cargo into the hold. "When we were out, looking for cargo-hauling deals, I saw lots of sleazy villains and opportunists skulking in the back alleys. And the not-so-back alleys. This station is rougher than it was the last time I came through here."

Leonidas was tempted to point out that the *empire* had likely ruled the last time Beck had visited. Of course the station had been safer and more orderly. The Alliance had been so busy overthrowing the throne that it hadn't worried about how well it could govern the system once it achieved its objective. But he didn't want to engage in a conversation with the security officer, so all he said was, "I've heard."

"I could go with you," Alisa said, still smiling at Leonidas.

He blinked slowly, perplexed as to why she made the offer. Something to do with his warrant?

"For my safety?" he asked.

She chuckled. "Yes, with my prodigious muscles and state-of-the-art weaponry—" she patted the bullet-slinging Etcher pistol in its holster under her jacket, "—I'll be your bodyguard."

"There's an image," Beck muttered. "Your head only comes up to his shoulders. Do you even weigh half as much as he does?"

Leonidas wanted to order Beck to trot up the ramp to unload the hoverboards and to butt out of his conversation with Alisa, but he wasn't a colonel anymore. Once, he had commanded a battalion and undertaken special missions for the emperor. Not anymore. He was nobody now. Except a man wanted for information he didn't have.

"I don't know," Alisa said. "We haven't jumped on a scale together and made comparisons. Why don't you get Mica to help load our cargo, Beck? She's got a hand tractor in engineering."

"Sure, Captain." He saluted, an Alliance army salute that came naturally to him, reminding Leonidas of what Beck and Alisa had been in the war, a noncommissioned officer and an officer. Alisa didn't act much like an officer, preferring flippancy and irreverence to stately shows of decorum and authority, so he could forget sometimes that she had been a captain and had flown ships against his people. Perhaps even against him.

"I just meant that I'd keep you company if you want it," Alisa told Leonidas as Beck ambled up the ramp, the hoverboards of crates barely fitting through the wide hatchway at the top. "You'll have to wait several hours while the smith repairs your armor, won't you? We could grab some dinner."

"I ate on board," Leonidas said before it occurred to him that she was making an offer of camaraderie rather than one of necessity.

In his youth, he would have caught that sooner, navigating the relationships between men and women without any more trouble than the average teenager, but twenty years with cyborg implants, in addition to the physical and biological changes the army had made to him, had left him a stranger to male-female relationships. He hoped to change that one day, perhaps even to have a family, but his quest to find an appropriate cybernetics specialist had been waylaid.

"Ah," Alisa said, her smile faltering. She turned to head past him and up the ramp.

"Coffee, perhaps?" Leonidas suggested.

"If I get a mocha this late at night, I'll be swinging from the catwalk," Alisa said, waving toward the elevated walkway in the cargo bay. Despite the words, she returned to his side and nodded toward the concourse. "Perhaps a decaf. Also, did you know that there's a shop in there that specializes in *nothing* but chocolate?" Her eyes gleamed. "It's open around the clock."

Leonidas didn't share her obsession with the sweet stuff, but he burned a lot of calories even when inactive, so he wasn't opposed to the occasional carbohydrate bomb. He subvocally ordered the case of armor to follow them as they left the ship. The earstar that hugged his lobe, awaiting his commands, relayed the order to the smart interface on the case, and it hummed along behind them.

The concourse was quieter than it had been during the day cycle when they had first landed, but the people they passed seemed more disreputable than the ones he'd observed then. Many wore hats and hoods that shadowed their faces, with few efforts made to conceal the BlazTeck firearms that they carried. Weapons had been illegal for civilians to carry, especially on ships and space stations, when the empire had maintained order.

More than one of those armed men eyed his armor case, but nobody approached him openly. A good set of combat armor was worth thousands, and even damaged, his would fetch a high price. But it had been issued by the imperial army, the crimson color of the case matching that of the armor inside, a color used predominantly by the men in the Cyborg Corps. Those who had served in the military, both imperial and Alliance, knew the meaning of that color, and many who hadn't knew it too. He doubted anyone here would be foolish enough to assault him.

Alisa cast a wistful look toward the restaurants and shops in the kitschy Castle Arcade, a wide walkway lined with faux cobblestones, the buildings to either side and on the levels above ensconced in gray brick. If any castles on Old Earth had flashing cloud lights in obnoxious colors such as these, it would be news to the historians. Leonidas supposed the chocolate shop was down there.

Presuming she would be fine with waiting to visit until after he dropped off his armor, he guided her to one of the floating bridges that created tunnels between the two massive cylinders that marked the different halves of the station, separating the shopping and entertainment region from the refinery that this station had first been built to house. The tech smith's shop was on that side.

The number of shoppers and passersby dwindled significantly as they stepped off the bridge and into a night-dimmed corridor. His ears, sharper than those of any unmodified human, caught the whisper of clothing rubbing together from around a corner at an intersection ahead. That wouldn't necessarily have alarmed him, but then he heard the snap of a battery pack being secured in a blazer rifle.

He shifted from walking beside Alisa to walking in front of her.

"Does this mean you're not open to hand-holding?" she asked.

He lifted a hand, hoping the gesture would be quelling. Her sense of humor came out at the oddest and most inappropriate times. Granted, she didn't have his hearing and likely did not sense the possible threat ahead.

Feet shuffled around the corner. The ceiling lamp over the intersection, already dimmed for night, flickered and went out. Suspicious timing.

Leonidas rested his hand on the butt of his destroyer, a deadly weapon some referred to as a hand cannon. It wasn't useful in stealth situations, but he had a feeling that making a statement might be ideal if muggers waited around the corner.

By the time he reached the intersection, his senses had informed him of three people waiting, two on one side, one on the other. The single person had light footfalls and sounded like someone small, perhaps a woman or a child. Leonidas drew his destroyer and with his left hand, removed a fluidwrap from his pocket. He wasn't as well-armed as he would be for going into battle, but with the warrant the Alliance had out for him, he had assumed he might run into trouble.

Before entering their line of sight, he glanced back at Alisa, this time lifting his palm in a stay-there gesture. Inappropriate humor or not, she had drawn her Etcher and appeared ready for a confrontation. That was good, but he had no desire for her to risk herself in some minor squabble.

Not making a sound, he burst around the corner. He threw the fluidwrap across the intersection at the smaller person while sprinting for the other two. He was tempted to shoot them, but they hadn't yet committed a crime. Also, he doubted the punishment for mugging was death on this station, and even if it was, he no longer had the authority to help enforce the laws.

Two big, fat tattooed men with long hair bound with beads scrambled back, their eyes widening. One carried an old shotgun more appropriate for hunting Arkadian ducks than men. The other had the blazer rifle Leonidas had heard being loaded.

He surged across the five meters between them and bowled the first man over, even as he registered that the second was lifting his arm to throw a fluidwrap of his own. Leonidas ducked as he hurled his first adversary aside, the ball-shaped projectile flying over his head, its energy netting unfurling too late. The shotgun clunked to the floor as the first man struck the wall so hard that he might have cracked his skull.

Leonidas realized he had used too much force, a constant problem for a cyborg capable of bending steel bars with his hands, but he did not feel much regret in this case. Realizing his net had missed, and perhaps what he was up against, the other man dropped his blazer and tried to back up, to flee.

He did not scurry away quickly enough to outrun a cyborg. Leonidas caught him around the neck and lifted him in the air, his feet dangling six inches above the floor. The man gasped and gurgled even though Leonidas was careful not to completely cut off his airway. His foe kicked futilely, the efforts so puny that Leonidas did not bother blocking them. His torso and thighs, enhanced with subcutaneous implants as well as ridges of hard muscle, could take a lot of abuse.

As he glanced toward the intersection to make sure his fluidwrap had, indeed, caught the third person—it had—the dangling man reached for a pistol holstered at his belt. Leonidas reacted instantly, tearing away the belt as well as the trousers it held up. He wouldn't normally rip off an opponent's pants, but he didn't want to hurt these people more than he already had and thought humiliation might do as much to end the fight as brutality.

"Are you done resisting?" Leonidas asked the man, chilling his voice to ice, an art he had mastered as an officer commanding hundreds of young, strong idiots.

His adversary's eyes grew round at the realization that his hairy legs were dangling, exposed to the alley and its occupants. Or maybe he realized that he was the only one capable of responding. His nearest ally was unconscious, and the young man on the other side of the intersection lay pinned by a net. The mugger's own net had flown uselessly wide and now plastered the wall, lighting it with electric blue tendrils that crackled and zapped. They would deliver a stun charge to a trapped person, but they had no effect on the wall.

"Leonidas?" Alisa asked from the corner, an odd note to her tone.

He looked to her, worried that she had spotted some other trouble. Her head and her firearm stuck around the corner, her gaze turned toward him.

"Am I disturbing you?" she asked, a smile quirking the corners of her lips. "I can leave you two alone if you want to take more of his clothes off."

Leonidas gave her a sour look. Of course she would make a joke. He should have known.

"I'm…done…resisting," his captured thug wheezed, Leonidas still using his throat as a handle by which to hold him up.

As he lowered the mugger to his feet, Alisa strode over to the one flattened on his back by the net. His features were hard to make out under the crackling blue energy of the net, but he looked young, fifteen or sixteen perhaps with an attempt at facial hair tufting his chin.

"What was the plan?" she asked him, tapping him on the chin with the muzzle of her Etcher. "Rob anyone who came this way?"

"Slavers are around," the boy said.

"On Starfall Station? Really? This used to be a respectable place."

"Always around," the boy mumbled, "and paying good right now."

"For cyborgs?" Alisa looked at Leonidas.

Leonidas barely glanced at them. He was searching his captive and removed a small pistol from his jacket pocket—amazing how a man with no belt or trousers could still be armed.

"For *women*," the boy said.

Surprise blossomed on Alisa's face.

"We were just going to *shoot* the cyborg." The boy's gaze slid toward Leonidas. "And take his armor."

"You'd just kill him? For no reason? Why, because he's not human?" Her tone had turned impressively frosty.

Leonidas watched her indignation with some bemusement since just a few weeks earlier, she'd been calling him cyborg and hadn't seemed to believe he was fully human. He did appreciate that once someone shifted from enemy to ally for her, she was loyal to that person. He hadn't experienced a lot of that from those outside of his unit, those who weren't cyborgs and didn't understand what it was like to be human, but different. Mostly, he encountered fear and uneasiness, even from men he had worked beside for years.

"Uh, because he had big guns," the boy said, wilting under her glower. He looked toward Leonidas, his expression hopeful, as if he might help him. Hardly.

Leonidas had been debating whether to let his captive go since the muggers hadn't actually managed to do anything to them, but that comment, along with the fact that they had wanted to sell Alisa to slavers, hardened his heart. He ripped off the man's shirt, drawing another look of surprise from Alisa, and tore it into strips. He used them to tie the mugger's ankles and wrists together, then moved on to the unconscious man to give him the same treatment.

"I suppose you'd find it unseemly if I made a joke about how you like to strip your captives and then tie them up."

"Yes." He didn't even know what she was implying. Something sexual, he had no doubt, but most such jokes went over his head.

"You're good to have along for a fight—or a mugging—but we need to work on your sense of humor."

"We?" After tying the first two men, Leonidas started for the third, but something on the ceiling behind the light fixture caught his eye. He berated himself for not noticing it earlier, but the fixture nearly blocked it.

"I'll help," Alisa said. "I like projects. In truth, I just want to see you laugh now and then."

"I laugh. When it's appropriate."

"You haven't laughed since I met you."

"We've been fighting enemies and fleeing for our lives since you met me."

"What about after we escaped from the pirates? Remember? Beck barbecued that bear meat. We were relaxing, chatting, and drinking Yumi's fermented tea since that was the closest thing we had to alcohol. Everyone was enjoying themselves, and Beck told jokes while he grilled."

"Beck isn't funny."

Alisa squinted at him.

Three suns, she didn't think Beck was a comedian, did she? Please.

"I laugh," Leonidas repeated sturdily.

"I don't believe you. Unless you do it alone in your cabin at night. Which I doubt, because I've heard you thumping around in there, presumably having nightmares."

He'd had an argument poised on his lips, a suggestion that maybe he *did* laugh when he was by himself in his cabin, but it froze before coming out. He hadn't realized that he made noise when he slept. That he had nightmares was no surprise—he remembered them well when he woke up with a jolt, memories of battles gone wrong and lost comrades and guilt rearing into his mind. But he felt chagrined to learn that others were also aware he had them.

Not knowing what to say, and certainly not wanting to linger on this topic, he returned his attention to the light fixture. He stood on tiptoes to pull an item down from the ceiling.

"What's that?" Alisa asked, thankfully changing the topic.

He flipped it to her. "A small mirror."

She caught it easily, perhaps not with a cyborg's enhanced reflexes but certainly with a pilot's reflexes. He'd seen her fly a few times when it counted, such as when they were being chased through asteroid belts, and she was good at her job.

"Low tech way to see who's coming, eh?" Alisa tossed it onto the boy's chest, shaking her head as she looked down at him. "Slavery. I'm not sure whether to be horrified or flattered. I would have thought I was too old to attract slavers."

Leonidas raised his eyebrows. He knew she had an eight-year-old daughter and guessed her to be in her early thirties. Since he was edging up on forty, he would hardly call someone in her thirties old. The muggers—slavers—probably hadn't looked beyond her face and the curve of her hips when determining her potential as a slave. While she wasn't gorgeous, she was attractive and had an appealing smile. Too bad she was usually mouthing off when she made that smile. The Alliance had probably encouraged mouthiness, considering it a promising trait in someone signing on to help overthrow the government.

"You're supposed to say something like, 'You look fabulous, Alisa, and you're not too old to attract slavers.'"

"You *want* to attract slavers?"

"No, that's not my point. Never mind. Are you collecting your net?"

"Yes." Leonidas stepped past her and found the casing for the ball, which had split open into several segments to release its electric cargo. He deactivated the energy aspect, then tugged the slender tendrils of the net off the supine figure. The boy leaped up and tried to dart off. Leonidas caught him by the collar of his shirt. As he proceeded to tie the kid up, he asked Alisa, "If I call the police, what are the odds that they'll get here before someone comes by and mugs our muggers?"

"If you call the police, someone will probably come for you, wanting to collect—" She cut herself off, glancing at the boy, who was listening. "They'll probably come for you," she finished.

He appreciated that she hadn't mentioned the warrant. Even if these three weren't a threat, who knew who they knew?

"I can call them," she said, slipping a comm unit off her belt. She never wore an earstar comm-computer, as was common. "No idea on the mugging the muggers part. Beck was right. The station seems rougher than the last time I was through here."

"I'll wager that the last time you were here, the empire controlled the station and maintained order." He hadn't brought it up with Beck, but he couldn't help himself this time. He supposed he wanted Alisa to see reality, to realize that she'd fought on the wrong side, that her people had made the system a worse place, not a better one.

Alisa grimaced. "Yes, the empire was excellent at maintaining order."

"That *order* meant you wouldn't be mugged on the way to a coffee shop."

"We're not on the way to a coffee shop. We're on the way to some smithy located on the dubious side of the station. Besides, under the old regime, I would have been arrested for walking around after curfew, and my gun would have had to stay on my ship, a ship that has no weapons of its own because the empire forbade civilians to be armed, even if they were lugging freight through pirate-infested space. Even you have to admit it's been inconvenient that we haven't had a way to defend ourselves this past month."

"Pirate-infested space was rare when the empire ruled, unless you were way out near the border worlds."

"People on those border worlds like freight delivered to them too. My mom and I had more than our share of run-ins when I was growing up on the *Nomad*."

"That was your mother's choice to go somewhere unsafe, to take a child somewhere unsafe." Leonidas couldn't stifle the distaste in his voice, though it was directed more toward his resentment that the Alliance had destroyed the empire without having anything sufficient to instate in its place. If the war had created a better universe, perhaps he could have accepted being on the losing side more easily, but it hadn't.

"My *mother*," Alisa said coolly, "flew freight because she couldn't stand the stifling rules of living on an imperial planet, which was *all* of them in the last century. She should have been allowed to defend herself out in the system."

"Rules exist for a reason. They keep people safe."

"*Safe.*" Her lip curled, and she said it as if it were a curse. "You can get arrested, be thrown in a jail cell, and be safe as a *bramisar* in its den, but you'll never see the stars again. People love to give up their freedoms for safety. Pretty soon, you can't walk where you want, when you want, and you might as well be a dog instead of a human being." She issued a disgusted noise somewhere between a grunt and a growl, then stalked down the corridor in the direction they had been headed before the attempted ambush.

"The Alliance is overflowing with freedom-seeking idealists," Leonidas called after her, though he doubted she was listening. "It takes a few pragmatists to run a government. You'll see. When the entire system collapses and your government is replaced by chaos, you'll see."

Alisa did not look back. Leonidas glared down at the tied-up muggers.

"You sure you don't want to let us go so we can catch her and sell her to slavers?" the boy asked.

Leonidas grunted and walked away, hoping Alisa would remember to comm the police to pick them up. If police even existed on Starfall Station anymore. Star fall, indeed.

———

Leonidas put out a hand to stop Alisa. They were in the wide corridor leading to the smithy—it was more like a street with buildings to either side, a high ceiling arching about thirty feet overhead. The area was very quiet, considering how many of the shops kept night hours. To their left, a window display showed all manner of netdiscs and personal comm assistants, and floating holosigns promised inexpensive repair rates. Two buildings ahead, the roll-up door of the smithy was closed, though a glowing sign shed light from the window beside it.

A faint odor reached Leonidas's nostrils, that of a butcher shop—or a battlefield.

"More muggers?" Alisa looked down at his hand.

"Perhaps," he said, scanning the buildings more intently than he had when they first turned onto the street.

"You've accused me of being someone whom trouble always finds, but I think it's even more likely to find you."

"I believe I said you're someone who *makes* trouble wherever she goes. You're quick to mouth off to people, even those it's unwise to be mouthy with."

"Like cranky cyborgs?" She smiled, her irritation from ten minutes earlier apparently forgotten.

After years of outranking most of his peers and having them defer to him, he was never quite sure how to handle her irreverence. This time, he said, "I'm not cranky," and regretted that it sounded petulant rather than authoritative.

Her smile only widened.

He sighed and walked down a maintenance passage between the computer repair building and the next structure, checking to see if the shops had back doors. He couldn't yet tell where that smell was coming from, but striding through the front entrance of the smithy might be unwise.

A waist-high, bug-shaped trash robot rolled through the alley that ran parallel to the street, sucking debris into its proboscis, incinerating it in its carapace, and shifting the ashes to a bin in the rear. It reminded him of the chase that he'd been on with Alisa and Dr. Dominguez in the sewers below the university library on Perun. They had temporarily escaped pursuit by catching a ride on an automated sewer-cleaning vehicle. He and Alisa had sat side by side in the cargo bed, their shoulders touching. It hadn't exactly been pleasant since they'd both stunk of the sewers, but she hadn't been mouthy then, perhaps being too tired to make quips. For some reason, the image came to mind now with a feeling of fondness. Odd.

His memories faded as he turned into the alley and saw the robot trundling toward a charred box lying on the floor. A hole burned in the side displayed destroyed interior circuit boards and wires.

"That's an imperial spy box, isn't it?" Alisa asked, stopping beside him.

His armor case stopped, too, just shy of bumping into his back.

Leonidas nodded. "Yes."

The boxes were usually floating through the air when one saw them, built-in cameras observing from above and sending the feed to police monitors.

"Guess the Alliance decided they didn't want to use them when they took over," Alisa said.

"No." Leonidas shook his head as the trash robot widened its nozzle and sucked the box in, the same way it had the other debris. "That was shot down today, not months ago when the Alliance took this station."

"Good point," she said quietly, looking up and down the dim alley. "Someone was doing something they didn't want observed, eh?"

"So it would seem."

Leonidas waited for the trash robot to incinerate the box and continue down the alley, then walked to the back door of the smithy. Unlike the vehicle-sized, roll-up door in the front, this was a simple door for humans. There were no windows on the back of the building, so he couldn't see inside, but he caught that butcher-shop scent again.

He paused, looking down at Alisa. "You may wish to wait outside."

"Oh?" Judging by the curiosity in her eyes, waiting outside wasn't what she had in mind.

Even though he had served with some female soldiers and knew they could be tough, his instinct was to protect women from gruesome experiences.

"I don't think my armor case will fit through this narrow doorway," he said. "Perhaps you could watch it for me."

"Afraid the trash bot will come along and suck it up? I don't think it'll fit inside its maw."

"Nevertheless, I'll purchase your chocolate beverage later if you wait here."

He thought that might draw an agreeable smile from her, but her eyes closed to suspicious slits. Still, she leaned her shoulder against the wall and nodded for him to go inside.

The door was locked with an old latch-and-bolt system, rather than with electronics. He gave a quick tug on the handle, snapping the mechanism. If he was wrong and nothing had happened inside, he would pay the smith for the damage.

The area he stepped into was dark, but his eyesight was better than human, and he could make out most of his surroundings. An aisle ran the length of the back wall, with tools, crates, and unidentifiable clutter rising over his head and blocking the view of most of the building. All manner of machinery towered at one end, a mix of modern and computerized with old-fashioned and antiquated. At the other end, laser smelting equipment dangled from a ceiling beam, the tip resting against an anvil and a rack of mallets of various sizes. Heat radiated from a furnace behind the equipment.

Leonidas stood quietly and listened before venturing away from the door. The scent of blood was stronger inside.

When he did not hear anything, he walked down the aisle and turned toward the front of the building. The holosign glowing in the window, proclaiming the business open, shed some extra light. To his eyes, it clearly illuminated the prone person lying on an open stretch of floor near a front counter and payment machine. It was a man, blood pooling on the floor next to him, a rivulet of it leading to a drain nearby. It had dried, but only partially. This hadn't happened long ago.

Though he shouldn't have disturbed a crime scene, curiosity drove him forward. He knelt, careful to avoid the blood, and rolled the body over. With his keen night sight, he easily saw the hole in the man's clothes. Something—most likely a knife—had punctured deep into his flesh, slipping between his ribs and piercing his heart. It had only taken one stab to kill him. Someone had either gotten lucky or had known exactly what he was doing.

A draft stirred the hair on the back of Leonidas's neck, the door he had used opening. He sniffed, then sighed as he caught Alisa's scent, a mix of simple, warm feminine skin and the lavender hand soap in the lav on the ship. She bumped against something in the dark, but otherwise moved quietly as she maneuvered through the shop toward the front of the building.

He turned to face her, his nose and ears having already determined that they were alone in the shop, aside from the dead man. Whoever had stabbed him had since left.

The holosign must have provided enough light for Alisa to see his outline in the front of the room, because she lifted a hand toward him. "Turns out your armor case fits through the door fine if you tilt it on its side."

"Ah." He stepped toward her, thinking she might not notice the body, the shadows being thicker along the floor. Maybe he could usher her away from it. But her gaze fell upon it before he reached her.

"Uh, not your work, I assume?"

She didn't appear overly squeamish about the body. He supposed he shouldn't be surprised. If she'd fought in the war, she must have seen plenty of death, even as a pilot.

"No," he said. "I believe this is Master Tech Camden Meliarakis, the owner of the smithy."

"The one who was going to fix your armor?"

"Yes. I spoke directly to him about six hours ago and made the nocturnal appointment." Leonidas lowered his voice to murmur just for his earstar, "Time?"

It responded by speaking a soft, "Twenty-three twenty-seven, Starfall Station time," into his ear.

"I'm three minutes early for my appointment," Leonidas told Alisa.

"Very punctual of you." Alisa frowned as the armor case floated to a stop beside her, almost bumping her arm, as if it wanted attention. Or maybe it wanted to know when the armor inside would be repaired.

Leonidas started to wonder who else he could contact for the job, but that made him feel selfish—and guilty. So he walked around the shop, thinking he might figure out what had happened. It wouldn't matter to the dead smith, but it would make Leonidas feel better about thinking of his own needs first. Besides, it was hard to forget that he'd had a hand in keeping the peace for a long time. It was hard to shed that responsibility. Granted, he'd been more of an interplanetary peacekeeper than a police officer, but he'd always fought to protect civilians.

"Shall I call the police again?" Alisa asked. "Or should we just disappear without touching anything? Reporting a mugging was one thing, but I'd hate to be detained because we were suspects in a murder. You, especially, shouldn't be caught here."

"No," Leonidas murmured, peering at the closed roll-up door. Since the lock in the back had been intact, he presumed the murderer had come in through the front. Given the shop's around-the-clock hours, the door had likely been unlocked at the time.

He confirmed that it was still open without touching anything. Leaving fingerprints behind wouldn't be a good idea for exactly the reason Alisa had alluded to. He did not need the Alliance adding civilian murders to the list of reasons they wanted him arrested.

"Unlocked," he said. "The murderer may have come in, pretending to be a customer. The smith was stabbed in the front, so he might have even known the person. At the least, I bet he didn't expect trouble."

As Leonidas moved away from the door for a closer look around the premises and the counter, he was aware of Alisa watching him.

"Are you going to attempt to solve the crime?" she asked.

"You don't approve?"

"Well, I don't mean to belittle this man's death, but you investigating it won't get your armor fixed, and I'm worried that if we're found here, you'll be in a lot of trouble." She walked to the window and peered out into the street, her gaze flicking upward, as if to look for spy boxes.

Leonidas could now guess why the one in the back had been shot down. Had the murderer gone out that way? So as not to be seen? Locking the door as he went?

"You don't think *you'll* be in trouble too?" he asked.

"Oh, I reckon my mouth could also get me into trouble—" Alisa flashed him a quick smile, though it appeared more distracted than heartfelt, "—but you're the one my people want."

"Your people."

"The Alliance people." She shrugged. "The ones with two hundred thousand tindarks on your…not your head, exactly, because they want you alive. That's one boon for you. I can't imagine less than an army taking you in alive. Even that army would need some tanks and armor-piercing rounds."

Cyborgs were not quite as invincible as that, but Leonidas did not correct her. No need to educate her on the various poisons and chemicals that could act on his unique mecho-biology. And it wasn't as if he was impervious to blazer bolts or bullets. In his armor, he nearly was, but that armor was in shambles now. He needed to get it fixed, one way or another. Was it selfish to hope the smith had an apprentice that he might contact? He leaned around the clerk's counter to eye the shelves and display screens.

"Hm, what is this?" Leonidas mused, pulling a large case out from behind the counter. The case was familiar, since one very similar to it floated in the middle of the room. This one was resting on the floor rather than hovering, but it was the same size as his.

"Combat armor?" Alisa asked.

"Red combat armor."

"You mean crimson," she said quietly. "And only cyborgs have that, right?"

"The color isn't—wasn't—forbidden in the private quarter, but it's somewhat infamous, yes, since it was issued to soldiers in the Cyborg Corps."

The case was unlocked, so Leonidas opened it, wondering if he would know the owner. He also wondered what had brought one of his people here after the war ended and the imperial army largely dissolved. He supposed Starfall Station was as likely a place as any to move on and look for work. He'd heard rumors that some of his cyborg colleagues had become mercenaries, others bodyguards and heads of security for wealthy civilians. It seemed demeaning employment after working for the empire for so many years, maintaining order and keeping the people safe. Though it was not as demeaning as piracy—he'd already run into one of his people engaged in that, planning to carve out an empire of his own in territory no longer being patrolled.

"Sergeant Lancer," Leonidas read off the plate fastened to the inside of the lid.

An image of a big farmer turned soldier came to mind. Sandy blond hair and freckles, a boyish look even after more than ten years in the army. Yes, Leonidas remembered him, and a twinge of excitement ran through him at the idea of reconnecting with someone from the unit. Even if Lancer had been along for many of the battles that were the fodder for Leonidas's nightmares, he still wanted to see the man. He hadn't had a chance to say a proper goodbye to anyone when the empire had lost and the unit had been disbanded. He had been too busy on a last mission for the emperor.

"Anyone you know?" Alisa asked.

"Yes, I remember him. We fought together on many occasions." Leonidas found a receipt on the top of the set of armor and read it. "This was just finished. He's scheduled to pick it up at midnight station time."

"That's not far off, but I'm not sure waiting here for him would be wise." Alisa leaned closer to the windowpane. "Someone's coming."

"Someone who looks like he might need the services of a smith? Or someone who might *be* a smith?" Leonidas hoped it would be the apprentice, though it might not help him if it was. The man would be too distraught over his master's death to fix armor tonight. Besides, Leonidas twitched at the idea of an apprentice handling his most prized possession—and one of the few possessions he had left. He would have to do some research to find out if anyone else on the station was qualified.

"Someone who looks like *she* might be here to investigate the death of a smith," Alisa said. "It's a woman, and she's wearing a police uniform."

"We better leave then." Leonidas nodded toward the back door.

"Don't forget your box."

"Never," he murmured.

The armor case floated after him as he moved away from the counter. He stepped past the body, experiencing a twinge of regret at leaving the smith's killer at large without trying to help, but it wasn't his responsibility to enforce order here, and he doubted the police would appreciate his assistance. Besides, if a patroller was on the way, she would be more useful here than he.

Leonidas held the back door open for Alisa and his case to exit. He heard someone lifting the roll-up door. He slipped outside, shutting the back door softly, noticing his bare hand on the knob. He should have taken more care not to leave fingerprints, but maybe it didn't matter. The Alliance was already after him. He'd probably be on the run for years to come. If they didn't catch him first.

Alisa did not make any jokes as they retraced their steps through the alley, and for that he was glad. He wasn't in a good mood and didn't want to make the effort to be good company. Uncranky company. His helplessness here on the station—in the system as a whole—grated on him more than it had in the previous months.

As Alisa turned up an alley heading toward the street, Leonidas paused, a ladder catching his eye. It led up the side of a warehouse to a third-story rooftop.

"Alisa," he said softly, waving for her to come back. He gave a subvocal command for the case to stay put by the side of the building, then told her, "Side trip."

"Oh? Somewhere exotic?" She arched an eyebrow toward the ladder.

"It depends on how exotic you consider rooftops."

"Not very," she said as he started up.

"Then this side trip may disappoint."

As he climbed, Leonidas listened for noises back at the smithy or out in the street. He did not hear anyone walking or talking, but if the policewoman had verified the existence of a body, a violently murdered body at that, she might have called for backup. He wondered how she had learned of the smith's death, since he hadn't seen a flashing alarm or anything of that nature.

Once he reached the top of the warehouse, he had to drop to his belly to crawl across it. The arched ceiling that had seemed high when down in the street, had its beginning at the wall behind the buildings, and it stretched only a few feet above the warehouse rooftop. Pipes and ducts rose in spots, too, further tightening the space as they disappeared into the station above. The hum of machinery reached his ears, reverberating through the rooftop. In spots, colorful graffiti adorned the ceiling.

He crawled to the far side of the warehouse so he could peer into the street. An inebriated couple crossed at an intersection several buildings away, leaning on each other and laughing too loudly. Targets for muggers, Leonidas supposed. He didn't yet see any other police, though he scanned the shadows closely in case others lurked in the recesses.

Alisa scooted up beside him, eyeing the white outline of a penis and balls graffitied above them. As a military officer, she had doubtlessly seen worse, but he found himself hoping that it was too dark for her normal human eyes to pick out the details.

"If I'd known you would bring me someplace so cozy, I would have brought a blanket and a picnic basket."

Apparently, she had better-than-average normal human eyes.

"Do you have one? A picnic basket?" He couldn't imagine her bare bones freighter possessing such comforts, not when it had been huddled in the back of a junkyard cavern a month earlier. The lavatories didn't even have towels, something that might have compensated for the fact that the body dryers only worked intermittently.

"Not presently, but for you, I would have bought one."

"I had no idea I rated special consideration."

"Yes, the specialness of braided wicker." She grinned at him, surprising him since he hadn't thought his comments that witty. "You're bantering with me. That's excellent. I have hope that you might one day laugh, after all."

He returned his attention to the street. With a man dead a few buildings down, Leonidas did not think this was the time for laughter. Or banter.

"Are we looking for anything in particular?" Alisa asked, not visibly chagrined by his lack of a response.

"Sergeant Lancer. His armor will be ready soon, and if it were me, I wouldn't be late to pick up such a precious item. He may have deliberately asked for a late-night pickup so he could avoid walking through the station during prime hours."

"Is there a warrant on *his* head too?"

"I don't know, but if he's toting a case of red armor around, people will know what he is. Most former imperial soldiers can change out of their uniforms and blend in. It's not so easy for cyborgs, even without the armor."

"You look completely human when you're not cut up with your implants showing." She waved to his arm, where he'd received such a cut a couple of weeks earlier. Dr. Dominguez had sealed it, leaving only the faintest of scars, one of many after so many years in the military. "An overly muscled human who spends four hours a day in the gym," she added, grinning again, "but a human."

"Overly?" He twitched an eyebrow.

Her grin widened. "Depends on your tastes, I suppose. I have a fondness for lanky scholars who appreciate my irreverent humor." Her grin faded, and he wondered if that described her late husband.

"Which is why you're on a rooftop, shoulder to shoulder with me," he said, thinking that responding to her banter might distract her from uncomfortable memories. The three gods knew he had his share of uncomfortable memories and understood about needing distractions.

To his surprise, her cheeks reddened. Someone else wouldn't have noticed in the shadows, but he had no trouble picking up the flush.

"I just wanted an excuse to go out for a mocha," she said, scooting closer to the edge of the building and peering into the street. "Will you be inviting your friend along if he shows up?"

That wasn't what he'd had in mind, though the image of Alisa walking arm-in-arm with a big, brawny cyborg on either side of her amused him for some reason. She wasn't that short of a woman, standing roughly five-foot-ten, but the top of her head only rose an inch over his shoulder, and he wasn't even that tall for a cyborg. The imperial army had enforced strict recruiting standards, picking men that had rated highly on athletic tests and had also already been physically imposing. They had been fussy about who they invested in for the expensive surgery necessary to turn a human into a cyborg—or killing machine, as Leonidas's recruiter had said all those years ago. He remembered being unimpressed by the rhetoric. Yet here he was.

"You wouldn't be intimidated by walking into a coffee shop with two cyborgs?" Leonidas asked, realizing she was looking at him and remembering that she had asked a question.

"Intimidated?" Her forehead crinkled.

He snorted. "Never mind. I forgot who I was talking to." He had yet to see her intimidated by anything, neither cyborgs turned pirates nor imperial warships on their tails. No matter who was after her, she was always ready to fling sarcasm like others flung bullets. "To answer your question, I want to keep him from walking in on a murder investigation where he might be turned into a suspect and held."

"Ah."

Alisa looked past him and toward the front of the smithy. "Is the police-woman still in there? I wonder how she knew to come looking. That body didn't report itself."

"She may have been sent to investigate the broken spy box," Leonidas said, though he thought it was interesting that Alisa, too, had noted that there hadn't been any alarms triggered.

"It was behind the building, not in it. She strode straight to the front door, didn't she?"

"You sound like you want to go peek in the window."

She raised a finger, looking interested in the idea, but then lowered it and shook her head. "No, I don't need to go looking for trouble any more than you do. We'll just wait for your friend and—" Alisa frowned. "There's not a possibility your friend is responsible for this, is there? What if he already came by, and the smith tried to gouge him for some reason? Because he was a cyborg, and the smith's loyalties were with the Alliance maybe."

Leonidas was shaking his head before she finished speaking. "First off, if he had come already, he wouldn't have left his armor behind. Second, a cyborg wouldn't have bothered with a knife when he could simply break a man's neck."

Alisa frowned down at his hand where it rested next to the lip of the rooftop. "Thanks for putting that image in my mind."

He regretted making the comment, not wanting her to feel uncomfortable around him. He had two brothers who'd never gotten over the fact that he'd given himself to the army, mind and body, twenty years earlier. After their mother died, he'd stopped going home. Family gatherings were awkward enough when everyone was…fully human.

A faint whir reached Leonidas's ears, and he squinted into the gloom at the back of the building. Something stirred in the shadows. He whipped out his destroyer, instantly locking onto the target. It wasn't a person—he would have seen that—but it took him a couple of seconds to figure out what the squarish thing bobbing along the far side of the roof was. A spy box. One that hadn't been shot. Yet.

Alisa probably wouldn't have heard or seen it if he hadn't been pointing his gun across the rooftop, but she followed his gaze and spotted it.

"You don't want to just break its neck?" She waved at his big handgun.

"If it had a neck, I'd be glad to do so," he murmured, keeping his voice low. The devices recorded audio as well as video. That had never bothered him when the imperial police had been monitoring the feeds, but it was different now.

After bobbing along the edge in the back, the spy box floated onto the rooftop, spinning slowly as it headed in their direction.

"They only deviate from their usual routes if they see something suspicious, right?" Alisa asked.

"That's my understanding. Apparently, we're being suspicious."

"We're just a couple looking for some privacy."

"On top of a warehouse?" Leonidas asked.

The cube floated closer, one of its lenses focusing on them.

"Don't get twitchy with those neck-breaking hands." Alisa scooted closer to him before he could ask her what that meant. She slung her arm across his shoulders and tossed a leg over his.

"What are you doing?" Leonidas whispered.

"*We're* canoodling," she murmured back. "And keeping it from getting a good look at our faces."

Leonidas decided that might, indeed, fool the spy box. It wasn't as if a sophisticated AI ran the devices. It had probably only come in this direction to investigate the missing unit in the fleet of spy boxes that patrolled the streets collecting footage.

He shifted onto his side, facing Alisa and resting a hand on her waist. It had been so long since he'd had sex—or even *canoodled*—that he found the intimacy awkward. Alisa ducked her chin to hide her face under her arm, and he did the same. Their foreheads brushed as she peeked under her sleeve to eye the spy box. He resisted the urge to pull back and put space between them. If he had met her eight months ago, he would have treated her as an enemy—and she surely would have done the same to him—but they were just people now, neither employed by their governments. Neither soldiers, not anymore. After all his years of service, that was hard to accept, but he forced himself to think of her as nothing more than the captain of the freighter he was riding on, a captain who had stuck up for him when the Alliance came looking for him, risking her own reputation—and her life—to help him escape. She deserved to be treated well, like a friend, or at least a fellow officer. Not that he'd made a practice of canoodling with the officers in his all-male cyborg unit. Fortunately, she smelled better than they did, that lavender scent teasing his nostrils.

The spy box floated to their side of the roof, pausing to hover just beyond Leonidas's feet.

"What's it doing?" Alisa muttered. "Watching to see if we take off our clothes?"

"Perhaps our ruse isn't fooling it."

"Perhaps it's a perv."

Alisa lifted her gaze to meet his and quirked her eyebrows. He wasn't sure if she wanted his opinion on the likelihood of robotic fetishes, or if she was checking to see if he appreciated her humor. Her suggestion that he didn't know how to laugh anymore trickled into his mind. If it was true, he knew it had nothing to do with his cyborg implants—he refused to believe those had altered his humanity in any way—and everything to do with the war. He'd once laughed with his comrades, not as often as some, perhaps, but he had laughed. Unfortunately, years of being on the losing side of a war, of having his people survive only to lose the frailer humans they had been protecting, had left him with guilt, regret, and the knowledge that he had failed. Humor did not tickle his inner spirit very often anymore, and he did not know how to fix that.

With a faint whirring sound, the box floated toward the rear of the rooftop. Leonidas lifted his head to watch it go while wondering if it had sent its footage to police headquarters and if the patroller investigating the smithy was even now being alerted to nearby spies. He still found it odd that only one person was poking around down there.

As the spy box drifted over the edge, Leonidas heard a click from the street, from the direction of the smithy. He whirled back to his stomach, shedding Alisa's arm. He was in time to see the top of a man's headful of short blond hair before the person disappeared inside, the rolling door dropping down behind him with a thud.

Cursing inwardly, Leonidas leaped over the edge of the roof. It might be too late to keep Sergeant Lancer from meeting the policewoman, but perhaps there was still time to help. The last thing he wanted was for one of his people to run afoul of the authorities here for no reason.

After sprinting to the smithy, Leonidas crouched to grab the latch on the bottom of the roll-up door, but he halted in shocked surprise as the faint odor of charred almonds reached his nose. He leaped back, crossing to the far side of the street, his instincts driving his reaction. He forced himself to stop, analyzing the ramifications and his options instead of sprinting several blocks to make sure he wouldn't inhale too much of that gas.

Tyranoadhuc gas.

At least two years had passed since anyone had used it against him, but he recognized the smell immediately. And he remembered being flat on his back in the middle of combat in a corridor on his ship, his mechanical implants frozen, even his eyes locked open, unable to blink as the gas affected every enhanced body part he owned. That day, his people had been caught unprepared, a secret betrayal turned into a surprise attack, and neither Leonidas nor his cyborg men had been able to take the time to don their combat armor, armor that would have filtered out the gas and protected them. He remembered the smug look of the female commander leading the Alliance troops as she had walked up to his side, looking down at him through the faceplate of her helmet, her left cheek and jaw shiny with an old burn she'd never had grafted. She'd pointed her rifle at his chest, and his instincts had screamed for him to move, but his body had refused to comply.

"Colonel Adler," she murmured. "We meet again." Instead of shooting, she had lifted her rifle to her shoulder, barely noticing the energy bolts flying past her, one even glancing off the shoulder of her dented green armor. "I think it will hurt you more to survive when your ship falls, when all of your people are killed. And I believe I shall tell you that one of your own officers was responsible for this betrayal. A Captain Morin. You know him, I'm certain. Cyborgs, it seems, are as amenable to bribes as human men."

She'd stalked past him without waiting for a response—not that he could have given one. It had taken nearly twenty minutes for that gas to wear off, an eternity in battle. Most of his people had been killed, including the senior command staff on the *Excelsior*, and he'd barely roused in time to grab his combat armor and make it to an escape pod.

LINDSAY BUROKER

"Leonidas?" Alisa asked softly from the corner of the building—she must have left the warehouse rooftop via that ladder and come around through the alley.

He shook the memories from his head and looked up and down the street, aware that they had consumed him so fully that he hadn't been paying attention to his surroundings. He could have been an easy target for someone with a grudge against cyborgs. Or for the person who had loosed that gas. The policewoman? She was probably a victim. Maybe someone else had slipped in while Leonidas had been distracted by the spy box? Or maybe he'd been mistaken about who had been entering the smithy? When he had spotted that blond hair, he had assumed it was Sergeant Lancer, but he hadn't seen the man's face.

"What's wrong?" Alisa whispered, jogging across the street.

Leonidas took a step toward the smithy, but halted and thrust his fingers through his hair in frustration. "I can't go in." He couldn't smell the gas from the middle of the street, but he knew his nose hadn't been mistaken. It wouldn't take much of a dose for him to be affected, and holding his breath wouldn't work. The potent stuff had such small molecules that it could enter the bloodstream through the skin. "Tyranoadhuc gas," he said, catching Alisa's puzzled expression.

"Ah." The puzzlement faded.

She recognized the name. He kept himself from asking if she had ever used the stuff, or piloted a team of soldiers who had used it, against his people. What was going on in that building now was more important than the past. If that *had* been Sergeant Lancer, he could be sprawled on the ground in there, helpless.

"It doesn't bother humans, right?" Alisa pulled out her Etcher. "I'll go in."

"No. This isn't your battle."

Her eyebrows rose. "I don't think it's your battle, either."

Not true. His unit might have been dissolved, but he would always consider the cyborgs who had served under his command as his people.

Explaining that would take too long. Instead, he lightly gripped her arm to keep her from crossing the street and said, "Stay here. I'll put my armor on."

242

He let go and sprinted for the case, tugging it into the alley so that he could dress with his back to the wall. Whatever was going on, it wasn't anything innocuous. They didn't sell that gas at the corner market. It could damage all computers and machinery, not just cyborg implants, and it was illegal for civilians to have it. Military supplies were tightly controlled, or at least they had been when the empire had been in charge.

Growling to himself, he stuffed his legs into the greaves as quickly as possible. Usually, they flexed and conformed around him automatically, fitting precisely and comfortably about his limbs, but every piece of his armor had taken damage during his escape from the Alliance, and some of the servos whined and grumbled as he manipulated them. Under the best circumstances, it took more than five minutes to suit up. Unfortunately, he dared not take any shortcuts. He needed the suit to be airtight before venturing in to deal with that gas. As airtight as it could be. Normally, it was spaceworthy, but he well remembered the leak he had sprung during his brief space walk on the way back to the freighter. That small hole shouldn't let in enough gas to affect him. He hoped.

Someone shouted, and a clatter arose inside the building. Cursing, Leonidas tried to dress faster. That had been a woman's voice. The police officer? Something crashed to the floor inside. He wished there were windows, but neither the side nor the back of the building had any, and getting his armor on was more important than running over half-dressed and peering through the front window. Or so he thought, until he heard the front door roll up quietly.

Alisa?

He lunged out of the alley, still fastening his torso armor around his body. "Don't go in," he barked.

It was too late. The street was empty.

———

It took another minute for Leonidas to get his helmet on and the rest of his charred and dented armor into place. An eternity. As soon as he could, he pulled up the roll-up door. He hadn't heard any more ominous noises from within—he'd heard nothing at all since Alisa disappeared inside. And that worried him.

He made himself open the door slowly, using all of his senses, as well as the ones augmented by the armor, to get a feel for what danger lay within. Whoever had set off that gas had come expecting to deal with cyborgs and would likely have more weapons that could affect him. Somehow, the person inside had anticipated that Leonidas would come. It must be some bounty hunter after him for the reward money—the gas would be perfect for someone who wanted to bring him in alive.

The faintest of footfalls came from the back of the smithy. Leonidas eased inside, putting his back to the wall. Data scrolled down the side of the glastica display of his faceplate, not interrupting his line of sight as it informed him that gas had been detected in the space. No kidding.

The same Open sign that had allowed Leonidas to see before was enough to glimpse the smith's body still on the floor near the counter, but there were too many crates and too much equipment in the way to see Alisa or whoever was making noise in the back. It might be she. But he was certain they weren't alone. He imagined the policewoman's body in an aisle somewhere while a powerful bounty hunter stalked Alisa, prepared to kill her for daring to intrude.

As he strode silently along the wall, Leonidas listened for sounds of distress—sounds of any kind at all. But the footfalls had halted.

The armor made his shoulders even broader than usual, so he had to pick his route carefully past machinery and tools. He did not want to bump or scrape against anything, nor knock anything over. Combat armor wasn't made for stealth, but he could step carefully, keeping his footfalls silent.

A gun cracked, black powder igniting. Alisa's Etcher. An instant later, a second weapon loosed a sizzling bolt of energy, the orange beam blasting out of the darkness at the rear of the building. It slammed into and *through* the wall it struck. Hand cannon.

Knowing Alisa didn't have such a weapon, Leonidas gave up stealth and sprang in the direction where the bolt had originated. He leaped over a fifteen-foot-high vat, hardly worrying if he landed on the ground or on something else.

As he dropped onto a stack of crates, he spotted Alisa and another woman. Alisa was charging, trying to bowl her opponent over before the hand cannon could fire again. Her foe leaped to the side while launching a kick. With surprising reflexes, Alisa reacted, dodging while grabbing the leg from the air. The other woman did something Leonidas couldn't see from his position, and they both tumbled to the ground, grappling with each other.

He crouched to spring over another stack of crates and to their aisle, but noticed something out of the corner of his eye and paused. A man lay on his back on the floor by the furnace. He wasn't moving. The face and blond hair were familiar. It *was* Sergeant Lancer. And he'd been shot in the chest with that hand cannon. He lay there bleeding, unable to even lift a hand to staunch the flow of blood.

The sound of a thump pulled Leonidas's attention back to the women. He jumped twenty feet to land in the aisle beside them. The woman—it was the one they had dismissed as a police officer earlier—had gained the advantage, rolling atop Alisa, her hand cannon clenched and ready to use.

She glanced toward Leonidas as he landed and shifted her aim. He reacted too quickly for her. He surged forward, grabbing her by the back of the uniform and hoisting her into the air. His knuckles brushed against something hard and skin-tight beneath her clothing—fitted body armor. It wasn't as tough as his combat armor, but it would deflect bullets and energy bolts from most hand weapons.

Furious about Sergeant Lancer, Leonidas hurled her across the room. Let the armor deflect *that*.

The woman hurtled toward a wall and should have crashed shoulder-first, but she twisted in the air with impressive agility. The soles of her feet struck the wall as she crouched deep to absorb the impact, and she sprang off before gravity dropped her to the ground. She landed lightly on her feet like a cat. A cat with a thief's set of impact boots.

"You're no police officer," Leonidas said, only pausing long enough to make sure Alisa wasn't gravely injured—she lifted her head and made a rude gesture toward their foe. Then he strode toward the woman.

"And *you're* the cyborg I'm after." She flicked a dismissive hand in Lancer's direction. "Why don't you take off your helmet and breathe deeply for me, Colonel?"

"Who are you?"

She grinned, not showing any sign of fear as he strode closer. "Someone who would love an extra two hundred thousand tindarks."

Instead of lifting her big hand cannon again, she flung a black ball at him, a fluidwrap. Leonidas fired one of the miniature blazers built into his armor. A beam of energy struck the ball just as it started to unfurl. The net never reached him, instead bursting into a tangled mess in the air.

Leonidas leaped toward the wall to avoid it and jumped off at an angle that took him straight toward her. She was already moving, dropping a pellet that exploded in smoke at her feet. As Leonidas landed, she dove to the side, rolling behind the furnace. He lost sight of her, the chemical-laced smoke interfering with his helmet's cameras and sensors as well as his eyes. Static burst across his helmet display.

It didn't matter. He anticipated her path, his ears telling him what his eyes could not. She was quiet, but not quiet enough. Her sleeve caught against the edge of the furnace, and he leaped, powerful legs taking him through the air faster than she could run. He landed behind her as she came out of the smoke, and grabbed her with both hands. Furious with the woman—the damned bounty hunter—for mistaking Lancer for him, Leonidas wrapped his hand around her neck even as she kicked backward, trying to fight him. He squeezed once, and bone snapped. She thrashed a few more times, then fell limp in his grip.

"The threat is gone," Leonidas said for Alisa's sake.

A soft groan came from the aisle behind him.

"Good." Alisa came into view as she staggered to her feet, grasping her ribs. "I nearly had her defeated, but a little help never hurts. Besides, I was holding back because I thought she really was a police—" She caught sight of the woman hanging from Leonidas's hand, and her humor evaporated, her face growing grim.

Leonidas did not respond. He dropped the woman and ran around the building, turning on all of the vent fans and opening the doors. As soon as he finished, he raced to Sergeant Lancer's side. His old comrade's eyes were open, his face scrunched with pain. He didn't seem to be able to turn his neck or move his hands yet, but his eyes were a window to his agony.

When Leonidas knelt beside him, Lancer smoothed his features, trying to hide the pain. His fingers twitched, as if in a salute. Saluting was the last thing he should be worrying about now. The hole in his chest was like a crater—that damned woman hadn't hesitated to fire, probably shooting him point blank as soon as the gas froze him in place. All he had been doing was coming to pick up his armor. He'd had no chance of defending himself.

Leonidas knew a fatal wound when he saw one, but he whispered, "Hospital," and a map with a flashing blip rose on his helmet's interior display. It was on the far side of the station from here. Leonidas growled and slipped his arms under Lancer's body, prepared to lift him up and carry him there.

Lancer winced and shook his head. "Too late for that, sir," he whispered, sadness and regret replacing the pain in his eyes. "Wasn't...alert. Didn't expect trouble here. Should have. Trouble everywhere. Not a good time...to be a cyborg." That regret seemed to deepen, as if he was talking about far more than his death, far more than this night.

"I know," Leonidas said, his voice thick. He was aware of all the blood on the floor, the blood still flowing from that wound. His sergeant was right. It was too late. Even if he sprinted to the hospital, they wouldn't make it in time. "I'm sorry, Sergeant. Todd," he corrected, remembering the man's first name from the personnel reports, even if he'd never used it. "She was after me, not you."

"Ah." Lancer's brows rose slightly. A mystery solved? "After she shot me...said I wasn't the...right one." His gaze flicked toward a hover pallet floating near the wall. The woman must have intended to roll Leonidas onto it to take him in. She'd just shot Lancer because—for no good reason, damn it. "Makes sense," Lancer added.

"Because I'm an ass that everyone wants to kill?" Leonidas asked, trying to smile, to make Lancer forget about his impending death, at least for a moment. He eased one of his hands out from under him and pulled off his helmet. To hells with the gas—he wanted his sergeant to see his eyes, not just the reflection of his own pained expression in the faceplate.

"Because you're *important*." Lancer managed the grin that Leonidas couldn't.

Leonidas snorted. "Hardly that. It's because the Alliance thinks I know where someone is, someone I haven't seen in six months." His throat closed up again, refusing to let him speak further. It was just as well. Lancer didn't need to know that his death had been for absolutely nothing. That the Alliance wanted Leonidas for information that was six months out of date and growing staler by the day.

"Sir?" Lancer whispered, his voice barely audible now. His fingers twitched again. "Will you—" He broke off and coughed, blood dripping from his mouth. His eyes closed, and Leonidas feared that was the end.

Leonidas clasped his hand. "What is it, Todd?"

His eyes did not open again, but Lancer's fingers wrapped around Leonidas's hand weakly. "Let my mother know I'm—let her know…what happened. Only make it sound heroic. At least…respectable."

Leonidas tried to swallow down the lump in his throat. "I will."

"Thank you, sir." Lancer managed another faint smile before taking his last breath, before dying in Leonidas's arms.

After a moment, Leonidas eased back, resting his man on the floor. He rose and stepped away, anger and frustration replacing his sorrow. He punched the wall, his armored fist knocking straight through it. He might have destroyed the whole place, but when he turned, thinking of kicking that hover pallet into pieces, he glimpsed Alisa standing near the front counter. She had risked herself to fight the bounty hunter, and none of his anger was for her, but he eyed her warily, anticipating some inappropriate display of humor.

"I think I understand now," she said quietly.

"What?"

"Why you don't laugh." She looked toward Lancer's body, then back to him, moisture glistening in her eyes. "Do you want me to wait outside?"

He groped for an answer. Did he? He needed to take care of the body, arrange to send Lancer home for a proper funeral if he could, and he still needed to find someone to fix his armor. This wasn't her mission. She'd just come along for a coffee.

Alisa walked over to him, eyeing *him* a little warily, then reached up and put her arms around his shoulders and leaned against his chest, not seeming to care that he was wearing his armor and covered in blood. He returned the hug, figuring he must look like he needed it. Maybe he did.

"I'm sorry," she said.

"Thank you."

She reached up, resting her hand against the back of his head, fingers lightly touching his hair. He'd never thought of himself as someone who needed comforting—he would go forward, dealing with the realities of being a soldier, as he always had—but he found himself appreciating having someone close. Having someone care. It almost startled him to realize that she did, considering what he was and especially considering he had pointed a gun at her chest the first time they met. She probably cared about a lot of things and just didn't let it show. Usually.

Alisa stepped back, resting the palm of her hand on his cheek before letting go. "I'll wait outside."

She looked over her shoulder at him, holding his gaze as she walked out the door. As he stood in the dark smithy, it slowly dawned on him that she had come along for reasons that had very little to do with coffee. He doubted he should encourage that, and didn't know how he felt about it, but he admitted that at least for now, it was good not to be alone.

THE END

Made in the USA
San Bernardino, CA
12 September 2016